D1509985

DEAR LAURA

DEAR LAURA

Jean Stubbs

STEIN AND DAY/*Publishers*/New York

First published in 1973
Copyright © 1973 by Jean Stubbs
Library of Congress Catalog Card No. 72-95551
All rights reserved
Designed by David Miller
Printed in the United States of America
Stein and Day/*Publishers*/7 East 48 Street, New York, N.Y. 10017
ISBN O-8128-1565-3

To my fellow conspirators,
Tess and George,
with all my thanks

I should like to thank the Borough Librarian of Merton, Mr. E. J. Adsett, F. L. A., and in particular Miss Lynn Evans and her staff at Wimbledon Park Branch Library. My vague request for "Anything you can find about the late Victorians" produced an avalanche of books, chosen with both imagination and discrimination, and my gratitude is endless.

CONTENTS

All happy families resemble each other,
each unhappy family is unhappy in its
own way.

Leo Tolstoy
Anna Karenina

INTRUSION

The villa, built in 1808, stood apart and slightly back from its neighbors on Wimbledon Common. In that dim February evening toward the end of the nineteenth century, it gleamed dully and then more radiantly as the lamplighter touched gas to flame and walked on.

From his vantage point at the far side of the Common, Dr. Padgett saw the whole establishment as a citadel in state of siege; or a doll's house in the distance, so minute were its appointments, so perfect its evolvement. He reined his pony to walking pace, and reflected.

He knew the barren regions of the attics, where the servants had their sleeping quarters, whose plain furniture was a medley of castoffs and poor relations to the richer pieces below. He knew each bedroom on the second floor, called there to consult a range of childhood ailments and to assist in the drama of childbirth. He was familiar with the dark ornate rooms on the first floor, where the Croziers entertained themselves and others. He had trodden the elegant staircase many times, carpeted in thick crimson Wilton, curving up and around a wall which was papered in heavy crimson flock.

Even now, he mused, Mrs. Crozier might be descending it, fresh from the hands of Kate Kipping. Fair head inclined to droop under so much trouble, fair arms glittering with husbandly tributes, black dress trailing and rustling from step to step. Down and down, to sit alone and stately in the somber dining room, to toy with the relentless march of courses.

He could picture Mrs. Hill, the cook, on the ground floor, moving deliberately from oven to table and back again, conducting an epicurean symphony; and the more rapid movements of the maids, starched caps perched saucily, black ribbons astir. And, sunk three feet below the ground, the cellars carried their army of provisions: regiments of bottled fruits and preserves, slabs of butter, wheels of cheese, sacks of sugar and flour, and the late Mr. Crozier's fine selection of wines and spirits.

"Ah, poor fellow!" Padgett murmured to himself. "He will never crack another bottle of that 1884 champagne again—and at seventy-two shillings the dozen that seems uncommonly hard. Well, well, well, well."

His pony had almost halted and the doctor sighed and stirred himself, for the thought of dinner at the Croziers' reminded him of his own.

I should not mind so much, he mused, if there were justice in this situation, but there is none. Such a respectable family, standing so high in the City and in their social circle. What damnable meddling with a gentleman's private affairs! What an unwarranted intrusion on *her* grief.

He flicked the reins on the pony's neck, and his trap bowled toward a less exclusive part of Wimbledon and a patient wife, whom he greeted with abstract affection.

"There is an inspector waiting to see you, my dear," she began, a little tremulous between distaste and curiosity. "I told him you had not yet dined but he said that time was no object. I did not know where to put him. I do not know where one does put a police inspector. But he is in the parlor. I offered him a glass of Madeira. I hope that was right? In any case he refused it. Shall you see him now or later?"

Dr. Padgett hesitated. He was hungry but the matter was important.

"I had better see him now," he replied at length. "Indeed, I shall not relish my dinner with a policeman in the house. A sorry business. In the parlor, my dear? Very well. And I shall take a glass of Madeira to keep out the cold, whether he wishes to join me or no."

One kept oneself above the common herd, cared for one's patients, provided for one's family, worshiped on Sunday, revered one's queen and country, and closed one's front door on the world. And, on a sudden, all was a chaos of scandal, and nothing would seem the same ever again.

What of *her* feelings? He was not an imaginative person but it seemed to him that the house no longer shielded her from the vulgar gaze, had been torn open.

"Inspector Lintott? I am Doctor Padgett. I understand you wish to speak to me?"

Intrusion, he thought. Intrusion.

The intrusion was stolid enough to give the impression of a foot wedged firmly against a closing door. The inspector intended to stay until he had got what he wanted, whatever that might be. His apologies were purely formal, his presence implacable.

"You have seen Mr. Fitzgerald, the family's solicitor, I believe?" said Padgett, switching the tails of his frock coat aside, sitting down in his armchair.

"Yes, sir. Earlier this evening. A very precise gentleman. Very *con*cise, too. He covered the professional side of this business as well as anybody could have done. It's the personal side that you might be able to advise me on, sir. You know the late Mr. Crozier's household from the viewpoint of a family doctor, which means intimately."

"I also respect my patients' privacy, and would not dream of betraying the confidences I regard as sacred."

"There *is* no privacy in a murder case," said Lintott bluntly, "or in a case of suicide. Whichever it may be. That's what I'm here to find out."

"The oath of Hippocrates—" Padgett began ponderously, and was checked.

"Three grains of morphine, to my mind," said Lintott, "is sufficient reason to set aside any oath that I know of, except a Bible oath when you swear to tell the truth, the whole truth, and nothing but the truth. And that's all I want, sir. Now I understand from Mrs. Padgett that you've had a long day and no dinner—which puts you in the same position as me—so I'll make this as quick and easy as I can. I hope you'll do the same."

Demolished, the doctor inclined his head, and set his hands palm to palm judiciously.

"Now how long have you known the family, sir?"

"Some fifteen years, if I recollect aright. Mr. Theodore Crozier had just married a girl—as she was then—of good family and great beauty, with money of her own, I understand. Her father was a Bristol merchant, name of Surrage. Both parents have died since. She is quite alone in the world, poor lady."

A pale oval above the mourning, pale head inclined, dining in solitary state beneath the three gas globes of the chandelier.

"You were the late Mr. Crozier's physician previous to his marriage, sir?"

"No, no. I was recommended to him. He had just set up house in Wimbledon. I believe he lived in rooms close to his business in the City before that. But, being newly married, he wished to have a physician close at hand. Naturally. A young wife. The expectation of a family. Also, he never enjoyed very good health himself."

"Something of a hypochondriac, judging from your statement at the inquest, sir. Am I right?"

"He was of a nervous disposition, Inspector," said Padgett coldly.

"And his wife? Is she of a nervous disposition also, sir?"

"Her constitution is a delicate one. Easily upset. Headaches, sleeplessness, and so on. Nothing organically wrong. A highly sensitive lady. We must spare her as much as possible."

"I see," said Lintott, seeing a great deal. "Would you have said they were happily married, sir?"

Padgett shifted in his chair and frowned.

"He was not an easy man," he said carefully, "but I should have always described him as a devoted husband and father. He provided for his family most liberally. The two boys are at Rugby, the little girl has a governess. No expense was ever spared. Mrs. Crozier, for instance, has what one might call an extravagant taste in dress. She must have cost him a pretty penny! But he was very proud of her appearance, quite indulged her. I do not blame him for that."

The wide straw hat, caught up on one side with a pink rose. Five pearl buttons harnessing the high collar of her blouse. The blown flower of her summer parasol. The bow glimpsed for a moment on one small shoe.

"Would you have called Mrs. Crozier a happy wife, sir?"

The soft cheek proffered dutifully, and quickly withdrawn. The anxiety underlying her soft voice. The sadness into which she lapsed when she was silent. One must not remember this. It might tell against her, who knows how? She must be protected from the eyes of the world, from prying, from further suffering.

"Mrs. Crozier is not of a light disposition," Padgett said awkwardly. "That is to say, in the bosom of her family. In society she is most agreeable. At home, as is right and proper, she is modest and quiet. Her late husband was a quiet gentleman. They seemed to suit admirably."

"You have known them for fifteen years," said Lintott. "Was he always the same? A quiet gentleman?"

"Always the same. Reserved, grave, some called him stern. But he was just. He required no more of his family than the standard he set himself."

"Perhaps it was too high?" Lintott suggested idly.

Padgett looked at him sharply, but the inspector's face was impassive.

"And was Mrs. Crozier a quiet and retiring person, when they were first married for instance, sir?"

"Naturally, a woman changes with the responsibility of a household. The charming frivolity of a girl of eighteen does not suit the dignity of a lady in her—good heavens!" Lintott waited. "Mrs. Crozier must be in her thirty-fourth year," said Padgett, amazed. "How times flies!"

"So the lady changed and the gentleman did not, sir?"

"I suppose you could put it like that, Inspector."

"I should be obliged if you would give me a list of the servants employed in and about the household, sir. Just names and duties, briefly. Servants," Lintott added drily, "often know more about their masters than the masters know."

Remote and beautiful, the white walls of the house were dissolving into dust. Behind them glimmered Laura Crozier. She had never appeared more vulnerable.

"There is Mrs. Hill, who acts as cook-housekeeper and has been with the family from the beginning. Then Miss Alice Nagle, the children's nurse, who was employed when their first child, Edmund, was born. A coachman, Henry Hann, inclined to the bottle, I am afraid. Kate Kipping, who acts as Mrs. Crozier's personal maid and also as parlormaid. Harriet Stutchbury, the housemaid. And I think they have a new kitchenmaid, but I cannot recollect the girl's name. It is not important."

"Thank you very much, sir. I shall not keep you above a few minutes more. There's one person I haven't mentioned yet. The late Mr. Crozier's brother. Mr. Titus Crozier. Quite the ladies' man by all accounts."

"I utterly repudiate any malicious gossip concerning Mrs. Crozier and her brother-in-law!" cried Padgett, with the only heat he had shown so far.

"Just so," said Lintott. "Only, it has been mentioned

and must be investigated, sir. What might your personal opinion of him be?"

Padgett replied stiffly, "Very charming. The antithesis of his late brother, in fact. Very popular. He lived with them, or at least he used the home as his background, for a number of years. When they were early married. The three of them were devoted," he cried, again with the same asperity. "I have never known two brothers so close. The late Mr. Crozier acted in the capacity of a father to Mr. Titus from the time of their own father's death. And being much of an age—I think he is one or two years older than Mrs. Crozier—Mr. Titus and she got on admirably. There was never a suspicion of scandal. In fact," said Padgett triumphantly, "I would have said that Mr. Titus was the link that held them together!"

"Fancy that," Lintott observed with immense satisfaction. "A strange marriage that requires a third party to keep it together!"

"I am fatigued, Inspector, and hungry," said Padgett, concerned, "and I may be choosing my words badly. I did not mean to imply anything of the sort."

"Well, sir, I'll leave you to the enjoyment of your dinner and go home to mine. There's just one thing I should like to mention, and I say this with all due respect. You certified the late Mr. Crozier as having died of a cerebral hemorrhage, yet the autopsy proved that he died of an overdose of morphine. I take it that the symptoms are pretty much the same?"

"They are, Inspector. And his medical and personal history was, of course, well known to me. I did not for a moment suspect morphine poisoning."

"Quite so," said Lintott, rising. "Appearances can be very misleading. That's the difference between your work and mine. Appearances mean nothing to me, sir. I take no account of them."

"Nevertheless, I trust you will deal with Mrs. Crozier in

as delicate a manner as possible. Speaking in the capacity of her medical adviser, I would caution you. She is a highly strung lady in a state of shock. I cannot be answerable for the consequences if your approach is too direct."

"I'll be as meek as a lamb with the lady," said Lintott mildly. "You needn't fear, sir."

And yet Dr. Padgett did fear, sitting in the lighted room until his wife reminded him twice that his soup was upon the table.

Only once, in the turmoil of mind which must seek some relief, did he attempt to communicate with Mrs. Padgett.

"I should have said that the late Mr. Crozier was devoted to his wife, would you not, my dear?"

She reflected, unsure how truthful one could be without overstepping the bounds of good manners.

"I always thought his behavior highly correct," she replied.

"And his treatment of Mrs. Crozier liberal almost to prodigality, my dear. Would you not have thought?"

Mrs. Padgett, who would never receive such material tributes, said wistfully, "Mr. Crozier gave her a most exquisite brooch on Christmas Day. She has many valuable pieces of jewelry. But, of course, she has set most of them aside for the mourning period as being unsuitable. Only jet, and pearls, and amethysts, and her diamond ring."

"Who could have known that this would be their last Christmas together? The time of goodwill toward all men, when one rejoices in the bosom of one's family. And then, a few weeks later . . . well, well, in the midst of life we are in death. Which among us knows when he shall be called?"

"Not *called*," said Mrs. Padgett rather too sharply, for Laura Crozier had never been a favorite with her. "Not *called*, surely?"

"Those who have laid violent hands upon themselves," mused Padgett, cutting up his mutton.

She did not answer, thinking, "Or those who have had hands laid violently upon them?"

PART ONE

OUTER WORLDS

1

*I know nothing like the petty grinding tyranny
of a good English family . . .*

Florence Nightingale

The weather had been finer than of late and there was no
ice on the mere, though the two boys had been hoping for it
since they arrived home for the Christmas holiday. Each
morning the grass upon the Common stood stiff with frost
and the ground rang beneath their boots, but by afternoon a
wet mist obscured the view. So the brothers lingered at the
drawing room windows, waiting an eternity of children's
time, obedient and subdued. They had, after all, said their
mother, been out that day and walked as far as the windmill
and fed the ducks on the pond. Now she rustled forward,
very fine and delicately scented in her best green watered
silk, to draw the curtains against a winter evening.

"Besides," she added, touching each son's head and
smiling, "it is Christmas day, and that should surely be
pleasure enough."

Edmund and Lindsey Crozier glanced at their father,
who sat reading yesterday's *Times,* wondering whether her
little sign of affection had been noted. For at fourteen and
twelve years old they were almost men, and Theodore
considered that she spoiled them.

"Their pleasure is not important," Theodore said into

the guilty silence, "since this is a religious festival and should be remembered as such. The fact that they have been generously—nay, lavishly—endowed with gifts should be regarded as their great good fortune and not their right. The poor," he continued, folding the newspaper neatly into one readable half column, "are always with us. It would be less than my duty if I did not remind you all of those less fortunate than yourselves. Do you comprehend me?"

"Yes, Papa," the boys chorused, with one last wistful look at the Common in the evening light.

"Then why do you not amuse yourselves instead of worrying Mama?"

"Play with your new toys," Laura whispered, giving them a little push toward the Christmas tree, "and say something appreciative about them to your Papa. Tell him how much you value his kindness."

She shut out temptation with a swish of blue wool brocade.

"They are not, in any case, merely toys," said Theodore, hearing and seeing everything without apparently lifting his eyes from the print. "That would be superfluity. Lindsey!" Suddenly pouncing on the younger lad as he set out a battle line of lead soldiers. "Do you know how our firm advertises Crozier's toys?"

The boy scrambled to his feet again and hooked his hands behind the back of his Norfolk jacket. He concentrated on the wax flowers imprisoned within a glass dome which stood upon the mantelshelf.

" 'Dolls that instill correct notions into the young mind,' " he began. " 'Merry games—and—pastimes . . .' "

" '. . . combining,' " Edmund whispered, and was checked by a look from his father.

"Pray continue, Lindsey," said Theodore Crozier, one forefinger on the line he had been reading.

" '. . . combining . . .' "

" 'Pleasure,' " Laura dared to suggest, and smiled brilliantly as though pleasure were her birthright.

"My dear Laura!"

"I beg your pardon, Theodore. The phrase is turned so adroitly."

" '. . . pleasure,' " Lindsey finished, helped by mouthings from his older brother, " 'with instruction.' "

"Exactly! Blanche!"

The child turned so quickly that she overset the dining table in her doll's house, and righted it as quickly.

"Yes, Papa?"

"Do you know what the advertisement means?"

"No, Papa." She had not been listening, as usual, rapt in her own world and talking quietly to each small perfect room as she set it out.

"It is a most extraordinary thing," said Theodore testily, "that when I spend time in the bosom of my family I am rewarded with so little attention!"

"My dear," Laura cried, sacrificing herself out of habit, "I wonder whether you could not look at the safety chain of my new brooch. I should not like to lose something so exquisite."

She moved toward him, presenting a white neck and shoulders for his attention. He examined both pieces of property.

"It is well enough," he said, of the enameled green heart pricked out with pearls, "and looks good upon you."

Released, she smiled at him, paused prettily so that he might admire her longer, and said, "How long should we wait tea for Titus?"

The deliberation of his hand bringing out the gold watch from his waistcoat pocket chilled her. But her smile remained wide and sweet. The three children sat in silence, their attention a tribute to the coming visitor.

"We shall not wait a minute after five o'clock." He

returned to his paper, saying fretfully, "This influenza is reaching epidemic proportions."

"I do not think it is a matter for great concern," Laura replied automatically, listening for the caller. "It is in Europe, after all."

"My dear Laura, Europe is only across the Channel."

"A stone's throw away," she agreed hastily.

"Twenty miles from Dover to Calais, to be precise—that is, if you wish to be precise."

"Indeed, you are quite right." She smoothed her long skirt and lifted both hands to her pale crown of hair. "My lack of precision is monstrous."

The children were merely playing with time now. Waiting, as she did, for the best surprise of the day. The sound of the lion's brass head on its brass base, the refined voice of the parlormaid, an answering laugh both deep and hearty, fetched them from the drawing room in a tumble. Titus was there, ruddy and bright from the cold, punching the boys—who punched him back with glee—swinging Blanche up in his arms, nodding to his elder brother, smiling at Laura.

"My dear Titus," cried Theodore, renouncing the influenza epidemic, "how delightful to see you. Come now, leave him be!" he said almost indulgently to his sons. "Sit down, dear boy, sit down."

While Blanche cried that Uncle Titus was not a boy, while the lads searched his pockets for sweets and found them, Titus let himself be pillaged without protest. A handsome man in his middle thirties, he was a total contrast to Theodore in appearance and temperament. Charming, and he knew that very well, with his thick chestnut hair and curling sideburns; possessed of a caressing voice, to coax his own way; having an adamantine courtesy to cover a volatile nature and a wary heart. So he allowed them to make much of him until they were weary, and then announced that his Christmas present was outside—to wring the last drop of excited affection.

"A Negretti and Zambra's magic lantern and slides," he whispered to his brother and sister-in-law. "Perhaps after tea?" Then turning to her, who stood in cool green splendor, he cried, "My dearest Laura, how very well you look! A new brooch? Let me guess. A gift from Theodore. His taste is impeccable."

The older man, gravely pleased, received the compliments due to his choice of wife and jewelry.

"Now if I could meet with a lady such as Laura," said Titus, laughing, keeping the conversation always on himself, "you would find a twin case to that of my brother—the happiest married man in England."

Composedly, her eyes fixed on him, her smile unfaltering, Laura rang the bell for tea.

Afterward, Henry Hann the coachman came in, flushed with more than one spirit of the season, and secured a sheet to the picture rail so that it acted as a screen. Titus took Blanche on his knee and let the boys rest their elbows on his shoulders, while Henry slipped the slides into place. Solemnly they stared at colored views of Venetian canals and Swiss mountains, exclaiming politely at their beauty. Respectfully they listened to Theodore's dissertation on the grandeur of Scotland, the wildness of Wales. Then obeying a summons of their mother's eyes they thanked Titus roundly. But he was up, setting Blanche in his chair, taking Henry's place at the magic lantern: a greater child than any of them.

"The best is yet to be!" said Titus, and looked at Laura.

"What further astonishments can there be?" she asked serenely. "What a tease you are, Titus!"

"Look!" he commanded them, fitting a particularly thick slide into the socket, and turning its little handle.

And there was a fat man asleep in a chair. Titus snored, raising a shout of laughter, and as he snored a mouse strolled straight into the fat man's yawn.

"Do it again, Uncle Titus. Do it again," cried Blanche, clasping her hands together.

Again he snored, and turned the handle. Again the mouse soared into the pink cavity. They were beside themselves with delight. Laura laughed almost as much as her children. Theodore relaxed his dignity sufficiently to say, "What a nonsensical idea, Titus!" but watched nevertheless. And when they were tired of the fat man and the mouse there was a thin man, on a penny-farthing bicycle, who pedaled ·faster and faster; and a policeman who knocked a ruffian on the head with his truncheon; and a dozen more farces.

"But however hard that gentleman pedals he always stays in the same place!" said Blanche, and plucked her bottom lip, puzzled.

"Well, of course he does," Titus replied. "He cannot cycle off the slide, Miss Goose!"

So that she ran to him, giggling, and hugged his legs and said he was the best uncle in the world.

"What did *you* give Papa for Christmas?" Titus asked, when the last curiosity was done to death, and Blanche's arms were fast about his neck.

"Two pen-wipers that I worked myself."

"*Two* pen-wipers. Papa will have to write a great deal, will he not?"

She ducked her head modestly, looking at Theodore.

"But Nanny had to wash them first, because of unpicking all the mistakes I made, and getting them dirty," she added honestly.

"Oh, but the mistakes are best of all, for one does not expect them. I shall order a pen-wiper from you that is full of mistakes, so that I can laugh over them."

"Papa does not approve of mistakes," said Blanche, "and would not find them funny."

"Who gave you this new dress, Miss Goose?" Titus asked, covering her statement tactfully.

"Mama. Mama made it herself, and she made the sash too."

"I shall ask her to make *me* a white muslin dress with a blue sash."

The boys roared in unison, but Blanche said shyly that the blue would match his eyes, and found herself the cause of greater amusement.

"And Mama embroidered that beautiful waistcoat for Papa, did she not? Do you suppose she would embroider one for me if I asked her very nicely?"

"No," said Blanche, twisting the string of corals around her neck, "because you are not Mama's husband."

And was bewildered by the hilarity of their response.

"What an accomplished Mama you have," cried Titus, as the laughter flagged.

His eyes courted Laura. She sat in her green bower of watered silk, her husband's gift at her breast, a slight flush on her cheeks.

"Yes, Laura does all these things well," said Theodore, "and with some tastefulness."

The vastness of Christmas lunch, the heaviness of Christmas tea, had sated appetite, and dinner was a lighter affair. Blanche, wayward of stomach, and only allowed to join the party as a special concession, cut everything up minutely and left most of it. The boys plied their knives and forks nobly. Laura ate little. But Titus and Theodore paid tribute to Mrs. Hill's culinary achievements without difficulty. Excellent trenchermen, they took their wine with each course, and were still ready for their decanter of port and walnuts afterward. The question of a pantomime occupied the rest of their attention. Should it be *Jack and the Beanstalk* with Dan Leno at Drury Lane, or *Cinderella* at Her Majesty's? Blanche would have preferred *Cinderella* and was too timid to press her claim. Laura smiled and let the discussion pass her by, and Titus and the boys won the day with Dan Leno.

"Shall you join us?" Titus asked his brother, who shook his head somberly. "Then may I escort Laura and the children?"

"It would be very good of you to do so."

"It will be my pleasure," said Titus frankly. "I am a boy myself where Dan Leno is concerned."

Conversation lagged. Blanche's fair head drooped with exhaustion. The boys grew silent. Laura rang for Nanny Nagle, who bobbed an iron curtsey and stood inexorably by the door. One by one, the children made a mute circuit of parents and uncle, giving and receiving goodnights. Then each picked up a candlestick from the table in the hall, and mounted the stairs under the guardianship of Nanny's eyes and tongue. The table was cleared and swept, the decanter set ceremoniously between the two men.

"I will leave you gentlemen to your port," said Laura softly.

Titus held the door wide as she passed by him, head slightly lowered. In the fragrance left behind her they lit their cigars and settled to serious matters. As they talked, the core of their working lives took shape and flowered abundantly. Crozier's, the great toy-makers, now in its third generation and growing in size and scope, was a future upon which they could live in some luxury.

"Though neither of my sons will be concerned in the business," said Theodore. "Edmund is intended for the medical profession, and Lindsey for the army. You must look about you for a shrewd manager when I am gone."

"Come, brother, at forty-eight you have many years ahead of you."

"I am not robust," said Theodore soberly, remembering the influenza epidemic.

Titus laughed.

"No one would think it," he said lightly, of the big well-fleshed frame. "You worry too much, brother."

"So Dr. Padgett tells me, and says that worry will not assist my blood pressure. I worry about the blood pressure, then."

"Console yourself with Crozier's profits. We have had the best sales of any Christmas so far—which brings me to a question of some personal import."

"The usual question, I suppose?"

Theodore spoke without rancor but his face was inflexible: a dark face which seemed never to have been young.

"Have you no chink in that armor of yours?" Titus asked reflectively. "I am not such a good accountant as yourself. Money slips by me. I do not know where it goes."

"My commitments are nevertheless greater," Theodore replied. "There are the boys at Rugby. Blanche must have a portion when she marries. I keep Laura in dress, which is no small item. She is another spendthrift. I have an establishment to maintain," and he looked about him with pride at the solid mahogany. "You are a bachelor, Titus, and can make no such claims."

"I am a bachelor and have other claims," said Titus easily. "Surely, brother, you did not save all your money until three-and-thirty, when you married, without the ladies' picking your purse now and again?"

A shadow over Theodore's face gave him pause.

"You are now a reformed bachelor, brother," said Titus, smiling, "and should help me to reform also."

"Laura has given musical evenings for you in plenty," Theodore replied with indulgence. "No lady seems to come up to your expectation. We have often talked this over, Laura and I."

"And what is Laura's considered opinion?"

"That you prefer your freedom to domestic delights."

"Well, we cannot all be patriarchs. You have responsibility enough for both of us."

"I began early. I played the father to you for many years when our own father died."

"For which I thank you from the bottom of my heart. You fetched me out of some sad scrapes."

He laid his hand for a moment on Theodore's shoulder in genuine affection.

"Well, well," said Theodore, suspicious of showing emotion, "you were young and foolish, and I have sown a few oats of my own. A man must be a man, after all."

They both smiled, secure in a world where men were paramount.

"But no more money?" Titus persisted, returning to the nub of the discussion.

"No more money. You must find less expensive pursuits and cut your coat according to the cloth."

"A dancer can be a devilish expensive pursuit."

His brother did not answer, brooding over the ash of his cigar.

"Then shall we join the lady?" Titus asked, good-natured as ever, though a frown of disappointment lingered.

"Would you care to amuse Laura for half an hour or so? I have papers to look into."

Titus rose with alacrity.

"I am ordered to amuse you while Theo works," said Titus. "An order which I find most charming."

Laura motioned him to sit down, and lifted the coffee-pot with a perceptible tremor. Switching his coattails aside, Titus sat at his ease and watched her fill two cups.

"Now how shall I amuse such beauty?" he inquired idly, ruminating.

"You have many accomplishments," said Laura demurely, "and amusing the ladies is one of them. I leave the choice of amusement to you."

"Shall I tell you the tale of your inebriated coachman and make you laugh? I like to hear you laugh."

"Poor Henry," said Laura. "I fear that he prefers strong drink to anything else in life."

"There are more heady pleasures."

She was silent, fingering her rings as he sipped.

"Did I tell you of the time that he worked for Lady Wareham? I am sure that I did, and I would not have you bored by repetition."

"I should like to hear it again."

"Well then, the gallant Henry Hann was entrusted with Lady Wareham's exceptionally plain daughter Augusta—whom no man would have married without a handsome dowry, poor girl! Good God, how very ugly she is! And Henry, overcome by the honor—and possibly the young lady's countenance—dosed himself with a quantity of raw spirit, and set out in red-nosed style on the driving seat of a fine equipage."

She was watching him covertly and he affected not to notice, reveling in her absorption.

"At first all was well. The horses minced along Hyde Park nicely. The lady shaded her charms with a parasol. Then, as the drink rose to his head, Henry licked his steeds into a fair trot. 'Not so fast, Hann!" cried the Honorable Augusta. He took no notice. Smartly, she whisked the parasol down, furled it, and poked him in the back. 'I ordered you to slow down, Hann!' she cried. That voice would drive any man to drink, let alone Henry."

"You should not speak so of any lady, Titus."

He grinned at her.

"But we are old friends, are we not, and may speak the truth?"

She drank her coffee and did not answer.

"Faster and faster went the horses," Titus continued, enjoying both Laura's discomfiture and his story. "And the faster they went the harder Henry laid on with his whip, in the grip of a very demon of drink and speed. They tore through the park like Jehu, and as they flashed by all the other carriages people began to shout and cry 'Stop! Stop!' and 'Help! Police!' You always smile at that point, Laura. Up rose the Honorable Augusta, parasol in hand, and began to lay it about Henry's back, crying, 'Mama! Papa! Police! Help!' And the more she struck him, the more he belabored the horses, and the harder they galloped!"

Laura threw back her head and laughed, and he laughed with her.

"On and on. Faster and faster. Henry's top hat had fallen off a long way back. The Honorable Augusta lost her bonnet and then her parasol, burst into tears, and fell back in the carriage, thrown from one side to the other. And then the demon disappeared and Henry Hann returned, penitent. He reined and checked the terrified beasts to a halt. It took him many a hundred yards to do that, I can tell you. They were in a fearful lather and so was the lady. And he turned the equipage about, and drove her home as meek as a lamb. The Honorable Augusta was carried in to Mama on a tide of smelling salts, and Henry received his immediate notice. Have I amused you, Laura?"

"Indeed," she cried, handkerchief to mouth, "indeed you have."

"Then may I beg another cup of coffee, in payment?"

He judged her to be indulgent and himself to be in favor.

"Laura, I have a request to make of you." She looked up, startled, and he gave a little deprecatory movement of the hand. "No, that is another matter to be spoken of at another time. I am devilish short of money, Laura, and must get it from somewhere. Will you not speak for me to Theo?"

"How do you run through it so fast?" she asked, very low.

"I hardly know myself. But I owe Marchmont at cards, and some tradesmen, and they are pressing me for payment."

"You promised me you would not gamble."

"I promised I should try—and so I did!"

"Have you not approached Theodore yourself?"

"To no purpose. I thought you would know how to persuade him otherwise. It will not be the first time you have petitioned him for me, on one count or another."

She stared at her rings.

"I have no influence over him."

"That I find impossible to believe. You have considerable influence over *me.*"

She lifted her head and looked directly at him.

"Not at cards, Titus," she said drily.

For a full minute each held the other's gaze: he admiring, she confronting. Then she looked away again.

"I shall see what I can do," she said without hope.

After a pause, Titus said, "The influenza begins to rage here as well as in Europe and in the United States of America. Lord Salisbury, I hear, is confined to Hatfield. I wonder if I shall catch it?"

She rose and paced slowly to the window, lifted a curtain and contemplated the Common at night. He knew, without seeing, how she held her head crowned by that ashen coronet, and how well the emerald watered silk set off her pallor. And she, struggling against tears, sensed the arrogance of his ease and his sureness of her.

"If I were ill again," said Titus, surveying the fire with half-closed eyes, "would you come again to nurse me like a kind sister-in-law?"

She was silent, very still at the window, and he twisted to see her.

"Would you, Laura?"

"I beg of you," she said to the empty dark, "to forget what should be forgotten."

His face changed.

"That is very hard," he replied. "Do you not find it so?"

"I find it both hard," said Laura, "and bitter."

Her sadness had wiped out his humor.

"I suppose," she continued, in sorrowful acceptance,

"that your money has been spent on ladies as well as cards? It is, perhaps, unmannerly of me to mention such a possibility, but there can hardly be any pretenses between us."

He took counsel of the fire again.

"Yes," he said at last, "both women and cards. But I appear to have developed a taste for someone who cannot be bought. So what matter?"

"I would rid myself of you with that knowledge."

As torn as herself, but adamant, Titus replied, "Try, Laura."

The entrance of Theodore acted as a restorative to them.

"You will catch cold at the window in that thin dress," said the master of the house. "Come to the fire, Laura. Titus, you should not allow her to stand in a draft."

"Ah, but I have no influence over her," said Titus carelessly. "Have I, Laura?"

She let the curtain fall and turned toward them, her smile lifted like a banner.

"None whatsoever," she replied, just as carelessly, and sat back in her chair to be admired, with the brooch glittering at her heart.

2

*On an occasion of this kind it becomes
more than a moral duty to speak one's mind.
It becomes a pleasure.*
　　　　Oscar Wilde
　　　　The Importance of Being Earnest

In the vast hot kitchen the servants settled to a supper of cold meats and pickles after the day's labors.

"There'll be nothink more from that quarter tonight," said Mrs. Hill, nodding at the bell board above the kitchen door. "Let me help you to a bite o' beef, Mr. Hann. I can recommend it." And she nodded to herself, and narrowed her eyes at the blade of the carving knife.

A woman of fifty, stout of body and high of color, she was a tribute to good cooking and heavy feeding, queening her tableful of deferential faces in contentment.

On her right hand sat Nanny Alice Nagle, who had been in the Croziers' service only one year less than herself, brought in to nurse Master Edmund, the firstborn child. She and Mrs. Hill were strong-minded women with a powerful sense of their own dignity, and they understood each other. The kitchen was the cook's province and the nursery belonged to the nanny. On their separate grounds they deferred to one another, but to the rest of the staff they presented an irresistible front. Should anyone offend either they could expect a united attack, larded with exclamations of horror and protestations of outraged disbelief.

On Cook's left hand sat Kate Kipping the parlormaid: small-boned, smooth-haired, with a ladylike aspect. Privately the others considered that she gave herself airs, but she commanded sufficient respect to keep their opinions unvoiced. By her side was Harriet Stutchbury, the housemaid, one of Cook's protégées: kindhearted, gullible, and awkward. Henry Hann, the coachman, took the foot of the table. Between himself and Nanny wriggled the latest of Cook's recruits, Annie Cox, an undersized child of thirteen, who played general factotum for the sum of ten pounds per annum and board.

"Another Christmas over and gone, Lord love us," Nanny Nagle observed, watching Cook's knife shear expertly through the baron of beef and deposit three red slices on her dinner plate.

"Ah, yes," said Mrs. Hill, shaking her head sadly, though her mind and eyes were on the carving, "and none of us getting any younger. Harriet, make yourself useful and cut the bread. Not too thick, neither. We aren't cannibals, I hope."

Harriet set a pair of rough hands to the task, without avail.

"Six year," said Mrs. Hill, with somber satisfaction, "has that girl been under my instructions, and can't keep the loaf straight. Six year. Cut another for Miss Nagle, Harriet, and give that slice to Annie. *She* don't mind."

"Glad to get it, missus," said Annie sincerely, anxious to oblige. "Fresh or stale, as my mam allus says."

Mrs. Hill put down her carving tools with some deliberation, and a tight silence descended. Annie, stricken sparrow, stopped with the uneven slice of bread at her mouth and stared round-eyed at the mountain of wrath.

"Have I been trained and training in my profession for

uppards of thirty-seven year this Michaelmas," said Cook terribly, "to be called *Missus* at my own table?"

"Shame on you," cried Nanny Nagle, "and put that bread back on your plate, Annie Cox, instead of gourmandizing in front of your betters."

"She don't know nothink," said Harriet Stutchbury kindly, remembering a hard apprenticeship under the same authority. "She don't do it a-purpose."

The child squirmed, scarlet-cheeked and grateful, and looked anxiously at her slice.

"I'll thank you to keep a civil tongue in your head, Harriet Stutchbury," cried the cook. "Mrs. Hill is my name, Annie, and Mrs. Hill I *will* be called," though it was purely a courtesy title due to her status, since she had never married. "Two week you've been in this gentleman's house, Annie Cox, and a-gazing at the food as if you never saw meat in your born days. What you do at home is no concern of mine," she added loftily, "but in my kitchen you learn your manners. Last served is last to start, and nobody starts afore grace. You say grace at home, I hope?"

"No, missus—Hill."

The quietness was dreadful. In awed delight and suspense the others waited.

"Take that plate to the scullery, miss," said the cook, "and light a candle to eat it by. I don't sit down to my meal with a heathen of a Christmas day. Get along with you, do!"

The child, relieved that she was not to be deprived of her food as well as their company, scrambled down from her chair.

"You've forgot somethink, miss," cried the cook grandly, pointing to her knife and fork.

Annie scurried back and collected the cutlery she was unused to wielding. But in the privacy of the cold scullery, with her two inches of candle, she delved her fingers here and there in the tidbits, glad to enjoy it in peace.

Alone among them, Kate Kipping ate sparingly and elegantly as her mistress did, and wiped her lips with her napkin after every mouthful.

"Lantern slides this evening, Mr. Hann?" said Mrs. Hill.

"Yes, ma'am, with Mr. Titus a-clowning."

"Ah, he's a merry gentleman," said Mrs. Hill drily. "Very free. I hope he behaves himself with you when you open the door, Kate."

The girl lifted an exceedingly self-possessed face.

"I know my place, I hope, Mrs. Hill."

"Ah yes, but does he? *That's* what I'm saying!" And the cook sucked a fragment of meat from her tooth reflectively.

Harriet, staunch to the chains that bound her, said, "He took a liberty with me, once, Mrs. Hill. That day as Kate was poorly."

"How do you mean, girl, a liberty?"

"Pinched my cheek, ma'am, and give me a bit of a squeeze."

"He's done a deal more than that in his time, I can tell you," said Mrs. Hill heavily.

The housemaid giggled nervously, misjudging her mentor.

"I'll have no light behavior here, Harriet Stutchbury," said the cook, very sharp. "Do you hear me?"

"Yes, ma'am. Begging your pardon, ma'am."

"Well, he never took liberties with me, and never shall," said Kate Kipping firmly. She glanced at the subdued housemaid. "A gentleman knows when he may and when he may not, and Mr. Titus is a gentleman."

"Excepting where a certain lady is concerned," said Nanny Nagle, raising her eyebrows significantly.

"Name no names, Miss Nagle," the cook replied. "Say what must be said, but name no names."

"Oh, we all know very well round this table," said the nanny. "Henry Hann could tell a tale or two, couldn't you, Mr. Hann?"

He paused in the midst of his eating, swallowed, and cleared his throat.

"What I say now I could say in a court of law," he began, and they all pulled their chairs nearer, except for Kate Kipping who mentally withdrew from a conversation she could not check. "And I lay it all at Mr. Titus's door. The mistress is a lady, and without Mr. Theodore I'd be in the workhouse."

"No, no," they cried, as his lower lip trembled. "Never in this world, Mr. Hann."

"Yes I should," he protested, shaking his head from side to side. "Owing to an unfortunate weakness of mine as is no secret. Though I promised Mr. Theodore as I'd be sober whenever I drove his lady. And so I was, stone cold sober, when Mr. Titus was took ill in the summer." He buttered his bread liberally. "She was with him nigh on two hours, and she'd clean forgot about me when she come out."

"Lor'!" cried Nanny Nagle, throwing up her hands. "Whatever do you mean, Mr. Hann?"

Although they had heard the tale, with variations, many times already.

"Mrs. Crozier comes out, a-pinning of her hat and a-drawing on of her gloves, and begins to walk along the street. So I calls out, 'Here I am, ma'am.' And she stops, as if she recollects somethink, and walks back and says, 'I did not see you, Henry.' "

"What ever did *you* say?" the cook asked, agog.

Some delicacy was evident in his reply.

"I said, 'Begging your pardon, ma'am. I must've drawed up too far back.' "

Kate Kipping lifted her head and looked at him, then looked down again at her locked fingers.

"Was she flushed up?" asked Nanny Nagle, on the flushed side herself with scandal.

"She had a good color, but it could have been the heat. It was a warm day," said Henry slowly, regretting the deathless popularity of his story.

"Fiddlesticks!" cried Nanny Nagle. "I'd call it shame if I didn't know her better."

[43]

"Whatever it was, and we don't know as it was what we think," said Henry with rough courtesy, "it was Mr. Titus's doing."

"A man is as he is," said Nanny Nagle, "and a woman should know that and keep herself pure."

"She *is* pure," cried Kate, firing up. "Purer than you, Miss Nagle, for thinking shame of her."

"Hoity-toity, Kate Kipping," said the cook. "We all know you set yourself up to be like her. Walking the Common of a Sunday in her hand-me-downs, acting the lady. I shouldn't be surprised, miss, if you didn't know more than you say. Thick as thieves together!"

"I know nothing, Mrs. Hill, and there's nothing to know. Mr. Titus is Mrs. Crozier's brother-in-law and a bachelor gentleman. It's only right that she should see to things for him when he's poorly."

"She's a secretive cat," said Nanny Nagle, pondering. "She dodges papers under her blotter when I come in too sudden. And she sits for hours in that bedroom of hers, writing in her diary. She keeps it locked up, too. And once, when Mr. Titus called on her in the afternoon, I found her with her eyes red and she turned away so as I couldn't see she'd been crying."

"I don't hardly like to think of the lady crying," said Henry guiltily, but Nanny Nagle was relishing the idea too much to be parted from it.

"The virtuous woman is far above rubies, the Good Book says. Life may be a vale of sorrow, but there's One Above as sees all. Poor folks can be good Christians, and rich folks no better than heathens. Take her worldly goods away from her and I could tell you what's left—though I wouldn't soil my lips on the word!"

Their stomachs were distended with fruit tart, but a cheeseboard was not refused. Appetites whetted by defamation, they set to willingly, except for Kate.

"She's thought about it, even if she hasn't done it," said

[44]

the nanny, wiping cream from her mouth and helping herself to a hunk of Cheddar and three pickled onions. "Sinned in her heart. *I* know her."

"Still," said the cook, disturbed by the vehemence of her ally's arguments, "there's no signs of anythink being wrong. It's eight year since Miss Blanche was born."

"There's ways and means," said the nanny. "He'd know even if she didn't."

"I don't like to think of Mrs. Crozier being upset," said Henry helplessly.

"Don't you?" cried Kate Kipping. "Then why do you say ill of her? I'll tell you who's no better than he should be, and that's Mr. Theodore. Why should there be talk of her and not of him? He's out at nights often enough, and it isn't work that keeps him, I'll swear to it. Because Mr. Titus called once or twice, expecting to see him, and Mrs. Crozier was by herself. Don't smile like that, Miss Nagle, I won't bear it!"

"Prove it, miss!"

"I can prove it, for I was clearing away the coffee, and Mr. Titus said, 'Where's Theo?' And the mistress said, 'I thought he was with you, in the city, on a matter of business.'"

"Ah, they fooled you, miss," said the nanny knowingly. "They're up to many a trick of that sort."

"No more they did, for he went ten minutes after, and she sat by herself until well on eleven o'clock. She hardly spoke a word while I was helping her to bed. Just after three in the morning—I heard the clock strike—the master let himself in."

"And where was you, to hear all this from the top of the house?"

"I'd left the attic door open, because the mistress looked ill and I wanted to hear if she called for me. I told you, if you remember, Harriet?" The housemaid nodded, for they shared the same room. "Well, I crept onto the landing and saw him down below, mounting the stairs. You call her secretive, Miss Nagle, but you should have seen *him.* Smiling to himself. Then he went in as solemn as a vicar, and she was awake, and for once she let fly. I could hear them quarreling and then her crying. And I say it's the master you should be gossiping about!"

"Gossiping?" cried Mrs. Hill, enraged. "You'll hear no gossip in this kitchen, Kate Kipping."

"What do you call this, then?"

Cook and parlormaid faced each other, the one with social, the other with moral, authority. After a brief pause, Mrs. Hill gave way and rescued her dignity in one sentence.

"Here," she cried, in loud good nature, "if we aren't a-talking away and forgetting that silly Annie Cox in the scullery!" She turned from Kate and shouted, "Annie! Annie! Come back here, you silly girl. You'll be froze to an icicle!"

The kitchenmaid, chilled in bone and pink of nose, emerged.

"And what do you mean by this sort of behavior, miss?" the cook said briskly. Then, as the child wondered what new outrage she had committed, Mrs. Hill gave her a little push toward the polished range. "Get yourself warmed on that stool. And, Harriet, cut her a piece o' pie. I daresay you like apple pie, don't you, Annie?"

"I ain't never had it, missus—Hill—as I recollect."

"Then eat up. Pour her a spoon o' cream on it, Harriet. I can see it'll take me a month o' Sundays to make anythink of *you,* Annie!"

The kitchenmaid, perplexed and comforted, applied herself to the pie.

"Come now, girls, let's clear these things off," said the cook, "and I'll read the cards."

"On a Christmas day, Mrs. Hill?" Harriet asked uncertainly.

"It ain't a Sunday, and it's nearly over anyway."

"Well, I thank you for one, Mrs. Hill," said the nanny. "It'll be an education and a pleasure to us all. Be quick now, you girls, for Mrs. Hill!"

Among the farthing novelettes in the kitchen drawer, underneath a book on the understanding of dreams, the cook found a sleazy pack of cards. Harriet washed up, Annie dried, and Kate whisked crumbs neatly and folded the cloth. Then Mrs. Hill, in her best black dress, shuffled and dealt the pack. Between the reading of teacups and the reading of cards lay a chasm of difference. Little fortunes to be found among the leaves shriveled in comparison to the magnificence of the public Armageddon predicted through pasteboard.

In the grip of fate, Mrs. Hill prophesied sufficient financial disaster, adultery, and peril to undermine the entire Britsh empire.

Upstairs, the two boys lay awake in the dark and reexplored the world that pressed hardest upon them. Lindsey had just completed his first term at Rugby and found it a rough baptism. Edmund, in his second year, contemplated the Scylla and Charybdis behind him and prepared to negotiate the rocks ahead. A dark, sturdy boy, with an uncanny resemblance to his father, he also possessed his father's silent stoicism. But Lindsey was his mother's son, delicate of frame and gentle of eyes. He could be emotionally pillaged, and Edmund feared for him. The fear and the knowledge were a double burden for a fourteen-year-old lad to bear, but he sought to smooth Lindsey's path.

"And keep clear of Heddleston as best you can," he continued.

"I thought him very kind," said Lindsey defensively. "He told me I could fag for him next year."

"Stick to Matthews," Edmund advised. "If you do well enough he will want to keep you. So shine his shoes and brew his tea as he likes it. Matthews is a good fellow."

"And is not Heddleston a good fellow? He is very hand-some, and he said I was a young sport, and let me hold his jacket when he boxed with Smith Major."

"I am the elder," said Edmund, pitting brotherly status against the charms of Heddleston, "so you must do as I say."

His lips compressed over the order. Lindsey turned a puzzled face toward his brother's bed, but Edmund was staring at the ceiling: determined and inscrutable.

"Go to sleep now, Lindsey," he said.

The boy closed his eyes obediently, but Edmund lay looking into the dark for more than an hour afterward, thinking over his father's words.

"I am astonished that any son of mine should think fit to complain that I had sent his brother to one of the best public schools in England. Rugby was my school and your Uncle Titus's school, and our father's before that." Paid for by a tide of toys, instructional for the young mind. "I tell you it will make a man of Lindsey. He is too *soft*, Edmund. Your mother has spoiled him and now he pays for her indulgence. What was your purpose in speaking to me of this matter? Did you think I should take him away? No, sir, not if it break him! So look to his welfare, sir, and see that he faces his problems like a man. That is all I have to say to you, Edmund." And as the boy went slowly to the door, "Do not think to persuade me through your mother. Women have no knowledge of men's affairs, and no wit for them. This is between the two of us. If you so much as speak to her of it I shall whip you. And it will do her no good to be worried. What can women do but weep? You would not like that."

"No, sir. You may trust me, sir."

Theodore had placed one hand on the lad's shoulder. But it was not seemly to convey how much he loved him. So he patted the Norfolk jacket briskly and bade him be gone.

Released from the tyranny of Nanny Nagle, Blanche drifted into sleep and became very small like Alice in Wonderland. In her dreams she entered the new doll's house, room by little room, and was mistress of it all and free in her possessions.

3

The latest and most illustrious victim of the influenza
is the Dowager-Empress Augusta, now in her 79th year.
The Times, January 6, 1890

New Year's day, 1890, began with a sleepy adagio of housemaid, parlormaid, and kitchenmaid, who yawned their way
downstairs at 6 A.M. Long before breakfast, busy hands had
swept and dusted the main rooms, cleaned grates and lit
fires, carried cans of hot and cold water to the bedrooms.
Mrs. Hill, fortified by a pot of strong tea and tremendous morning dignity, presided over the range, the best
model of its kind and a Crabtree's Patent Kitchener. Annie
Cox had skinned two knuckles polishing it mirror-black
with Zebo. Now it simmered beneath the encumbrance of a
Victorian breakfast. Porridge heaved fitfully. Bacon,
kidneys, sausages sizzled. A kedgeree—Mr. Theodore's
favorite dish—was kept hot. Prunes cooled for the children.
Harriet toasted her face and the bread. A mess of scrambled
eggs lay under a silver cover. Cold meats and piping chops
were served up for the sidetable.

Tongue between teeth, Annie fetched china from the
dresser and counted rows of cutlery. In the parlor, Kate
Kipping made the setting as immaculate as herself. An

eight-day clock, purchased from Messrs. Benson & Co. of Ludgate Hill, ticked blandly upon the kitchen wall, in complete harmony with the cook. And she, marshaling her little army, gave orders and issued reprimands out of an experience which, in its way, resembled genius.

"Missus Hill got eyes in the back of her head," Annie Cox whispered woefully to Harriet, but not low enough.

"And ears to hear, miss. Take your fingers off of them sausages. Ain't you seen food afore?"

"Not near so much, Missus Hill. I'm one of fourteen and my dad's a docker."

Mrs. Hill sniffed. Her origins were higher, since her father had kept his own bakery and she had never known hunger.

"They breeds like rabbits," said Nanny Nagle, entering the kitchen in starched virtue. "It's disgraceful. Fancy having a horde of children like that, with neither bread in their mouths nor blankets to their backs! The cradle in your house must be fair wore out, Annie Cox!"

"We ain't got a cradle, Miss Nagle," said Annie unwisely. "My dad fetches a banana cask from the docks and cuts it in half, and my mam sets a bit of blanket in it. But there ain't a better mam in all the world"—goaded by their exclamations of horror—"nor a nicer baby than our Jonnie. No there ain't!" she finished rebelliously.

"Well, Annie, you can buy him somethink out of your first wages," said Harriet kindly, for she came of a large family herself and had been put into service for the same reasons as the kitchenmaid: not enough room or provision at home and a driving need for such small wages as she could earn.

"Five minutes of eight o'clock," cried Mrs. Hill, in a voice that sounded the attack.

The family were coming downstairs, Laura on her husband's arm and the children following, into the parlor papered with tropical birds roosting on improbable foliage.

[51]

His dependents assembled, Theodore took out his gold hunter watch, waited until the hand reached the hour, and rang the bell.

"Ready?" said Mrs. Hill, and led her staff into the presence.

Neat and quick, Kate drew the Bible from the curtained recess at the bottom of the sideboard and set it before the master. He chose his text from the Book of Proverbs.

"The preparations of the heart belong to man: But the answer of the tongue is from the Lord."

They listened respectfully, heads bowed. A flock of black dresses and white caps and aprons, with Henry Hann bringing up the rear in sober gray. Then all knelt in prayer and remained in silence for a minute after Theodore had finished.

Mrs. Hill, helped to her feet by the maids, nodded briskly to her cohorts. They disappeared as unobtrusively as they had come, to be replaced by Kate with a trayful of porridge and prunes. Laura ate little as usual: too busy preventing the children from disturbing her husband, who sat behind his *Times.* Blanche was in trouble with her prunes, and the boys scuffed their boots on the chair legs until frowned to quietness. Theodore cleared his throat.

"The funeral of Mr. Robert Browning is reported at great length today," he observed. "Should you like to hear about it? It is exceptionally well expressed, Laura."

"I should like that above all things, if you would be so good. The children, too"—motioning them to attention—"would like to listen."

" 'Yesterday the remains of the late Mr. Browning were removed from his residence in De Vere Gardens, Kensington, where they had lain since their arrival from Florence, and were deposited, in the presence of a large and distinguished company of mourners in Poet's Corner, Westminster Abbey . . .' "

Blanche dreamed, Edmund and Lindsey spooned up their porridge silently, Laura moved slowly with the cortege, and Theodore read clearly and deliberately from the columns.

" '. . . wreaths so numerous that they had to be carried separately . . . of ferns, laurels and evergreens, white roses, lilies, hyacinths, violets, myrtles and red flowers . . .' "

When our two souls stand up erect and strong, she thought, *Face to face.*

" 'Lord Tennyson, Sir Frederic Leighton, Sir John Millais, Mr. Alma Tadema . . . coffin of Venetian design in light polished wood . . .' "

What bitter wrong Can the earth do to us, that we should not long Be here contented?

" 'The inscription on the brass plate read: Robert Browning, Born May 7, 1812. Died December 12, 1889 . . .' "

Think. In mounting higher. The angels would press on us and aspire To drop some golden orb of perfect song Into our deep, dear silence.

" 'When it is said,' " continued Theodore, his voice resonant, " 'that all that is mortal of Mr. Browning lies near to Dryden, to Chaucer, and to Cowley, the scene will rise as a picture in the mind of every intelligent Englishman and of many thousands of English-speaking people all over the world.' "

Let us stay Rather on earth. Beloved—where the unfit Contrarious moods of men recoil away . . .

"Among others unable to be present were Mr. Gladstone, Lord Salisbury, Sir Robert Peel, and the Duke of Bedford, I see. I suppose they cannot *all* have the influenza, do you think, Laura? Laura?"

"Of course not, Theodore."

"But do you know? I cannot recall seeing anything except Lord Salisbury's ailment reported. Perhaps I have missed it. Of course, since he is the Prime Minister they would naturally mention . . ."

Oh, let your influenza rage, she thought, and read on— and let me be.

"Ah! I have missed the service. It was catching Lord Salisbury's name ahead of me that made me . . . They began with the chanting of the Ninetieth Psalm, set to Purcell's music. 'Lord, thou hast been our refuge.' That must have sounded very fine. 'Then Dr. Bridge had set to music for the occasion the beautiful lines of Mrs. Browning *What would we give to our beloved? . . .*' "

A place to stand and love in for a day, With darkness and the death-hour rounding it.

"So passes a great poet," said Theodore, looking around at his family.

And a great lover, and a great love affair, Laura thought.

Theodore reached for his handkerchief and sneezed explosively. She watched him in hatred. Suddenly the patriarch had dwindled to an anxious huddle.

"Paris records the highest number of deaths from influenza so far," he cried, seeking reassurance. "Cases have had to be postponed in the law courts because barristers are unwell. And pulmonary, bronchial, and laryngeal complications have appeared. It is the same all over Europe. Laura!"

"You need not trouble yourself, I am sure, my dear."

"Look at the paper!" he cried, shaking it at her. "Look at the reports! Vienna, Berlin, Brussels, Copenhagen, Rome, Sofia, Munich. How can you tell me not to trouble myself?"

"I believe that Mrs. Hill put too much pepper on the kidneys, and that is why you sneezed, Theodore. You have no other symptoms."

He pushed his plate fretfully away.

"I shall not ride to the City this morning," he said, martyred. "Henry must take me in the carriage. He will be back before you require it yourself."

"Yes, yes, I think that best. To risk the inclemency of the present weather upon a horse would be unwise indeed."

He replied, staring at the list of deaths, "It is this weather that breeds influenza. Mild for the time of year. A green winter and a full churchyard, they say."

She did not answer, knowing the time of reprieve was at hand, when she might see him off and the children occupied, and Kate would bring her a slice of freshly toasted bread to eat in comfort.

On January 2 temporary hospitals were set up at Würz-burg, forty thousand cases were reported at Munich, theaters and schools closed. But Lord Salisbury passed a good night at Hatfield, and there was a decided abatement in feverish symptoms. He took solid nourishment for the first time in a week and walked up and down some of the corridors. Queen Victoria and the Prince of Wales requested that the latest information should be telegraphed to them morning and evening.

On January 3, in Vienna, between forty and fifty people were dying every day. Budapest was hit badly. And, to augment Theodore's unease, the *Times* obituary for 1889 on page 5 was exceptionally long: one and a half columns, containing many names of note and distinction.

On January 4 the railways and postal and telegraph services were affected in Holland, owing to the number of sick workers. In Paris 378 policemen had succumbed to the disease and 357 in New York. Switzerland and Spain con-tributed to the death dance. In England a remarkably springlike element in the air attracted the European disaster.

In an effort to distract her husband's preoccupation with his health, Laura took some pains to read up about the Forest-gate district school fire, which had roused public indignation and a public inquiry. But the twenty-six chil-dren, suffocated to death on the top floor of a building without an alarm bell or watchman, their doors locked, could not move him beyond mere comment.

"It has never been compulsory up to the present time to provide means of exit from the danger of fire. Some good may come from this lamentable occurrence. Have you seen that the Dowager-Empress Augusta is prostrated in Berlin? I fear she will not recover. She is very infirm and of a great age."

He was willing himself toward the ax. Its blade gleamed menacingly on January 8 as the Empress died and was proclaimed "a sphere of gracious and womanly ministra-tion." Its blade fell the following day, when a serious spread of influenza was reported in most districts of London. Out of 1900 telegraph boys, 222 were off duty, and the disease was now described as "Russian influenza." As Henry assisted his master into the brougham, bought from Hart's in New Bond Street, Theodore invited affliction.

Laura reckoned she had about three hours before he was brought home again. So she suggested that the parlor table be set with newspapers and the three children paint their picture books. There was some delay as Blanche was arrayed in a Holland pinafore and cautioned by Nanny not to get dirty. But eventually two fair heads and one dark one pored over their tasks, and all was peaceful.

From her desk, Laura inspected the day's menu and made up her accounts. Upstairs, Harriet stripped beds and tidied rooms, supplying each with its proper complement of soap, clean towels, candles, and writing paper, and wished she were Kate Kipping. Sighing for the lighter tasks of acting lady's maid to Laura, and answering the front door in a frilled cap and apron, she made her way down to Mrs. Hill and hard labor.

Annie Cox was in trouble again, performing a legion of mean tasks under a hail of scolding.

"And when you've finished scrubbing that passage to my satisfaction," Mrs. Hill cried, "you can start a-carrying the coals. And don't you so much as spill a speck o' dust or you'll answer for it! What are you about, Kate?"

But this was simply the habit of authority, since Kate knew very well what she was about and needed no supervision.

"Mrs. Crozier's coffee, Mrs. Hill."

"Make us a big pot of tea when Kate takes that tray in, Harriet," said the cook. "We must keep our strength up, I hope. She'll be in the parlor until lunch—unless she goes to her room. Did she order the bedroom fire to be lit?"

"Yes, Mrs. Hill," said Harriet. "She said as Mr. Crozier warn't well and might be back early."

Kate lifted her eyebrows but said nothing.

"He worrits hisself to death," said Mrs. Hill. "A kinder gentleman never breathed, but he don't half worrit."

"He frightens me," Annie Cox confided, wiping her hands on the sacking that served her as an apron.

"So he should, if ever he sees you. And he shouldn't see you neither, except at prayers. Your place isn't in the house. Let me see that passage! It's well enough," mollified. "I can tell you've done scrubbing at any rate."

"Oh yes, missus—Hill—since I were eight year old. I used to go up Lavender Hill with our Nellie and we did the steps there. We didn't get no pay if they wasn't spotless."

"I used to be a step girl," Harriet confided, unmindful of her dignity. "Did you, Kate?"

Kate held out her hands without comment. Almost as white and pretty as Laura's, they had done no rough work.

"Lady Muck!" Harriet whispered to Annie, and ached for gentility.

"Send for Dr. Padgett at once!" cried Theodore, helped in by the cabbie. "I fear I have caught that confounded illness. Here, my man, here's something for yourself to keep out the cold. Do not come too near, Laura. I do not want you to be ill, too!"

"The bed is aired and a fire lit," she replied, glad to keep her distance, leading the way.

His sickness oppressed her, and she seemed as stricken as he, her natural buoyancy of carriage gone.

"You are very pale," he accused her, anxious that no one should divide his dominion of ill health.

"It is usual in me, Theodore. I feel very well."

"I shall require the most careful and constant nursing, if

I have the influenza. You understand that? My blood pressure. My bronchial weakness. That murmur of the heart which Padgett treats so lightly—send for him! The Empress Augusta had the finest physicians in Europe. She died, you know, Laura. Laura, are you listening?"

"She was very old and very enfeebled, Theodore. You are in your prime."

"I am not as strong as I look, nor as Padgett seems to think," he cried petulantly. "Ask Nanny to fetch me a cordial, a hot cordial. She is a *good* nurse," he added, accusing Laura, who was never as tender on these occasions as he could wish.

Groaning gently, as the doctor questioned and examined, Theodore was received into the arms of the epidemic.

"Now, ma'am," Padgett counseled, in the privacy of the drawing room, "we must take care of you as well. This is a highly infectious and contagious disease, and possibly cannot be kept away from you all, but we must do our best. I advise you to sleep in a separate room, and order your servants to keep Mr. Crozier's utensils apart from those used by the rest of the household. And do not distress yourself unduly. Nature heals, ma'am, nature heals. He should be up and about in a week, though convalescence will take far longer—particularly as he tends to coddle himself. Beef tea and dry toast, as soon as he can take nourishment. Otherwise, warmth, rest and hot cordials. And keep the newspapers from him. He will harm himself far more, brooding over the mortality rate, than the sickness will harm him. Distract him as much as you can. Keep him optimistic."

"I shall endeavor to do so," knowing how ineffectual those endeavors could be.

He looked at her sharply, drawing on his leather gloves.

"How are you keeping?"

"I have slept better since you prescribed the capsules, though I do not wake up as quickly as I could wish."

"One cannot have everything, ma'am. A little drowsiness in the morning is fair exchange for a night's rest. And the headaches?"

"The powders ease them."

"You suffer from a nervous disposition, ma'am. So do not let your husband's illness overburden you. Mr. Crozier has great confidence in Miss Nagle. Let her divide the nursing with you. And you have two maids that can watch by him, turn and turn about. You must get your sleep."

Satisfied that he had done what he could, the doctor picked up his bag, and Kate Kipping curtsied as she opened the front door.

"Take it from an old medical practitioner, ma'am," Padgett said cheerfully, as he climbed into his trap, "Mr. Crozier will be up and about in a week. Do not alarm yourself."

He lifted his hat, flicked the reins on the pony's neck, and was off at a spanking trot to his next patient. A handbell rang furiously from the main bedroom.

"Well?" Theodore demanded. "What does he say? Whispering downstairs. I must know the worst."

"Indeed," said Laura gently, tucking the blankets a little tighter, "he tells me you are pretty well."

"Pretty well, Mrs. Crozier? With a temperature of one hundred and two?"

"Dr. Padgett told me it was not a virulent attack, and you would feel better presently. But you must rest undisturbed. I shall get Harriet to make me up the bed in the guest room."

"You must leave your door open in case I should need you."

"Certainly I shall," she soothed him.

"And Titus must keep in touch daily," he rambled fretfully. "He must come every evening and keep me informed."

She hesitated, saying, "Surely he need not. It is a long way to and from the City. He knows the business, Theodore."

"A journey I have performed daily without complaint—or comment from you—these many years. Do not argue with me. It makes my head worse."

"Do you require anything more at the moment, Theodore?"

"I require you to sit with me until I sleep."

Her head moved in question toward a book on the table by the bed.

"No, no, no, no. Not to read, to sit with me, Laura. To sit."

She sat, hands folded in her lap, and watched him drift uncomfortably away from her.

4

If I leave all for thee, wilt thou exchange
And be all to me?
                    Elizabeth Barrett Browning
                    Sonnets from the Portuguese

Her father had had two faces: one he presented to the
world, correct and fastidious, the other warm for her. Even
as a child she knew that her mother disappointed him,
though Mrs. Surrage was always elegant. Even as a child she
knew how to reach him for herself, and assumed that all
men were made in his image. With women she was less easy,
accounting them rivals or disciplinarians. And since she was
an only child, and they kept her very close, she found
friendship a difficult business. Life was simpler, confined to
one love and a social audience who could be charmed and
forgotten. Because she sought to please him in all things she
was considered a good girl, though the obedience was
merely a means to a greater end.

   He was fond of music and she learned to play for him
with some accomplishment. He loved poetry and she
learned to read and recite it to him. He admired beauty and
she practiced a hundred little graces to capture his praise.
He had no use for intellect in a woman, so she neglected
even the modest requirements of a female education at

home. He was generous with money, and she spent it. He was unwise and prodigal in his loving, and she responded. He molded her into the ideal he had never possessed, and she put aside anything that might mar the surface which delighted him.

The other side of his life held no interest for her: the finance, the constant striving for achievement, the long-headed, hard-headed fight for supremacy in an age which flung business tentacles farther and farther into an expanding empire. Only, she understood him to be powerful and enjoyed the fruits of that power.

In his turn he lavished imagination as well as affection upon her, entering into her most childish pursuits with an indulgence that roused his wife's criticism. Every absence from her, however brief, brought a gift back: a musical box, a toy theater, a string of coral beads, a wax doll. Whenever she was ill she woke up to a nonsense letter tucked beneath the candlestick. He could not bear her to be punished, though he was quick to let her know if she displeased his notion of her.

Constant erosion wears away even rock. Mrs. Surrage, who had married well and wanted nothing more of love than an establishment, finally left them to themselves. As Laura grew older her mother grew apart, sometimes using her as an intermediary, often envious, occasionally angry. Father and daughter had made an art of loving, a fantasy world in which all is well so long as the lover and the beloved are one. Of the real world Laura knew nothing and expected everything.

She came out at the age of eighteen and the dream flared awake. She danced with countless phantoms of her father, and he laughed them away.

"Too young, Laura. Besides, he is the third son. We must find someone who can keep you in the manner to which you are accustomed."

"A dull dog, my love, in spite of his fortune."

"Too old, Laura. He has a son the same age as yourself."

"In love with you? Impudent young rascal. Besides, they are all in love with you. So they should be. So they should be."

Dancing through a season, faster and faster, her mother's fan faltering as she espied a good match, her father's fingers tapping fretfully as he turned each possibility aside. And then Theodore Augustus Sydney Crozier, in his middle thirties, head of Crozier's Toys, leading her gravely into the waltz.

"He is interested in you, Laura," said her mother, snapping the fan shut, "and he is eminently suitable. Well bred, the right age, and capable of setting you up in a fine establishment. Think of that, my dear. London, the capital city. Your own house. A wide social circle."

Still Laura was undecided, wanting to spin time out and out, ever returning from each conquest.

"We cannot afford another season as lavish as this one," Mrs. Surrage said sharply. "And we cannot afford to have three seasons, in any case. Besides, if you are not engaged soon, people will think that no one has offered."

"What do you think, Papa?" Laura asked.

"You must make up your own mind, my love," he answered, jealous that she should consider leaving him, knowing that she must.

"But what shall I do?" she cried, who had never made a decision in her life, except between one colored ribbon and another.

Her father got up suddenly and left the room, shutting the door angrily behind him. In command of the field, for the first time in her marriage, Mrs. Surrage marshaled her arguments.

"Mr. Crozier will make an excellent husband, Laura. Your papa, naturally, wishes you to be quite certain before you encourage the gentleman any further. But if you keep him waiting too long he may lose interest. Besides, what possible objection could you have to him?"

"I do not know him very well, Mama."

"He has called here regularly. He has escorted you to various entertainments and had conversation with you. He has spoken to me at great length and with admirable sincerity. I have nothing but good to say of his conduct, his background, and his character."

"He has not said anything to me of an—affectionate—nature, Mama."

"Leave such nonsense to boys like that subaltern. You may be sure that if Mr. Crozier did not admire you he would not be interested. Besides, for a woman, love comes after marriage. You cannot expect to know a man until you are married to him, Laura. Good heavens, if a lady allowed every gentleman to pay court to her in the way you seem to expect, her reputation would be ruined."

"I will not be hurried, Mama," Laura said obstinately.

Her old ally was waiting to hear the verdict, face set, eyes cold. To him she ran, wilful, certain of her hold on him.

"I will not be hurried, Papa. I must have time to think."

He was allive again, triumphant, teasing, all-powerful.

"Of course you shall, my love. All the time you wish. Do you hear, Jane? I will not have my daughter married against her inclinations."

Mrs. Surrage said nothing. She and Theodore Crozier had much in common. They wished to look well in the eyes of the world, and they knew that marriages were made not in heaven but on earth.

His courtship was tenacious, correct. Backed by Mrs. Surrage, who imputed heaven knew what feminine fancies to his somber presence, Theodore progressed. She was clever enough to realize that Laura's imagination must be captured, and interpreted his reserve as restraint, working upon her daughter's romanticism with fearful skill.

"Mr. Crozier is a gentleman who says little and feels all the more strongly, Laura dearest. And what authority he has! How he worships you, my love! One can see what pride he takes in your appearance."

So the girl set her charms and graces before him, like jewels to be admired, and certainly·he was proud to have her on his arm. She began to seek out his preferences, to explore this strange territory which was to be her new life. As her interest in Theodore Crozier increased, her father diminished. As he diminished, the image of Crozier filled her horizon.

She created a fresh picture, another story, with herself at its center, with her husband always in attendance as her father had been. But this was greater, richer, infinitely better, since Theodore would be her lover also. Her knowledge of the physical relationship stopped short, mouth on mouth, and she lacked curiosity to pursue it further, assuming that all would be made clear in its own time.

Over her dreaming head the masculine struggle for property rights reached an inevitable conclusion. Laura's five hundred a year was invested in the firm of Crozier's Toys, to be used at her future husband's discretion. Certainly, Walter Surrage made sure that the capital could not be touched; and provision in case of Theodore's death, and Laura's allowance, and settlements on her possible children, were all satisfactorily concluded. But at the end of all the discussions and legalities one inescapable fact remained: she had exchanged her father's dominion for that of her husband, one luxurious cage for another.

On the eve of the wedding, Mrs. Surrage attempted to explain something she had been unable to comprehend herself. She spoke, in confusion of mind and heart, of the duty a wife owed. She said it was not necessary for a lady to do more than remain obedient and passive and think of better things. She promised the joys of children in return, and waxed enthusiastic over Laura's future wardrobe and status. Then, her own duty done, she kissed her daughter's cheek perhaps more tenderly than she had ever kissed it before, and wished her happiness.

"Say goodnight to Papa," she added, kinder now that her victorious rival would be forever removed. "He is devoted to you, dearest."

So Laura drifted down to the library to wind her arms around his defeat. They had nothing to say to each other, but she sat opposite him for half an hour while he enjoyed his brandy and cigar in silence. He thought only of her, and she thought of Theodore. Then he roused himself, seeing time now and for always as an enemy, and counseled an early night.

As she reached the door he cried, "He must take good care of you, you know, Laura. I have done all *I* can!" As though Theodore's behavior rested entirely on her.

Knowing him so acutely, translating the admonishment into concern, she replied lightly, "If he does not then I shall come home to you, Papa."

But he was a man of his word, and that word had been irrevocably given.

"You belong to your husband now," he said sternly. "Your home is with him. Let us have no nonsense on that score, Laura. You understand me?"

Wounded, drooping, she trailed back to the comfort of his arms.

"There, there, there," he said, casting the mantle of protection about her for the last time. "You will be happy with him. I do not know why I spoke as I did. We are fatigued with preparations for this fine wedding of yours. And where has all the money come from, miss?"

She knew the answer to this old and constant question. He had laid it so often at her feet, a tribute that required another tribute.

[66]

"From you, Papa! Dearest Papa!"

"Gentlemen make different approaches, so I under-stand," Mrs. Surrage had said. "They are inclined to think much of what seems distasteful to us. Mr. Crozier may trouble you with poetry, or with poetic allusions. Bear with him in this, and above all do not reject his advances."

Laura was drunk on unspoken words.

"Give and take is an excellent maxim, my dear. If a gentleman's passion appears inexplicable think of the chil-dren. They are our crown, Laura, and our reason for existence."

Laura was ready to be swept on any tide.

"At least, it is soon over," said Mrs. Surrage.

She was correct about this, at any rate. Theodore, who looked splendid in his impeccable suiting, was a terrifying figure of fun in his nightshirt. He did not trouble her with poetry, with passionate embraces, or with much explana-tion. Simply, he said that there were certain duties to be performed between man and wife, and executed them with a lack of consideration that appalled her, who had always been coaxed and cosseted.

Laura trailed back from her honeymoon, listless and pregnant. Theodore, glad to be back in the business he understood, left her in her new household with Titus for company. At twenty, already getting into scrapes at medical school, Titus was the only friend she had. Young and foolish and beautiful, they clung together under the dark protection of Theodore's authority. Mrs. Hill, fortunately for Laura, was content to pay lip service to this guileless mistress provided she held the reins of house and kitchen, so they got on famously from the outset. But when Titus returned to the university Laura suffered isolation.

The birth of Edmund found her as unprepared for motherhood as she had been for marriage. In a nightmare of pain and embarrassment she reached out her hands for succor, and felt them clasped.

"Oh, help me!" she cried, over and over again.

"Now, now, now, my dear lady," said Dr. Padgett, "it will soon be over."

His fatherly manner, his kindness, and the chloroform set him in her mind on the level of the divine. She found it very comforting to be slightly ill from time to time, afterward. She and he made a little fetish of her headaches and indispositions: a substitute for love.

Theodore abstained from his marital duties, apparently without difficulty, for a few months after Edmund's birth. Then, according to some inner dictate, he committed solitary acts of violence until she was with child again. The second confinement was easier, but between dread of labor and nausea at the prospect of intercourse, Laura threw up so many symptoms that Dr. Padgett spoke to Theodore of her delicate constitution, and won her a long respite.

Blanche Victoria Crozier was born four years later, after Laura had ceased expecting any happiness with her husband. He did not come to see her until the following morning, and his inspection of the baby was perfunctory. Weak and sick, she realized that she had disappointed him, though she did not know how. The explanation was given as briefly and brutally as any of his physical connections.

"I have two sons," he said, as though they were no part of her, "and that is enough. Their education will be costly, but worthwhile. I consider that my duty as a father is fulfilled."

Strapped in the corset which prevented her from any but the most restricted movements, entering on the six weeks of compulsory convalescence, Laura indicated the white organdy cot with a flutter of one hand.

"See how pretty she is, Theodore, even for such a young child."

"You must rest now," he pronounced. "I shall not disturb you further, Laura."

Nor did he. The next six years found them sharing the same bed like two strangers who are anxious to have no contact. The pattern was set: rigid, sterile, meaningless. He had beaten down any shows of affection early in their marriage. Sure of herself, practiced in the arts of charming, she required a sterner snubbing than mere indifference. He administered this also.

"Really, Laura, such behavior is not only childish, it is distasteful. Do not touch me, if you please!"

So even the warmth of proximity was rejected. But appearances were paramount. He set his cold lips to her cheek each morning and each evening, put cold hand beneath her elbow to guide her. Knowing the emptiness beneath the show, she came to dread this too. Sometimes, in a fit of perversity, he would inflict his attentions upon her in order to enjoy the shrinking.

The seasons turned, the years passed. Dr. Padgett recommended sea air. She paced deserted promenades, sat in vacant hotels, took water cures. Her thoughts turned increasingly upon her childhood, when love seemed to be her birthright, but that lover had retreated into old age and silence. There was no returning. When he died she wept bitterly and only Titus showed kindness. Only Titus was allowed to show kindness, for Theodore was jealous. He permitted compliments at a safe distance, callers who did not stay too long, friends who showed no sign of becoming confidantes.

Because he was devoted to his brother he did not mind him, and Titus's influence became absolute. At first he leaned on Laura, who played the mother. Then they were children together and equal. Finally, understanding her, divining the situation, he began to make love to her. Her response, in spite of herself, worried and exalted him. She made a brave attempt to interpret their relationship as the movement of soul toward soul. He helped her to fail. Fifteen years of emotional and physical deprivation completed the conquest.

In those two hours at his rooms, while Henry Hann absentmindedly flicked flies from the horses' necks, Laura endeavored to feel repulsion and could not. All that her mother had told her, and all she had learned from Theodore, was proved false. Her inability to control either herself or him terrified her. The remembrance of her behavior was agony, the compulsion degrading. Shaken, humiliated, she avoided seeing him for a week afterward, and then found herself beset by a need she had overlooked. She had thought that if she could put the incident behind her she might go back to their former relationship. Instead, she longed to discover the new one, to build stone on shameful stone, and achieve what? And she could not.

The experience sharpened all her senses. She became aware of Theodore as a man, and watched him. For years she had thanked God whenever her husband left the house, and clutched her privacy to herself if he was kept late in the City. Now she wondered why he was late, and noticed discrepancies. She would have shrieked for help, whatever the consequences, however iron-strong the proprieties, if he had used her as his wife. But she could not bear the thought of infidelity on his part.

She had been bitterly cheated, and desired that the cheat should be cheated also. If they were bonded even to death he must not go free, for that left her more sad and solitary than ever before. She required him to be unfulfilled with her, since his was the sin of omission.

The letter from Titus brought one sorry ray of comfort. He, too, had been scorched and wished to burn. She tore it up, weeping, and threw the pieces in her wastepaper basket.

Later, frightened of discovery, she went back to her room to retrieve them but they were gone. There was no reason to suppose that Harriet would know the difference between these and any other torn papers, and Kate's loyalty was complete. Yet now and again she regretted that she had not set a match to them and so rendered her mind easy.

Now, sitting obediently beside her sleeping husband, she said very softly to herself, "I should have died before I met him, and then all this need not have been."

5

*Laurel is green for a season, and love
is sweet for a day;
But love grows bitter with treason,
and laurel outlives not May.*
                    Algernon Charles Swinburne
                    The Triumph of Time

Sufficiently improved to render their lives tedious, Theodore insisted on hearing all the details of the epidemic: tutting sympathetically. Oppressed, Laura settled him down for a couple of hours, and retired to her parlor.

It was a quiet time of day, while her staff recuperated from their morning labors and were not yet involved with the evening meal. The cook snored by the range. Harriet exchanged whispered reminiscences with Annie Cox. Henry Hann drank, unwanted, in his room over the stable. In the linen room, Kate's needle was dexterous with the lace on Laura's dressing jacket. Nanny Nagle, her afternoon free, met Sergeant Malone, with whom she had had an understanding for years, and gossiped as he twirled his mustaches and swaggered by her side. The boys were back at school, and Blanche had been taken to Mr. Barnum's circus at Olympia with a party of small friends. Here, Sam Lockhart's six extraordinary and wonderful performing elephants, just arrived from the Continent, especially and exclusively engaged at enormous cost, enchanted their young audience.

The book of poems slipped from Laura's lap as she slept, and she returned it with a start and smoothed the page.

> Go from me. Yet I feel that I shall stand
> Henceforward in thy shadow. Nevermore
> Alone upon the threshold of my door
> Of individual life . . .

The doorbell brought Laura to her feet, then she sat again and slid the book beneath a cushion.

"Are you at home, ma'am?" Kate Kipping asked quietly, popping a frilled cap around the parlor door. "I thought I had best ask first, in case you were resting."

"No, Kate, thank you. I am not at home."

"Very well, ma'am." She paused. "Suppose it should be Mr. Titus, ma'am?"

"He will not come before this evening. But would you say that I have a headache? He will have come to see Mr. Crozier."

"Yes, ma'am."

The bell rang again, imperiously, and Laura reclined on one elbow, listening to the murmur of voices, the sharp closing of the door.

"Excuse me, ma'am," said Kate, evidently disturbed, "but it was a strange lady, with these," and she held out a package, robustly wrapped in brown paper and sealed with red wax. "The lady would not leave her name, ma'am, and she said I was only to give this into Mr. Crozier's hands. But, seeing he was resting, I thought it best to bring it to you."

Laura took the package and read the directions carefully.

"What did the lady say, Kate?"

"She said it was private business and could I deliver it to the master personally. I took the liberty to say that the master was still abed poorly, and could it not be given to Mr. Titus since it was business? But she said it was a confidential matter for Mr. Theodore."

Laura turned the package over and over. Her husband's name was underlined twice in red ink, and printed very large and stiff.

"How strange she did not give her name. What was the lady like?"

"The lady was not exactly a lady, ma'am," said Kate cautiously.

"I do not comprehend you."

"Well, ma'am," said Kate, coming closer, "she seemed modest and refined enough at first sight, but her dress was not quite . . . and she wore a heavy veil as if she did not want me to see her face. But perhaps her complexion was poor, ma'am."

"A working girl?"

"Why no, ma'am. Her dress was a deal too showy for that. And her voice, ma'am, the way she spoke. Very mincing, and then downright common when she spoke fast. And she smelled of patchouli, quite strong."

A tacit understanding lay between them. Kate had given all the information she could, and Laura had interpreted it. Now both must render the information outwardly acceptable.

"I think it must have been one of Mr. Crozier's new clerks, Kate. If she was trying to better herself she would perhaps try to make a good impression. We must not be uncharitable if she failed. She would be too shy, possibly, to leave her name."

"Yes, ma'am, that would explain it. I hope I did right to bring the package to you."

"You were quite right, Kate. I shall see that Mr. Crozier receives it as soon as he wakes. You may bring me tea here at a half after four. Miss Blanche will not be home until six o'clock."

Alone, she read and reread the printing, felt and shook the package. It remained inscrutably sealed, and she neither would nor could open it without detection. Kate had referred to it as "these," and Laura now tried the parcel for flexibility. Letters, probably. These. Letters. For about twenty minutes she sat thinking, then mounted the staircase with more resolution than usual.

"I was sleeping," her husband complained. "Can I have no peace in this household?"

"We have been married for fifteen years, Mr. Crozier," said Laura, her pride and dignity damaged, "and I think you will agree that I have been a dutiful wife."

He sat up amazed, nightcap askew.

"Well, ma'am, that is a matter of opinion. But what of it? Is this"—and he waved an arm at the William Morris wallpaper—"not evidence enough of my indulgence? I told you it would tire the eyes. We should have been wiser to buy a flocked paper," and he glared at the pomegranates.

"I have endeavored to please you," Laura persisted, "and very often against my inclination—sometimes against my personal belief. I had not expected to be insulted in this fashion!" And she flicked the packet on the bed.

Annoyed, confused, he reached for a paper knife and began to prize off the seals: face set against her.

"Before you open it, since you appear to think it of little import," said Laura, one hand at her throat, "I must tell you that it was delivered by a woman of doubtful respectability, who wished it to be given only into your hands and described it as confidential business."

He laid down the paper knife and looked at her.

"She was heavily veiled, so Kate told me. Her clothes, her manner, her speech, proclaimed her to be something other than one of your clerks. Yet she dressed too showily for an ordinary working girl. Furthermore, she was most secretive. She did not leave her name, and she implored Kate to deliver this package direct to you."

[75]

"Then why did Kate not do as she was told?"

Because she was loyal to me.

"Because she knew you were resting, and so entrusted it naturally to your wife. And why should your wife not be trusted?"

He was as white as herself now, tapping the package thoughtfully.

"This is private business, Laura, and I must be careful."

"You must be *secretive!*" she cried, casting off years of restraint. "Who is this woman? She stank of cheap perfume. What is her name? What is she to you? Why are you away in the evenings? Do you go to her? Do you? I know you are not always at business. Titus came once, expecting to find you at home, when you told me you were together."

"Be silent!" he said furiously. "I will not be questioned in this manner. I have told you this is private business. I have rivals, you know. I have—enemies, even. I employ—certain people—people you would not receive—to watch over certain aspects of my business. So that you can dress as you do, among other things," and he gestured at the fine lace blouse and black tailored skirt, at the great cameo pinned to her high collar. "My duties toward you, Mrs. Crozier, are fulfilled. I beg you to remember your duty toward me. Obedience was one of your vows, if you recollect."

She was weeping, beside herself. He watched her, angry and puzzled.

"Then open it, in God's name," she begged, reaching for the handkerchief tucked at her waist. "Open it while I am here, and show me that I am wrong."

His fingers lingered over the package and withdrew. His expression hardened.

"You forget yourself, madam. I do not have to prove my honor. It is absolute. Now please to go."

She stared at him over the handkerchief.

"You do not care what I suspect?" she asked, astonished.

"You are not yourself, Laura. I suggest that you lie down for an hour with the blinds drawn, and come to your senses."

"You would leave me, perhaps to the end of our lives together, not knowing what this person meant to you?"

"I order you to leave this room."

"You do not care enough for me even to confide in me?" she said.

It was a revelation. Dark and withdrawn, he considered his wife and the package.

"Mrs. Crozier, it is *seldom*—I hope, in most cases, *never*—that a husband finds it necessary to speak to his wife as I must. When we first married I observed some lightness in your nature which I set down as girlish folly, and which I am happy to say has since been eradicated."

"Lightness?"

"A tendency to foolish behavior. You were pure and innocent. I know that. But there are certain duties which—I express myself as delicately as possible—must be performed between husband and wife. They are duties, madam, not pleasures. One does not marry for pleasure."

Colorless, she sat down in a chair and observed him with cold self-possession. Heedless of her moods, unless they disquieted him, he spoke half to her and half to himself, his eyes upon the package.

"One marries in the sight of God for the purpose of procreation. I am grateful to you, Mrs. Crozier, for my two sons, who will—now they are out of your spoiling—be of some consequence in life. The British empire is the greatest the world has ever known. Edmund and Lindsey will be dedicated to its service. I can think of no finer goal."

"You have a daughter, too," said Laura bitterly.

"Whose tastes, I hope, may not become as extravagant as your own."

"Surely you wish me to dress becomingly, and according to your station?"

"But not so expensively, madam. Your milliner's bills alone are beyond everything!"

"Wait!" she said, dangerously quiet. "Let us not interrupt this sermon on my duties, Mr. Crozier, by dragging in a milliner's bill for which you have twice reprimanded me already. So I have given you two sons and burdened you with a daughter? I keep your home as it should be kept. May I not ask for a little affection and trust in return?"

"You had both, and a measure of respect which I do not wish to lose—though your behavior puts it in some peril, madam."

She swept the packet from the bed with one blow of the hand, and it lay between them like a reproach.

"I have *nothing*," she cried, "*nothing*. And I hoped for so much."

Regarding her steadfastly, he issued a command.

"Control yourself, madam. You are hysterical. You do not know what you are saying."

"Duties," she cried. "Duties. No tenderness, no true kindness, no understanding. Do you suppose that Mr. Browning spoke of duties to his wife? He spoke of love, Mr. Crozier. *I* loved you when we were married."

"I thought we had dispelled this nonsense," he said, displeased. "A lady, Mrs. Crozier, a *lady* should be concerned with decorous and modest behavior. I do not ask for poetic phrases and lavish demonstrations. I do not wish them. I do not require them. The conversation is closed, and I shall endeavor to forget that it ever took place."

Her arms fell to her sides.

"You have spoiled yourself with weeping," he added dispassionately. "Do not allow the servants to see you in such a wild condition. Now please go."

Submissively, wretchedly, she dried her eyes and cheeks. Inclined her head, beaten. Then, with her hand on the doorknob, she paused. Torn between fear and misery, the misery came uppermost.

"How can you bear to live as we do?" she whispered. "How can you endure it?"

Waiting for her to be gone, he spoke to the looking glass on the wall. In it they were mirrored: she bruised, he adamant.

"I am at a loss to discern your meaning, Mrs. Crozier. I suggest that you are not yourself."

6

Let's contend no more, Love,
Strive nor weep . . .
> Robert Browning
> *A Woman's Last Word*

Laura had moved into the guest room while the influenza lasted, and Kate found her there an hour later, crouched over the unlit grate.

"I took your tea to the parlor, ma'am. It's going cold," she said, affecting not to notice Laura's brooding posture. "It's starting to rain again, ma'am, but still mild for the time of year."

She pretended to be busy with the immaculate bedspread.

"Come downstairs in the warm, ma'am, do. You'll catch your death up here. Or shall I get Harriet to light the fire for you, and bring you a cup upstairs and you can lay down for a while?"

"I want no tea, Kate. You may dress me early for dinner. I shall rest in the parlor."

Kate rang the bell, and ordered Harriet to fetch up the copper cans of water, and then set a match to the fire herself.

"Shall you wear the watered silk, ma'am, to cheer your-self up a bit?" she asked. "The master's illness has fair worn you out. Or shall you have the blue velvet? You favor blue better than green to my mind."

"The blue will do well enough, thank you, Kate. Oh, do not bang those jugs down so, Harriet! You know how I suffer with my head!"

"Downstairs with you, Harriet," Kate whispered sharply. "What kind of lady's maid will you ever make, with your stupid clatter? Come, ma'am," encouragingly, "and I'll brush your hair. And Mrs. Hill would like to know shall Mr. Titus be stopping to his dinner? And Miss Nagle says should Miss Blanche come downstairs, being so late home this evening?"

"I cannot endure any more noise today," said Laura suddenly. "Let Miss Blanche go to bed after she has had her tea. I will come up and say good night to her. She can tell me about the circus tomorrow. And, Kate, since Mr. Titus is coming such a way to your master, I feel I must invite him to dinner. In spite of my headache. Perhaps it will have eased by then. Give me one of my powders, if you please, and a glass of water."

"Here, let me hold the glass for you, ma'am. You're all of a tremble. You've caught a chill, sure enough, sitting here in the cold."

"You had better tell Mrs. Hill," Laura said, remembering the volatile nature of her guest, "that Mr. Titus will not be staying, of course, if he has made other arrangements. Tell her I regret the inconvenience."

"Yes, ma'am. But it's easy to lay another place at table, and Mrs. Hill always cooks sufficient for extra visitors. That will be a bit of company for you after all the worry."

They savored the early-evening ritual, culminating with the brushing and piling of Laura's pale hair. Under Kate's skillful hands and quiet chatter, Laura recovered some of her spirits and all of her beauty. She was no less sad when she swept into the drawing room, but physically more buoyant. Titus bowed gallantly.

"You look so hearty!" she said, cheered by his good health, and she held out her hand. "I have a commission for you."

She moved gracefully to her chair, speaking over her shoulder, smiling. They had long been able to conduct a conversation without seeming to notice each other more than was needful. And though they were now alone they observed all the proprieties, so that no ears might hear or eyes note anything out of the ordinary. But they could not dissolve the magnetism that was like a third presence in the room.

"Your commands are my delight, Laura. What sort of commission? Do you require me to fetch the moon down for my charming niece, or for yourself?"

"Do not be so ridiculous," said Laura indulgently. "It is much more important than that. And almost as difficult and delicate."

"Indeed? You intrigue me. Pray avail yourself of my services."

"Shall you take a glass of Madeira? I will pour it myself?"

"It will taste a thousand times as sweet."

She handed him the glass, saying composedly, "I believe that Theodore has a mistress. I wish you to tax him with the knowledge, and then tell me."

As quick and composed as herself, he replied, "On what grounds do you base this accusation?"

"I think I shall drink Madeira, too," she said aloud, hearing Harriet's knock. And watched her mend the fire, and sipped.

"He has a mistress," she repeated, when the door closed, and told him of that afternoon's visitor.

"My dear Laura," said Titus, sitting opposite, crossing his legs, "what purpose would a confrontation serve?"

"I must know. It is my right to know."

"To quieten a guilty conscience, perhaps?"

She flushed. Then raised her glass steadily, and sipped steadily. Head on one side, Titus admired her.

"My dear Laura, even if this were true, what can you expect from your husband but a gentlemanly apology? Surely you are not imagining that this knowledge will give you some moral hold over him?"

"I know my position very well," she said vehemently. "I have no father or brother to speak for me, and no other home to which I can go. But I must know the truth. I will not let him treat me so. I will not."

"You are naturally distracted," Titus said idly, "and unable to weigh the situation with any degree of objectivity. Let me play the devil's advocate, Laura. If Theodore is amusing himself elsewhere—though I trust you not to betray my partiality for the lady's side of the argument—you may seek amusement on your own account. Provided you are discreet, and that should not be difficult. It is all in the family."

"I have asked a favor of you. I beg you to grant it. That is all I have to say. Except, that if you have no other engagement this evening I should welcome your company at dinner."

He shrugged, finished his wine, kissed her hand, and sought his brother's presence, while she stared into the fire as though it held some counsel, if only she could fathom it.

"I have had a most extraordinary interview with Laura," Theodore burst out, before Titus could inquire after his health. "I really think I must speak to Padgett about her. Perhaps she is run down again and needs a month of sea air. Still, at this time of the year, she would get no benefit from it. I do not understand her."

"Nevertheless, you seem remarkably improved, brother."

"I have learned to bear my cross," said Theodore sententiously. "I promised to cherish Laura in sickness.

What troubles me is the constancy of her complaints, and then their diversity. First her head, then her digestion, then sleeplessness, nerves, hysteria. What ails her?"

"She appears to believe that a lady of dubious morals has returned your love letters," said Titus, hands in pockets, and he sat on the end of the bed.

"Head full of romantic nonsense," Theodore grumbled. "Laura's behavior passes all comprehension at times. If you had seen her this afternoon you would have been astonished. She was—possessed."

"You do astonish me. And is there not a word of truth in this rumor? Was the dubious lady with the package a figment of Kate's imagination?"

"Come, brother, a man is not obliged to confess everything. A wife with any proper feeling would affect not to notice. Laura is too fond of her own way."

"Are not all the ladies? At any rate, this one returned your letters, I take it?"

Theodore hesitated.

"You amaze me," said Titus, grinning. "Such a pillar of rectitude, such a staunch supporter of God, queen, and country! I had thought you incorruptible. But you must set yourself right with Laura, if you will allow me to advise you. She is highly strung and inclined to be impulsive. Not devoid of one male relative—though at the moment she bewails the fact that her father is dead, and cannot use a horsewhip on her faithless husband. It would be a confounded nuisance if an enraged uncle made inquiries. Laura's portion is not inconsiderable, and invested in the firm."

"She would not so risk herself and me."

"Do not be too sure. Laura is capable of more than perhaps you reckon."

Theodore said tetchily, "Well, what would you have me do? No one is so close to both of us as you, Titus. Indeed"—and he laid a hand on his brother's shoulder—"I have always been able to say more to you than to anyone else, the last few years. It has been a lonely road, Titus, and often a dark one."

"Ah! One cannot speak to real ladies—charming as they are—as one can speak to a man. It is a pity that good women are so dull, and bad women so infernally cunning. One is caught between a yawn and a risk. A man does not know which way to turn at such times. Come, brother, you can confide in me, and I will make all well again. Have you paid for the letters, or did the lady return them out of sheer good will?"

He watched the struggle on his brother's face, with amusement and some compassion.

"You keep such a devilish tight rein on yourself, Theo," he observed kindly. "For God's sake, man, get yourself out of this entanglement and find a ballet dancer. I know the alleys of London as well as any tomcat. If you need eyes to guide you, use mine. For though you have acted the father to me, and I do not forget that, in some ways you seem younger than I."

"You do not know me as well as you imagine," said Theodore, pondering. He had made up his mind. "I confess I have been—unwise."

"Damned foolish," said Titus gaily. "Never put anything on paper, brother. Give them jewels, suppers, pay their bills or their rent, pay court, but never write it down. How much did she want?"

"A sizable sum, but not an impossible one. She has brought some half dozen letters, and retained the others, to persuade me. They are set on a scandal if I do not pay. I cannot afford a scandal. The difficulty is that I am bedfast for the time being."

Titus's expression was unreadable.

"There is more than one person involved, then?"

"A—protector."

"Good God," said Titus, horrified. "What a scrape!"

"This woman's visit was an indication that they mean to make it a bad business. If a female of her sort dares to knock at a respectable man's own front door—"

"You may use me as an intermediary."

"I thank you. But this affair I must, and shall, deal with myself."

"I see!" He smote the bedpost, thinking. "I should advise you, even more strongly, to set yourself right with Laura. We cannot fight on all sides at once. If she should write to her uncle . . ."

Theodore lifted his shoulders and let them drop, defeated.

"Tell Laura, then," he said with difficulty, and his face was as stern as if she were present, "that the lapse was single, and of small significance. That I was tempted and I fell. Such things do happen. Tell her, I was more sinned against than sinning."

"Eve proffered an apple," Titus suggested genially. "They do, you know!"

"Put it as you will. You say these things so much better than I."

"I should say something else, as well, with your permission."

"And what is that?"

"Ask her forgiveness," said Titus.

The silence between them was shattered by the sound of the dinner gong.

"I do not expect to hear any more of this matter from Laura," Theodore commanded. "Everything must be as it was between us, henceforth."

"And how was that?" Titus asked, rising.

"A fair and honorable arrangement."

"One tires, of course, of any woman in time," said Titus, puzzled. "At least, I do. Or I have done so far. But Laura has always seemed to me—judging her purely as my brother's wife—to be all that most men would desire.

"People do compliment me upon her," Theodore replied,

"and she is charming in company. But the spectator's view is a faulty one. I say this to you, when I would say it to no one else. I know Laura very well, and her temperament mars anything in her which I might have found attractive."

"You surprise me. I have always admired her spirit."

"A rebellious and a foolish one. It is a wife's duty to be submissive to her husband."

"I should have thought," said Titus, musing, "that a man of some persuasiveness could make Laura biddable enough."

"She is intractable."

Titus looked at him curiously.

"Forgive me," he said, "but what was the lady like who wrung those highly dangerous love letters from you?"

"Ah, that!" Theodore replied heavily. "That was a very different affair. A very different affair. Let us not speak of it again."

"Man errs," said Titus lightly, drinking his wine, "and woman forgives him ever."

"I do not forgive him. I do not and shall not."

"He has admitted his fault handsomely. He humbles himself before you. What more do you want, Laura?"

The food untouched upon her plate, she said, "Retribution."

"You combine the best qualities of both good and bad women. I love you for all of them."

She sat stricken, and pushed aside her dinner.

"Tell me," Titus continued easily, "did you ever love him?"

"At first I did. I thought him everything" She clasped her hands together upon the table before her, remembering. "I thought him wise and strong and handsome. I listened to him. Tried to please him. And then nothing. Coldness and misery."

"Still, you are jealous of this sordid little *affaire*. There must be some feeling left."

"Jealous?" she cried. "I am not jealous. I am *envious*."

He stared at her, astonished.

"You may smoke a cigar over your coffee, if you wish," said Laura, rising and ringing the bell. "I do not find them in the least objectionable. I am expected to do so, I know, but I do not."

He offered his arm, and they sauntered to the drawing room, while Harriet cleared the plates and glanced after them.

"Envious?" Titus repeated, interested.

"Why should he have a freedom that I am denied?" she asked forcibly. "Why should he keep a mistress, discard her, say he is sorry—and all is well? How dare he send me a message, ordering everything to be as it has been between us, henceforth?"

"That is the way of the world, Laura."

"It is unfair," she said to herself. "It is so unfair."

"I have offered you an alternative. One that you did not find unpleasant."

"I do not wish a temporary and dishonorable arrangement," she cried, turning on him. "Besides, how can you? You are his brother and he loves you. And you, in your fashion, love him. How can you use him so?"

Regarding the tip of his cigar he replied, "How can *you*?" And tapped the ash into a silver tray.

She was quiet again, her anger ebbing.

"He wrote her love letters," she said softly. "What must she have meant to him? He never wrote so to me. And Kate said she stank of cheap scent and was not a lady. What did he write, I wonder? Did he speak to her of duty and submissiveness?"

"I should think not, on the whole," said Titus, ironic. "He seems to have made a perfect fool of himself for once. The love letters amaze me."

"You have read them?" she asked quickly.

"No. Nor do I need to. The usual maundering."

"Like the one you wrote to me?"

His face changed.

Carefully, he replied, "The aberration of a moment. Did you destroy it?"

"Of course. I tore it to pieces."

"Very small ones, I trust?"

"I do not recollect. I expect so. It did not matter. I remember every word. Does that please you?"

Quietly, he replied, "Very much."

"Then cherish the thought of it," she said hopelessly, "as I do."

"Did I maunder nicely?" he asked, at last.

"Almost as nicely as Mr. Browning." She smiled suddenly, and said, "I wish we could be again as we were in the beginning, Titus. You were a boy with me, then, and we basked in Theodore's protection and were each other's confidants."

"The days of sweet and twenty. Did you love me then, Laura?"

"Very much, even when you got into such scrapes. Especially when you got into scrapes, I daresay, for you came to me first. But not as I do now."

"And when did we put away childish things?"

They were at one, somewhere in the past, looking for a signpost they had not noticed, or had ignored.

"When Blanche was born," Laura said, seeming to speak at random, "Theodore had waited all day in his study. He did not come to see me, or her, though she was pretty even as a newly born baby. Afterward, I discovered why. She was a daughter, another expense to him. He loves his sons only. He told me that he regarded my duty as done, and no doubt thought I should be relieved to hear it. As I was."

"A cold brute," said Titus reflectively. "This business of the letters puzzles me. He sought his pleasures secretively. I wonder why he troubled to marry if the gutters served him so much better."

Laura laughed, genuinely amused.

"He married because marriage is expected of a good citizen. Theodore cares very much what the world thinks of him. I was considered a catch on the marriage market. Eighteen years old with five hundred a year of my own, born of a prosperous merchant family in Bristol, and regarded as something of a beauty. He, too, was highly marketable."

She was bitter, remembering.

"I thought him very handsome. Grave and clever. Eminently capable of caring for me and protecting me. He kept a part of the bargain. He set me up in an elegant establishment within reach of London. He gave me financial security and a position that might occasion envy in most women. He gave me nothing else."

"The fire is low," said Titus. "Shall I ring for more coals?"

"No. Let it die. It is almost ten o'clock. You must go soon." She continued, "Yes, it was after Blanche was born. I can guess what he must have said to Dr. Padgett. 'I am aware that I have a daughter, and that my wife and she are doing well. I do not wish to see the child. If anyone should need me I am in my study.' My pride was hurt. I had not wanted him, but I did not like to think that he no longer wanted me at all."

Titus smiled and she smiled back at him in pure friendship, as they shared her little flash of vanity.

"Oh yes," she went on, though he had said nothing. "Vanity and pride are two vices we have in common, you and I. Then, gradually, I found I was free. Free from him, free from the terror of childbearing. I began to look about me, to read poetry and novels again, to take an interest in world affairs. You helped me in this! I was only twenty-five and I could breathe a little."

He lit another cigar, watching and listening. Older, harder, infinitely more attractive than the pretty boy to whom she had played mother in the early years of her marriage.

"That was when I began to put away childish things," said Laura. "I read the poems of Robert Browning, of Elizabeth Barrett. I thought them somehow shameless and yet pure. I knew, though I was not supposed to know, something of your own wild life. Once I asked Theodore. He told me there were two kinds of love, the sacred and the profane. Then he commanded the subject to be closed, henceforth, as this latest subject must be closed. I knew the sacred to be a dead and wretched thing. I knew nothing of the profane. I knew also that, in some way, the Brownings had combined them"

"It was unwise," said Titus, kindly enough, "to turn from one brother to the other, in search of further knowledge."

"Do you think I did not comprehend that? I say more. I should never have turned to you on my own account. Yours was the first step. Was it not?"

"A long and arduous one. I have never taken so much time over anyone else. My indisposition served me in the end. You were a loving nurse."

She mused over the dying fire, indifferent now either to teasing or to cruelty.

"No, it happened before then," she said. "These things happen in the mind, randomly, suddenly, and take root. It was in the hall," she realized. "You had come very late, in some usual difficulty, and Theodore went down to let you in. Even though he was so angry, he still loved you, and he said—to cover up this dubious weakness—'Titus, you are a confounded nuisance!' "

"And I said, 'Then throw me out. I deserve nothing better!' "

"I was standing at the top of the stairs and you looked up, seeking support. And I could not help laughing. And Theodore smiled at you, and at me, as he so rarely smiles. We were happy, for once, the three of us. You had snow on your cape."

"You wore a white wrapper, edged with lace."

"Yes. That was when."

Titus extinguished his cigar. Humbly he went over to her and raised her hands to his lips.

" 'Let's contend no more, Love, strive nor weep,' " he said into her palms. " 'All be as before, Love—only sleep.' "

She did not answer, reclining in her chair, two long years away. So he touched her cold cheek lightly, bade her good night, and let himself out.

7

Home is the girl's prison and the woman's workhouse.
George Bernard Shaw
Man and Superman

Theodore exploited the furthest limits of his illness, and clutched upon postinfluenzal depression with all the talent of a professional hypochondriac. His return to business was accompanied by martyrdom, and his homecomings by outbursts of bad temper. Even Titus's good nature was strained to capacity, though his gift for ignoring life's annoyances served him nobly.

February came in, cold, frosty, foggy, mirroring the present relationship between the Croziers. Together they agreed, without saying so, to let a little sunshine play upon them in the form of Titus, who was always ready to entertain.

Kate Kipping had succumbed to the influenza, and Annie Cox rose from her own flock mattress to help out Harriet. Nanny Nagle and Blanche had shared the illness: the one in great discontent, the other with patient acceptance. But Mrs. Hill soldiered on, upholstered by her excellent catering; and, as Henry said of himself, the demon drink kept all other demons off. Harriet, red-cheeked and hearty, waited on at the dinner which should have brought an evening's harmony to the household.

"Where is Kate?" Theodore demanded, over Harriet's willing head.

"She is still abed, Theodore."

"Stuff and nonsense. Coddling herself because you spoil her. Watch what you are doing, girl!" As Harriet spilled the brown Windsor soup. "Take that back to the kitchen. I will not drink soup from a slopped plate."

"Come, brother," said Titus cheerfully. "You frighten her into further feats of clumsiness—and the poor wench is clumsy enough already, God knows. Her hands are not so pretty as Kate's, either!"

"I beg of you, Theodore," Laura pleaded, though with an edge to the plea that brought Theodore's head up, "do not so discompose Harriet that we have no dinner at all. Mrs. Hill has gone to some pains, and the girl does her best."

"Which is not nearly good enough. She has been here some years. Harriet, how long have you been with us?" As she returned, scarlet from a kitchen scolding as well as a dining room one.

"Six, sir."

"And have you not learned to wait at table correctly in all that time? If you cannot manage without help, fetch someone else from downstairs."

"Whom would you like?" Laura asked, dangerously serene. "Mrs. Hill or Annie Cox the kitchenmaid?"

"Please, ma'am," murmured poor Harriet. "I don't think as Annie would be suitable."

"No more do I. Carry this soup plate very carefully, if you please."

Theodore drank from it in suppressed anger, glancing at his wife.

"You are not taking anything, I see, Laura. Are you feeling unwell?"

"I rarely feel well, but I have not caught the influenza, if that is what worries you, Theodore."

"I saw a most capital show at the Egyptian Hall the other week," said Titus. "It was the Moore and Burgess Minstrels, and the theater is now illumined throughout by electric light. You would have laughed so much, Laura. There was a gloriously funny sketch, called the Phour Phunny Phellows. The *f* spelled as *ph*. Really capital!"

"I do not care for such things," said Theodore. "Take this plate away, girl, and hurry. Is Kate not well enough to get up for an evening, Laura?"

"She has scarcely been abed four days. You took a fortnight, if you remember. She will get up tomorrow, Theodore."

The soup plates were slippery, and Harriet made the mistake of setting the tureen on top of them, from which perch it slithered gracefully to the carpet.

"I cannot have this. I really cannot. Fetch that other girl from the kitchen to help this one. And tell her to bring a damp cloth or there will be a mark in the carpet. It is a very good Indian carpet. I will not have it marked."

"Bring Annie, Harriet, but let her stay outside the door during the serving," whispered Laura.

Ducking her head to hide her tears, the housemaid retreated.

"I was fortunate to hear something you would have liked very well," Titus interposed. "Sir Charles Hallé and his Manchester Band performed most agreeably in the St. James's Hall on February 7. It was a final appearance before he departed for Australia on tour."

Theodore did not answer, tapping his fingers on the table, watching for the maids.

"They gave the Concerto for Two Violins, in D minor, Laura. The one you like so much, by Bach. And there was the *Peer Gynt Suite*. And the *Eroica*."

"How elegant!" she cried, watching Theodore watch for trouble.

Annie Cox crept in, paralyzed by the presence of the great and powerful, with a wet cloth in her red hands. Under Theodore's outraged eyes she cleaned the soup from the carpet, bobbed a curtsy, and disappeared.

"Is that the kitchenmaid, Laura?"

"Certainly it is the kitchenmaid. We do not employ anyone else."

He motioned Harriet to go out, and she, carrying a saddle of mutton, collided with Annie and put the joint in some peril. Together, they trembled in the hall, waiting for orders.

"I dislike your tone, Mrs. Crozier," said Theodore softly. "I dislike it exceedingly. I beg you to change it, madam, or you and I will disagree."

She opened her mouth to answer him, was silenced by a rapid movement of Titus's hand, and closed it.

"Now, if you are in a correct frame of mind, madam, we will continue with dinner. Harriet!"

Had the tension been less, or humor stronger, the efforts of Harriet and Annie would have caused more amusement than the Phour Phunny Phellows. As it was, Laura ceased to eat at all, and Theodore's progress was punctuated by exclamations of disgust. Alone among them, Titus struggled against a desire to laugh.

"It is like a concerto for two violins that are out of tune!" he ventured, as they went for the castle puddings.

Laura and Theodore stared past him, unhearing, into their two dark separate worlds. He shrugged, and wiped a drop of gravy from the cloth.

"Mr. Tree and the Haymarket Theatre Company are appearing at the Crystal Palace in *A Man's Shadow*, Laura. It has had enormous success. I must take you both to see it."

"That would be most delightful," she replied, colorless with anger.

"Or Imre Kiralfy's *Nero* is still on, and much praised. Let us arrange an evening."

"I thought we *had* arranged an evening, at my house," cried Theodore to his wife. "But apparently Mrs. Crozier is unable to order her servants properly."

"I will not bear this!" she answered, casting down her napkin. "You have spoiled what little appetite I had. I ask you to excuse me."

"Sit down, madam!" Theodore shouted. "Sit down. I order you!"

For a moment she looked as though she would faint, then sat again. During the remainder of the meal, which she did not eat, she watched Harriet upset Theodore's castle pudding on its side and spill the egg custard, without comment. Titus made no more effort to stem the flood of his brother's bad temper. The maids got through as best they could, and breathed relief as they set down the decanter of port and the dish of walnuts.

"May I go now?" Laura asked, and walked trembling to her drawing room.

"I beg pardon, ma'am," Harriet whispered, managing the coffee cups without disaster. "I do beg pardon. I meant to do like Kate. I did indeed."

"It is of no consequence. We are all a little upset by the illness in the house. You may go now, Harriet. Please to congratulate Mrs. Hill on the dinner."

"Yes, ma'am. Thank you, ma'am."

Titus and Theodore were not ten minutes over their port. He had thought of a fresh humiliation, and was anxious to put it into execution.

"Mrs. Crozier," he said, over his cup, "you are still in the guest room"

"I thought it best until all the infection is cleared."

"You say you are not ill, and Padgett tells me one cannot catch the influenza twice. You must come back to your own bedroom as is right and proper."

"Very well," she replied slowly. "I will ask Kate to move my things tomorrow, if that is what you wish."

"I wish you to have your things moved at once. Tonight."

It was open war, and she stared about her for an answer or an ally.

"Why, brother, you must curb your ardor," said Titus gaily and unwisely. "Your staff has shortcomings enough at the moment, without making a muddle of two bedrooms. Besides, they will be at their own supper—unless Harriet dropped that mutton on the stairs!"

Theodore rang the bell.

"Harriet, fetch Mrs. Crozier's toilet articles and clothes from the guest room and put them in the main bedroom."

She had been eating, and wiped her mouth quickly on her sleeve.

"Yes, sir. Anythink else, sir?"

"Get that girl Annie to put more coals on the fire. I feel the cold!"

"I do not think I can survive Annie's attention with the coals," said Titus humorously.

"Out!" Theodore shouted, and Harriet ran. "I will not be plagued by your wit, sir," he cried to Titus. "It is ill enough that I must be plagued by my wife's bad management and her undutiful attitude toward me."

"You must forgive me," said Titus, as pale as Laura, "but your own attitude leaves so much to be desired. I find it monstrous to witness you humiliating Laura in front of me. You have never been a warm man, brother, and you have often been a stern one, but never so discourteous."

"Do not quarrel, pray, upon my account!" Her distress was evident. "If you should quarrel with Titus, where could I find a friend?" she asked her husband. "He is the only friend you allow me. If anyone seems in my favor you find an excuse to dismiss them. It has always been so. I am surrounded by acquaintances whom I dare not know. What life is worth such a price?"

Relieved to be spared the necessity of annihilating Titus, Theodore turned upon the property he did not care for and could annihilate at leisure.

"You are not fit to choose your own friends," he cried. "Your notions of propriety are hazardous in the extreme. Who knows what rag, tag, and bobtail you would introduce into my house if I let you? I will not be flouted."

"I wish that I were dead," she wept. "I wish I could die."

"My heart is racing," he murmured to himself. "I must not let her distress me. Laura! I had better lie down. Go upstairs and see that those maids are out of our room. I coughed all morning, because of the fog. I may have bronchitis. I do not feel at all well. Perhaps Padgett is wrong and one can catch the influenza twice. Laura, control yourself, and attend to me if you please. In sickness and in health, you said, until death us do part . . ."

"And what was all that about?" Mrs. Hill demanded, rather greasy with the mutton.

"Ooh, such goings-on as you never did see," said Harriet, sitting down to her food, which had been kept warm on the range. "They've had a row to end all rows, and the master's in bed with the mistress running up and down after him, and Mr. Titus a-smoking his cigar and staring in the fire. I never heard the like, did you, Annie?"

All eyes and bones, the kitchenmaid nodded and then shook her head.

"I'd best send some more coffee in, when they've settled down," said Mrs. Hill comfortably. "How's Kate, Harriet?"

"She would get up, when she heard I was a-moving Mrs. Crozier's things. What between her fussing over every fold, and the master shouting, and the mistress crying, I didn't

[99]

know where to turn. Kate says as she'll take the mistress's tea tomorrow."

"*They'll* be well away, then," observed Nanny Nagle, nodding in the direction of the drawing room. "Left to theirselves."

"You wouldn't say that, Miss Nagle, if you could see the upset. They don't sit still above a quarter of an hour. Mr. Titus has been up twice already, and the mistress goes every so often, a-soothing of the master down."

"I'll send some more coffee in," said the cook. "Eat up, Harriet, and then you can take it. It'll be a long time afore they let *you* wait on them again, my girl. I can prophesy that without a card on the table!"

8

—What sort of doctor is he?
—Oh, well, I don't know very much
about his ability; but he's got a
very good bedside manner!
                    Punch, 1884

"How does he seem after that outburst?" Titus asked.

"Fretful, but quieter," said Laura, very white. "I have promised him that I will attend him myself. Only the sight of my misery at such times really appeases him." She sauntered the length of the room and brooded at the window. "So I shall leave you every so often," she added drily, pacing the carpet again. "How often do you think he requires to feel his power over me? Every half hour? Perhaps every twenty minutes, until he sleeps, since he has been so deeply disturbed. Yes, every twenty minutes should be sufficient reminder of my duty toward him. I must go upstairs every twenty minutes like a devoted wife."

He was concerned with more than her wretchedness.

"I had better not stay long this evening, Laura. There is no point in making further trouble between the three of us."

"As you think best. Titus, I should like to thank you," and she laid a hand on his sleeve. "You spoke for me."

He covered her hand with his, absently, but the frown still lay between his brows. She divined that he was regretting his chivalry, and her gratitude became irony.

"I fear that even my championship is of small account in his eyes," said Titus, restless.

"It was of no account at all—except to me. Perhaps you had better see him before you go, and make amends?"

His face cleared. Relaxed and gay, sure of his charm, he reached for the decanter of port.

"This should ameliorate matters considerably! And it will help him to sleep." He turned at the door, and read the bleakness in her eyes. "I shall not take back what I said, Laura."

She replied. "Of course not, Titus, I understand perfectly."

He was back again in a few minutes: boyish, self-deprecating.

"I forgot the glasses!" he cried, and quoting Dickens's Miss Mowcher added, " 'Ain't I volatile?' " with a grin, seizing two of Theodore's best Waterford.

She neither looked at nor answered him, watching the clock.

"Mrs. Hill says, ma'am, excusing me coming in like this," said Harriet, who had hoped to find her mistress locked in a wild embrace, "that would you be wanting some more coffee?"

"Yes, if you please, Harriet. I shall be sitting here until Mr. Crozier goes to sleep. And, should Miss Nagle offer to watch by him, you might tell her that he expressly asked *me* to do so. Oh, Harriet, that is Mr. Titus coming down the stairs now. You might see him out."

Hauling on his greatcoat, settling its handsome cape, back in favor at what cost of flattery and betrayal?

"I have left the decanter by his bed. The port seems to have made him sleepy and that is all to the good. There is little the matter with him—"

"You may go, Harriet!" Laura ordered, seeing her evident interest.

"I daresay he has another of those heavy colds coming on him, though he swears it is the influenza and the bronchitis and his heart and his liver, and the Lord above knows what else. But there is little the matter in my opinion."

"I can tell you what is the matter with him," said Laura bitterly. "A cold heart and a black temper, and there is no curing either."

Seeing that they were alone he bent to kiss her cheek, but she averted it.

"We are not observed," he said softly, courting her with a smile.

"A kiss can betray, nevertheless."

He looked at her quickly, flushed up, and let himself out without a word. Alone with the coffee, Laura poured herself a cup until her self-appointed time for humiliation came about. Then she trailed up the stairs again.

"The port has made me thirsty!" Theodore complained.

But he seemed a little more subdued. It was a grumble, not a tirade. She poured water and helped him to drink.

"What time is it?"

"Ten o'clock. Titus has gone home. How do you feel now?" she asked, with the correct amount of deference due to his condition.

"I feel as though I could sleep, but there is a heaviness about me, a languor. I fear I have a heavy cold coming on—unless it is something more serious."

"I daresay it is nothing at all but the weakness left over from the influenza, and the wine you have taken this evening, Theodore."

"Perhaps you are right. If I am no better tomorrow you must send for Padgett!"

"Of course, Theodore!" She hesitated, needing the little privacy of her empty drawing room, knowing it must be sacrificed also if he required it. "Do you wish me to sit by you?"

"No, no, no. I wish to be undisturbed. But you must come up as you promised. You must not go to sleep until I am settled."

In relief, she said, "I shall come up to see how you are. You need not fear I shall fail in that respect."

He mumbled something and turned on his side.

"If you will mend the fire, Harriet," said Laura, as the housemaid appeared at the bend of the staircase, "you may go to bed. You may all go to bed. I shall require nothing more tonight. I shall not retire until Mr. Crozier is comfortable."

"Very well, ma'am. How is the master, ma'am?"

"He seems more easy now, Harriet."

Her vigil ticked around the clock, and she observed it punctiliously, treasuring the hours on her own even when Theodore obviously slept. Shortly before midnight she turned down the lamps and mounted the stairs for the last time that evening. With some difficulty she undressed herself, but was balked by the obstacle of her stays. After two or three ineffectual attempts to unlace them she slipped on her wrapper and sought the attic, knocking softly. Harriet's voice answered her from the dark.

"I am afraid I cannot manage to undress without some assistance," Laura whispered. "I forgot, with Mr. Crozier being indisposed, that I should need help."

Harriet crept out of a hard bed and shivered up to Laura, red hands more awkward than usual. But she longed to be a lady's maid, and Kate was fortunately asleep.

"Hold on to the post, ma'am," she whispered. "I should've thought, but I didn't."

Both women held their breath. Harriet pulled valiantly. The laces spread into freedom, and both women breathed out.

"Thank you, Harriet. I am much obliged. I can manage now."

The maid crawled into bed again, and dreamed of promotion. Laura finished undressing in the warmth of her room, one ear cocked for Theodore's state of repose. He had been fairly restless, even in his first sleep, and though he seemed less so his breathing sounded noisy and distressed. Reluctantly, Laura trailed across the carpet and bent over him.

"What? What?" he grumbled.

"Are you not comfortable, Theodore?"

His eyes opened and he stared dully at the mane of pale hair, the pale face, and reached clumsily for her hand. She shrank back, clutching the wrapper to her breasts.

"My—head. My—head," he said, slurring the words.

Obediently, she laid a cool palm on his forehead.

"You have no temperature. Does it ache?"

"Dazed—feel—dazed. Thirsty."

She gave him water.

"You are half asleep, that is all. Have you any pain, Theodore?"

"Arms—heavy—legs—like—lead."

"It is nothing that a good sleep will not cure," she said, in soft desperation. "You should not have disturbed yourself so."

"Blood—pressure—Padgett warned—me—send—for Padgett."

"Do take one of my sleeping capsules, Theodore. Then if you cannot sleep we will send for the doctor."

She opened her little leather box and shook out one of two remaining pills. He did not resist her as she raised him and gave him more water to drink. But he mumbled and rolled his head from side to side as though it troubled him.

"Sit—by—me," he whispered, his fingers gripping her arm.

Huddled in the chair, she sat for an hour before disengaging her cramped hand. He had destroyed the little strength she gathered by being alone. She sought to regain it, and moved over to her writing desk. Until the clock struck two she wrote purposefully, earnestly, finding some comfort in her diary. Then she locked it up again, buried the key in a little bowl of potpourri, and blew out the candle, shivering from her vigil. His breathing seemed regular enough, but noisy. Satisfied that he would not now wake and disturb her, she felt for her glass of water and swallowed the other capsule. She could sleep in the armchair, in peace.

Kate was letting in the cold light of day when Laura opened her eyes.

. "Are you well, Kate?"

"Yes, ma'am. A bit on the weak side, but fair to middling. Your tea, ma'am, and your dressing jacket."

To the question of the maid's raised eyebrows, Laura shook her head. She intended to let Theodore snore on while she drank her tea in peace. So Kate poured out one cup and let her muse undisturbed. As the hot liquid woke her, she was aware that the snores were too frequent to be natural.

All the color had left his face. The night's beard growth stood out against a dusky pallor. Strong nose jutted. Eyes seemed sunk into stained sockets. Laboring breath fluttered blue lips. A thread of saliva, trickling from his mouth, had dried on his chin. Laura pressed the bell and kept her finger on it until Kate ran in.

"Quickly," Laura cried. "Send Henry for Dr. Padgett. Your master is very ill."

Then she sank into the chair by his side, hands over mouth, and stared at the deathly mask. She was still sitting there, white and frozen, when the doctor arrived.

"Here, Kate," he said, assisting Laura to rise. "Help your

mistress, will you? Brandy, girl, brandy. And warm clothes. Good God, madam, we cannot have you catching cold."

"I shall not go. I cannot go. Until you tell me," Laura whispered. "He is gravely ill, is he not?"

Kate wrapped a Shetland shawl about her and held her arm. Minutely, Padgett examined the unconscious man. Lifted the sunken lids and peered. Felt for the toiling heartbeat. Laid down the leaden limbs. Covered him gently. Nanny Nagle was waiting, wordless, by the door.

"A severe cerebral hemorrhage," he pronounced. "Take a good hold of your mistress, Kate! No hope, I'm afraid. Miss Nagle, I want you to sit by him while I am downstairs with Mrs. Crozier. Ring if you see any change. And where is Henry Hann? We must send for Mr. Crozier's brother at once. Mrs. Crozier will need all the support we can give her." He took her other arm. She seemed not to hear him, and he spoke across her as though she were indeed deaf. "A nervous disposition, Miss Nagle, suffers acutely at times like these. She was always highly strung."

Shock had anesthetized Laura. She drank the brandy they gave her and answered his questions with terrible calm.

"When did you observe this change in him?" Dr. Padgett asked. "I should judge that he must have been in this condition for some hours."

"Last night," she admitted with difficulty, "he complained of a heaviness in the limbs. He wanted to send for you. But I thought—"

"Yes, yes. He was inclined to worry unduly. You must not blame yourself if, for once, there was cause to worry."

"But I gave him one of my sleeping capsules," Laura said. "I did it for the best. I wanted him to sleep. I wanted to sleep myself. I blame myself."

She had so often wished him dead, but the reality appalled her. "I blame myself," she repeated.

The doctor sat by her, patting her hand, saying, "Fiddlesticks, ma'am! Fiddlesticks! The capsules were mild enough. One could not hurt him. Nothing could have hurt him."

He did not add that if she had sent for him straightway he might have done something. He knew the Croziers too well to blame the one or further distress the other.

"Your husband was inclined to cry wolf, ma'am," he said kindly. "You were not to know better. Do not fret yourself. Kate, stay with your mistress. Miss Nagle is with your master. Whom may I order to see to the child? Until Mr. Titus comes we are without a head."

"Mrs. Hill, sir, will see to everything. Should I tell her?"

"If you please, Kate, if you please. And hurry back."

Then he exerted his particular talent of giving confidence to the patient. Indeed, it was the only talent he possessed, for he was inclined to rely upon nature's powers of healing, and looked askance at newfangled notions. Had the queen herself not set an example of using chloroform for childbirth he would have opposed that too. But his sturdy body and deep voice, his simple character and good heart, were a form of medicine, and he did not stint the dose. Had anyone told him he was a little in love withLaura he would have been horrified and incredulous. As a respectable husband and practitioner such emotions were forbidden by the laws of God and man. As he abided by rules he set down his concern for Mrs. Crozier as paternal benevolence. Only, it was pleasant to speak to that troubled mouth and tumbled fall of hair, and hold those soft hands between his own.

Theodore never recovered consciousness. Loosing his grasp upon worldly goods, he sought oblivion and that deity in whose name he had reigned over his household. Downstairs, Henry Hann muffled the knocker with a black silk scarf and Harriet drew down the blinds. Kitchen chatter was subdued, and related only to the work in hand. Blanche sat silently, deprived of amusement, and suffered the *ennui* that normally attended Sundays only. Outside, under a winter sky, the Common was alive with elegant perambulators and starched nursemaids. Children bowled hoops, played hopscotch, shouted, and were reprimanded. And round the Common gleamed the house fronts: representatives of the good order that prevailed over one quarter of the earth's surface, and was called the British empire.

Laura turned distractedly from one to another person about the deathbed, and gave way to a storm of tears and self-reproach. Titus, troubled, hesitated to go near her but would have preferred to comfort.

"Come, sir," said Dr. Padgett, drawing a sheet over the stern face, "a brother's sorrow, though deep indeed, cannot be so great as that of wife for husband. Take Mrs. Crozier downstairs and offer her what solace you can. It is a good thing," he added to Alice Nagle, "that they were all so close. Mr. Titus will be a tower of strength to that poor lady."

Disapproval crackled from every crease of Nanny's apron. She sniffed loudly.

"You and Mrs. Hill must order the house between you for a while," he continued. "I fear that Mrs. Crozier's delicate constitution may have been overstrained. Watch her closely, and send for me if she seems more than commonly disturbed."

"Kate will watch her, sir," said Nanny Nagle stiffly. "Kate is the only one that you could call close to the mistress—among the staff, that is."

The funeral was of ostentatious magnificence. Titus, mindful of his brother's position, ordered it as Theodore himself would have done. Mutes, lifting black-edged handkerchiefs to their eyes, carrying long black staves, walked on either side of the procession. A dozen carriages followed the hearse. Across the Common they moved in stately measure. The subdued jingle of harness, the shuffle of feet, the restrained rumble of wheels, were a saraband to the dead. Within the glass-walled hearse the great walnut coffin rested beneath a mound of doomed flowers, which seemed to shiver in the winter afternoon as though they knew that the approach of night would wither them. In the first carriage, driven sadly and soberly by Henry Hann, Laura and Titus sat very straight-backed opposite the three straight-backed children. All was a rich unrelieved black, from the drooping plumes upon the horses' heads to the veil over Laura's face. The horses themselves were chosen for their silky somber coats, and trained to walk mournfully. Even the swish of a long tail, the flick of a long mane, was understated, never indulged. No hint of light or sparkle marred the cortege.

As they passed, men stopped and uncovered their heads, standing in silent respect. Women composed their features into masks of sympathy. Children stared openmouthed, solemn-eyed, at the terrible splendor of man's end. In St. Mary's churchyard the gravediggers blew upon their freezing hands and stamped their feet for warmth upon the freezing ground.

"Ashes to ashes and dust to dust . . ."

The silver trowel of earth in Laura's gloved hand.

". . . Resurrection to Eternal Life."

She had fainted, overcome by emotion and tight lacing. Murmurs of pleasurable concern, a waving of smelling salts, brought her wanly round. She had become the widow absolute: bereft of protection, prostrated with grief. It was all very sad, strangely satisfying, and very proper.

9

*An Englishman thinks he is moral
when he is only uncomfortable.*
George Bernard Shaw
Man and Superman

Dr. Padgett sat a long time with the letter in his hand, then folded and placed it with the other two in his breast pocket. Unsigned, printed in strong square capitals by someone unaccustomed to expressing himself literally, it had been posted in Wimbledon. The wording was brief, the meaning plain, the implications far-reaching.

Should he consult Mrs. Padgett? That stout good lady who had shared his bed and presided over her table for a quarter of a century? No, a woman's judgment in these matters would be faulty. He imagined her throwing up her hands, taking one side or the other according to her caprice, then gossiping over teacups.

He had discounted the first anonymous note, but preserved it out of uneasiness. The second disturbed him more profoundly. The third forced him to action. Normally he would have consulted Titus, as head of the Crozier family, but Titus was one of the parties named. It must be another man: cautious, trustworthy, objective. The Croziers' family solicitor, perhaps?

"My love," said Dr. Padgett, to the lady of his house, "I shall be away for half an hour or so. If there should be any urgent call I am with Mr. Fitzgerald."

Who was a small sharp man with large ears and an inquiring mind: a fox terrier of a person, bent on hunting out.

"I had thought," said Padgett to him, troubled, "that you could have printed a warning letter in *The Times*—or something of that sort?"

"Not a bit of it, my good sir. Not a bit of it. No, indeed. We must fetch this matter into the open."

"Poor Mrs. Crozier. Quite enough distress already. A nervous disposition. Further trouble to be strictly avoided."

"You speak as a medical man, sir, and quite rightly. I as a legal one, also rightly. And I can assure you that there is nothing here to be hushed up or smoothed over. Tongues are wagging, sir. They will wag the harder if we do not snip them short!"

"Then what do you advise, sir?"

"We must put these notes into the hands of Scotland Yard, sir, without delay. It will mean an exhumation. You are sure of the cause of Mr. Crozier's death, of course?"

"No doubt of it, sir. The late Mr. Crozier suffered from high blood pressure and his temperament was a gnawing one. How often have I warned him that worry could accomplish what the constitution might not? Ah, well. Take it from me, sir, postinfluenzal weakness coupled to an outburst of rage brought on that hemorrhage. Nature, sir, can work against us as well as for us. She didn't care to be badgered, sir, and she struck back! I would swear to that on my father's Bible—God rest him!"

"Then my client and your patient can come to no harm. Scotland Yard, sir, will not only clear the lady's name—and that of her brother-in-law—but may even track down the scurrilous villain who impugns their honor. Scotland Yard are uncommon sharp on ruffians, I hear. Eager hounds, sir, eager hounds. Glad to track down."

"The shock will prostrate her," Padgett mourned. "I would have spared her if I could."

"So would I, sir," said Fitzgerald, so busy over his morsel that he would not have let go for worlds. "But we must—in your own jargon—prescribe sour medicine to effect a cure."

Dr. Padgett smoothed the nap of his top hat.

"Would you accompany me, sir, to call upon Mr. Crozier and the lady? I feel we really cannot go straight to the police without informing them of our intention first?"

Fitzgerald consulted his fob watch with some complacency, and restored it to his waistcoat pocket in satisfaction.

"This evening at nine o'clock, then? We shall all have dined. Should you ask them if we might wait upon them, or shall I?"

"I will call as I pass," said the doctor. "I have done so frequently since her husband died. Mrs. Crozier's spirits are not as high as I could wish. I will not have her unduly alarmed if I can help it."

Titus was in great good humor when they arrived. He had dined well, and felt confident that Laura as a widow would be more amenable than Laura as a wife. True, she seemed subdued still, but she had lost her sadness. As head of the family, guardian of his late brother's children, and her official protector, the field was open and he prepared to wait. But he kept his cheerfulness within the bounds of decorum, disguising it as courtesy.

"My dear madam," Padgett began, while Fitzgerald sat up sharp and smiling. "I beg you to compose yourself. This is a shocking matter, but not irrevocably so—eh, my dear sir?"

"Certainly not," said Fitzgerald, head on one side, watching everyone. "Merely a distasteful formality, madam."

"I was not aware, Mrs. Crozier—how could I be?—that you had enemies," Padgett murmured. "But even unspotted virtue and peerless womanhood, it appears, may rouse vile envy in the human breast—"

"Get on with it, man, get on with it!" cried the solicitor tetchily, as Laura fingered her jet choker and grew paler.

"I have received three anonymous letters," said Padgett, glancing angrily at his colleague, "over which I took the liberty of consulting Mr. Fitzgerald. Like myself, he utterly denounces and repudiates these abominable slanders. But he feels they cannot be ignored."

Laura did not speak, only motioned him to continue, and sat very still.

"The first that came," Padgett mumbled, unfolding it and endeavoring to translate it into acceptable terms, "suggested that your late husband was poisoned by Mr. Titus Crozier in order that he could benefit by the terms of the will—"

"Which allows you full financial control over the family firm, you will recollect, my dear sir—subject to certain restrictions, of course!" Fitzgerald intercepted, giving Titus a very bright look.

Laura breathed quickly, and touched her jet as though it could ward off evil.

"The second, my dear madam," Padgett continued, embarrassed, "and I pray you to forgive me for being forced to mention such a matter, suggested that you and Mr. Titus were more closely acquainted—than relatives by marriage should be."

Fitzgerald eyed them, head tilted, no longer smiling. Laura shaded her eyes from the glare of the fire.

"Should I ring for your maid, madam?" Padgett asked anxiously.

"Please do not trouble," she replied clearly. "I am perfectly well. I am deeply shocked, and astonished, but I am perfectly well."

"The third," Padgett stated, "put together both villainous suggestions, and accused you and Mr. Titus of—of—

really I do not know how to express myself in the presence of a lady—of—"

"Adultery and murder," said Fitzgerald roundly, and noted the effect of his words.

Titus stood up and rested one arm on the mantelshelf, one patent-leather shoe on the fender, looking down at the flames. Laura drew a long breath, reached for her fan, and waved it languidly to and fro.

"I sincerely regret the necessity of this intrusion," said Padgett, agitated. "I do assure you that never, in all the years I have practiced, have I come across so monstrous an infamy. Such a slander!"

Laura snapped her fan shut.

"As head of the family," she said quietly, "Mr. Crozier must answer you. It is hardly my place to say what should or should not be done. Nor would I know how to advise anyone."

Even Fitzgerald was mollified by her behavior, resolute and yet modest.

"Very proper," he said, "very right and proper, Mrs. Crozier. Well, sir?" to Titus, who was not nearly so well in command of himself. "What do you think of this libel? Libel, sir, not slander," he added to Padgett. "Libel is written, slander is spoken. We must get our facts correctly, I think."

"I need hardly say that there is no word of truth in any of these statements, I take it?" Titus began.

"No sir, there is no need!" cried the doctor.

Fitzgerald made a gesture which might, or might not, have concurred with this remark.

"Is there no way in which the writer may be found and silenced?"

"I know of none, except through the police," Fitzgerald replied.

"Are there no private people who might be employed for such a purpose?"

"What, sir? Pursue them secretly and lay yourself open to blackmail? That would be a pretty pickle!"

"Laura," said Titus, "I am afraid that there is talk ahead of us, in any case, whatever we do," and he ventured to look at her.

Nothing could be divined from her expression. She looked back at him as calmly as though the three letters had never been written: as a sister-in-law looks at a brother-in-law she has known for fifteen years. Affectionately, trustfully, frankly.

"One can bear anything if one knows the truth," she answered, and spread out her fan and admired its ivories.

"Then take them to Scotland Yard," said Titus, "and be damned to them! I crave your pardon, Laura—I forgot myself."

She inclined a graceful head.

"I commend your decision, sir," said Fitzgerald drily. "I regret the need for it."

"And I, too. I, too. My dear Mrs. Crozier, should I not ring for Kate? The shock—the grievous upset to your nervous system."

"I can suffer no more than I have done," she replied coldly. "There comes an end even to suffering, I find."

"By the bye," said Fitzgerald, at the door, "this will mean an exhumation, I am afraid. You do realize that?"

She stared at him, and what little color she possessed left her face.

"Oh, certainly," said Fitzgerald, rocking on his heels. "There has been accusation of poisoning. They *must* exhume."

She rose, reached out a hand as if for help, and pitched to the carpet before even Padgett could fuss forward. In the melee of bell-ringing, hurrying maids, burning feathers, and sal volatile, three conscience-stricken men watched Laura revive into tears.

"I gave him one of my capsules," she wept, "they will arrest me. I can never forgive myself."

Dr. Padgett, fanning her ardently, concealed a smile and shook his head. Titus and Fitzgerald stared at each other.

"My dear sirs," said Padgett, so relieved by her second confession that he could have laughed aloud, "the capsule contained one sixth grain of quinine and the same of morphine. I have told the lady already that this could have made no difference to the illness from which Mr. Crozier died, one way or the other. But it really is extremely difficult—when the ladies get a notion in their heads . . ."

A touched amusement wiped the evening clean.

"I beg you to excuse me," Laura whispered from the sofa, and the shelter of Kate's arm, "I have not been myself of late."

They exchanged smiles. She was everything they could have wished her to be: beautiful, frail, loving, and most charmingly foolish.

The funeral had been majestic. The exhumation was shameful. Apart from occasional admonitions and directions, it proceeded in silence. A cold wind reddened noses and ruffled cloaks and greatcoats as the coffin jolted into light of day again. The two gravediggers wiped their faces with the corner of their neckerchiefs, cleaned grimed hands on nankeen breeches, touched their caps, and pocketed a tip apiece. An unpleasant business. Beneath the scratched wood, in fearful corruption, lay evidence of guilt or innocence.

"Sooner the doctor than me," said one gravedigger to the other, as they filled in the cavity. "I don't mind a-burying of them, but a-cutting up of them after is nasty!"

The other man spat, as though the too-sweet stench were in his mouth instead of his nostrils.

At the morgue, the forensic surgeon carried out his task methodically, delicately, accurately, and made his report.

The body contained a lethal dose of morphine. Three grains had dispatched Theodore Augustus Sydney Crozier to his Maker.

"Have you any notion, ma'am, where or when your late husband might have obtained such a quantity of morphine?" Padgett asked.

She stared for a full minute out of her drawing-room window.

"I should have spoken earlier," she said at last, "but I wanted to avoid a scandal, and I may have thus mistakenly involved myself in a greater one. I had a full bottle of the tablets you prescribed for me, since I was at the end of the others. When I fetched the bottle out, the night after Theodore's death, I found it empty. Would they be sufficient to furnish such a dose?"

"Yes, ma'am," said Padgett gravely, "they would. It is a pity," he added, "that you did not think fit to confide this matter to me. It will not look well, coming after the postmortem, I fear. Why did you not do so?"

She replied simply and truthfully, "Because I was afraid."

PART TWO

INNER

WORLDS

10

*We have had the morality of submission
and that of chivalry; but the time
is now come for the morality of justice.*
John Stuart Mill
The Subjection of Women

"Now, ma'am," said Dr. Padgett, outside the courtroom, "this is merely a formality. You shall be troubled as little as possible, I assure you. Everyone knows the true state of affairs, and their sympathy is with you in your tragic loss. I have no doubt whatsoever that your late husband, overcome by personal worries and the depressive mood induced by his illness, took his own life."

The thought of this made him grave, and then another and a graver thought occurred to him.

"Do you not think, Mr. Crozier," he said anxiously, to Titus, "that *I* should escort this lady? In view of the rumors, I mean."

"No sir," Titus replied firmly. "I discount and despise the rumors. The lady is my late brother's widow and as such entitled to my protection. I shall not truckle to gossip."

"Well spoken," Padgett murmured. "Most nobly put, my dear sir."

He opened the door upon a little sea of turned heads and

curious eyes. Laura pulled down her black veil and accepted Titus's arm.

"Are you not well, Laura?" he asked quietly, feeling her hand tremble.

"I wish I were not on view, that is all. I wish we could have avoided this."

The coroner stilled the whispers smartly with his hammer, and began to state the case. With an attention to detail tedious enough to have won Theodore's approval, the facts were disclosed. Once again, the deceased patriarch trod the dreary round of influenza under the guidance of Dr. Padgett. In his anxiety to be of help to Laura, the doctor brought up examples of every ailment Theodore had suffered. His high blood pressure and temperamental liver were exposed to the public. The murmur at his heart was revived. His tendency to pulmonary disorders racked them. When his last pessimistic state of mind had wearied everybody present, Padgett stepped down, satisfied that he had done his duty to the living if not to the dead.

"I regret to have to question you, Mrs. Crozier," said the coroner, consulting his notes, "but I shall not keep you longer than I can help. Being closest to the deceased you will be able to throw further light on these sad circumstances."

Laura waited. On the black crown of her hat, a pierced black bird spread his wings until the tail tips touched the wide brim.

"Mrs. Crozier, do you know of any reason, other than postinfluenzal depression, why your late husband should have taken his own life?"

"None, sir."

"You were happy together, I believe?"

"Yes, sir."

"You know, of course, of the existence of three anonymous letters? Yes. Well, I do not like to ask a lady to comment upon such libelous notes, but was there any truth in any of them?"

"No, sir," Laura replied firmly.

"He left no farewell note of any kind?"

"I have not found anything."

"There is a great deal of mystery to my mind, in this case," the coroner continued, after a pause. "If there had been no scurrilous letters, or if no poison had been found in the body, or if there had been some kind of last note—there would be less difficulty. But this is not a satisfactory state of affairs, ma'am, as I am sure you will agree. Are you positive that you know of no other reason, Mrs. Crozier?"

Laura considered, pressed her lips together, then again said, "No, sir."

"Very well, ma'am. I thank you. Mr. Titus Crozier."

Titus, bereft of his usual ruddy color and exuberance, nevertheless held himself smartly. And though he was in deepest mourning, his tailor had not failed him.

"I think you and I shall be frank with each other, sir," said the coroner abruptly, "and so spare the lady further questioning. Are you in debt?"

"I have one or two small bills unpaid," said Titus, easily enough. "Tradespeople can be impatient. I owe a friend something at cards, too."

"I see, sir. What sum of money would *you* describe as small?"

"I do not recollect the exact sum."

"Come, sir. This court is not concerned with halfpence. We can discover the amount if necessary. How much would you guess—to save public time and expense?"

Titus said reluctantly, "About eight hundred pounds."

"I should not have called that a small sum. Where would you have got it from, sir?"

"I asked my late brother to consider raising my salary. I have a position to maintain, and he always regarded me as an invaluable asset to the firm."

"In what way invaluable, sir?"

"My late brother was the businessman. I possess what one might call a flair for buying."

"And for spending," said the coroner, and raised a ripple that might have been laughter, but for the seriousness of the occasion. "Did your late brother refuse this advancement?"

"I am afraid he did."

"So where would you have got this small sum?"

"I suppose I should have borrowed it, from a money-lender. I do not wish my private affairs to be discussed in public," Titus added, ruffled, "so I am prepared to write down the amount of my annual salary on a piece of paper for your own eyes. You will see that—though I should have been somewhat straitened for a few months—it was possible to pay the debts in full."

The coroner wrote deliberately, and then read what he had written.

"I am quite satisfied, Mr. Crozier, on that point. You need not trouble to confide in me. Are the finances of the firm in good order?"

"In excellent order," said Titus, relieved to give good news for a change.

"Thank you. Now, sir, why should there be rumors of a warmer relationship than was proper with Mrs. Crozier?"

Titus pondered, one hand in the breast of his cutaway jacket.

"I was so frequently at the house, of course," he said, as though thinking of the matter for the first time. "My late brother acted *in loco parentis* for me, from when I was a boy. At the time of his marriage, he and my sister-in-law were good enough to accept me as part of their household. I was, and am, on amiable terms with her. I cannot conjecture how such rumors start."

"Did you visit Mrs. Crozier, perhaps, when her husband was not at home?"

"Occasionally. Why should I not? I have two fine nephews and a charming niece. I am regarded as an indulgent uncle. My visits were quite open. You may question my sister-in-law's servants if you doubt my word."

The coroner shook his head.

"Has Mrs. Crozier ever called upon *you* without her late husband?"

"Only when I was unwell. I am a bachelor, sir," said Titus, smiling, "and bachelors are sad creatures in the clutch of sickness. My sister-in-law was merciful enough—at her late husband's express wish, I may add—to see that I wanted for no comforts to aid my recovery."

"Have you ever escorted Mrs. Crozier to—say—the theater, or to supper, without her late husband?"

"Very probably. Yes, I suppose I have. If so, that was again with my late brother's permission. I have often taken Mrs. Crozier and her children to the pantomime and so on—but perhaps that is not what you wish to know?"

His good-humored replies took the tension, and some excitement, from the courtroom.

"Mr. Crozier, would you say that this marriage was a happy one?"

"Yes, sir. My late brother was extremely proud of his wife. She wanted for nothing. In his turn, I may say that he enjoyed all the benefits of a comfortable home and a devoted companion."

"They had had no major disagreements—particularly of late?"

It was Titus's turn to pause, but at length he said he knew of none. The coroner's pen sputtered on for a while before he laid it petulantly down.

"This is a highly important matter, Mr. Crozier. A gentleman has met his death, if not by his own hand then by that of another. I find the reason put forward by Dr. Padgett very thin. Very thin, indeed. I find it difficult to believe that a happily married man of considerable means, and a thriving business, swallows his wife's sleeping capsules simply because he has had the influenza. I had the influenza myself, sir, as did many a hundred other men—but my courtroom is not crowded with dead bodies in consequence!"

He regarded Laura's drooping black bird and Titus's returned color with some asperity.

"If you can furnish me with no better reason," he said briefly, "I must refer this case to a higher authority."

Titus looked imploringly at Laura, who looked back and then slowly nodded.

"We did not wish to bring the matter to public attention," Titus began in a low voice. The watchers became alert. "It is purely a personal family affair, which will cast a slur upon my late brother's otherwise unblemished reputation, and inflict fresh grief upon his widow."

The coroner placed the tips of his fingers together.

"I am very sorry for that, Mr. Crozier, but this is a public inquiry. I should advise you to clear such rumors as you can, for both your sakes, with whatever means are at your disposal."

Titus took a deep breath and folded his black kid-gloved hands one upon the other.

"A short time ago, sir, some letters were delivered by a lady who declined to leave her name, with directions to the parlormaid to deliver them personally into my late brother's hands. Knowing he was resting, and feeling that husband and wife were in each other's full confidence, the maid gave them to my sister-in-law. The lady who brought the letters was not the sort of person with whom our family would have enjoyed social intimacy, and Mrs. Crozier was suspicious. Distressed by the secrecy, she charged her husband with an indiscretion. He declined to comment, and out of her trouble she begged me to aid her.

"Mrs. Crozier has no male relative alive, other than an aged uncle. She had no one else to turn to, and was greatly upset. My late brother confessed to me that he had indeed been foolish. He assured me that the connection was at an end, and the fault would not be committed again."

Appalled, Dr. Padgett patted Laura's doeskin glove. But it might have covered marble for all the attention she paid to him.

"My late brother humbly asked his wife's forgiveness, and she did forgive him in a most noble and womanly fashion. They were fully reconciled."

The quietness in the courtroom was disturbed by the coroner's busy pen.

"But surely, Mr. Crozier," he said, returning persistently to the fray, "you are not suggesting—since they had made their peace—that the late gentleman then killed himself out of remorse? That would be pointless. Do you not agree?"

Titus said resolutely, "My sister-in-law is unaware of a further fact in connection with this matter. Her husband was being blackmailed. Not all the letters had been returned."

Laura lifted her head suddenly and stared at him.

"My late brother was gravely worried, and he dreaded scandal."

"I *will* have silence, if you please," cried the coroner, and emphasized his words with the hammer. "Well, sir, this puts a very different complexion on the affair. Are you able to produce these letters?"

Laura's voice, too high, said, "I believe them to have been burned."

"How do you know that, ma'am?"

"I saw a quantity of ashes in the grate, the day after they were delivered."

"Can any of your maids testify to that, Mrs. Crozier?"

"I do not know. They may. They may very well not have noticed. Why should they? We frequently burned spoiled papers on the fire."

"Pray do not agitate yourself, ma'am," whispered Padgett, but she rose, shaking.

"This is inhuman!" she cried to the assembly. "It is too

cruel. Am I to lose everything? Honor and respect and peace of mind, and now a memory that should have remained sacred to me?"

Cries of "Shame!" were directed at the coroner.

She reached for her cloak, but it had snarled on the leg of the chair. She pulled at it ineffectually until Padgett released it for her.

"Do not come near me!" she said peremptorily, as Titus and the doctor came to her assistance. "You have done your duty, sir!" Turning to the coroner. "You have found out a truth I would have concealed. I *knew* my late husband took his life. I thought it was from remorse. I found the empty bottle and I said nothing. If that is a criminal offense then imprison me. I sought to protect his reputation. I trusted in God to pardon his offense."

Her articulation was too precise, her voice too brittle.

The spectators were on their feet, craning to see her.

"Leave me! Leave me!" she commanded imperiously, and the small black gloves gestured away those who would have helped her. "If my husband were here he would not allow me to be so used. Is this how you deal with a woman who lacks protection?"

"Shame on you, sir!" shouted an elderly gentleman from the back of the room, and he shook his rolled umbrella at the coroner.

The hammer beat on the table in vain.

"What is to become of me?" Laura wept, and wrung her hands. "Where shall I go?"

She rallied, taking courage from the outraged sympathy about her.

"Let me pass!" she cried. "All has been spoiled that might have been left to me. I dare not even accept the support of a brother's arm. But my sons will know how you dealt with me, when they are older. When they are older."

"Stand near me, Sergeant Wilson, if you please," said the coroner nervously. "And look as stern as you can. Take out your truncheon if necessary. Only as a threat, mind!"

Over the tumult, Titus shouted, "I repudiate these vile rumors. I offer this lady my protection. My brother would have wished it." Infuriated with the lot of them, he cried, "And be damned to you!"

Sated, they stood aside as he and Dr. Padgett left the room, and murmured compassionately over the weeping woman they supported. The coroner's hammer reminded them that all was not done. He cleared his throat diffidently.

"The evidence is not yet adequate enough to form any conclusions. I shall adjourn this inquiry until further details are available."

Then he retreated, closely followed by Sergeant Wilson.

11

Ev'ry member of the force
Has a watch and chain, of course;
If you want to know the time,
Ask a P'liceman!
                    E. W. Rogers
                    Ask a P'liceman

Inspector John Joseph Lintott of Scotland Yard was a man whom the Croziers would not have known socially. He seemed a dull dog at first view; his graying hair parted in the middle and smoothed mercilessly down, his mutton-chop whiskers furled against flat cheeks. Quiet of dress and manner, his respectability could not be doubted, but he was no gentleman. One suspected that he came of an honest family who took advantage of every opportunity offered—and there had not been many. A man without style, yet of considerable shrewdness, he enjoyed some eminence in his little circle at the Yard. He lacked influential connections and would therefore not rise to the best positions. He never pandered to the curiosity of newspaper reporters, and therefore lacked publicity. In fact, he was one of those excellent and unsung persons who are the spine of any authority: a man who asked no more of his work than the enjoyment of doing it well, and accepting a modest salary in return.

He had risen from the ranks slowly, and knew the dark side of London. He tapped sources which his superiors found noisome, except when they took credit for rooting them out. In thirty years of police service he reckoned he had seen everything, could not be surprised, and seldom was. He treated his inferiors with a mixture of good nature and jocular bullying. His terrible patience, his reluctance to reach an easy conclusion, his acute perception, were backed by an indomitable nature. One might kill Lintott, but one would never deter him.

Yet each man has his weakness, and the inspector's underbelly—so to speak—lay in his family. They were also his secret strength. He kept them securely tucked away in Richmond, and rejoiced in their anonymity. For they were very ordinary, these beloved ones, except in his eyes. Without them he would have been merely a nose on the scent, a hollow man. With them in his background he trod surely on streets that his constables only paraded in pairs.

He was as familiar with the swarming warrens of Whitechapel, the squalor of Devil's Acre and Drury Lane, and the breeding slums of the dock area, as with his Richmond cottage. He could shine his bull's-eye lantern into the cellars of the greatest criminal slum in Britain: St. Giles Rockery, known as the Holy Land, which sprawled from New Oxford Street to St. Giles High Street. They knew him: the coiners, pickpockets, footpads, cardsharpers, ponces, prostitutes, beggars and housebreakers, kidsmen and shoplifters. And he knew them and could speak their jargon as easily as they did themselves.

"What's this then, Dollie?" he would cry, snatching up a warm heap of partly feathered poultry, "been beak-hunting?" Or, "Flying the blue pigeon again, Charlie?" as he came upon a quantity of roof lead. "Don't gammon me, lad!" But with the filthy children, who shrank into shadows, he could be kind. "Here's a mag apiece!" he would say, distributing halfpence among them. "Now, mizzle! And if I catch a one of you smatterhauling or buzzing or griddling I'll have you on the cockchafer! Hook it! And mind what I say."

They minded, but could no more have altered the pattern of their lives than they could have eased their hunger. London was two cities and two worlds: the one glittering, the other in perpetual darkness. Between them both, the police force strove to keep some semblance of order and justice.

Lintott's respectful voice, the way he held his Bollinger hard felt hat to his chest, soothed Laura.

"I have called at an awkward hour, Mrs. Crozier," he suggested, seeing that she was taking tea in the parlor.

His years, his gray head, his air of competence, even though he was not a gentleman, brought out the child in her. He was reminded of his younger daughter, in disgrace over some slight misdemeanor, silently begging for his intercession. But the elegance of her carriage, the composure of her voice and gestures, were those of a woman well versed in social behavior.

"Do not mention it, Inspector Lintott. I shall ring for another cup, and perhaps you will join me?"

He hesitated only for an instant, summing her up as a charmer and therefore suspect on that score alone. Then spoke briskly.

"On no account, ma'am. I have no wish to disturb you. But I should be obliged if I could have a word or two with your servants."

She detected a snub and withdrew into hauteur: wounded.

"My servants know nothing more than has been reported of the inquest."

She ached at the recollection of their names and private lives spread out in *The Times* and less mentionable newspapers.

Having put her in her place, Lintott twisted his hat with becoming modesty.

"A mere formality, Mrs. Crozier. A half hour would suffice, with your permission."

Firmness underlay his deference.

"I begin to dread the expression 'a mere formality,' " said Laura, attempting lightness. "Whenever anyone uses it something fearful follows."

He stood, politely unmoved.

"You may ask *me* anything you please, Inspector. I am afraid the inquest distressed me, but I have quite recovered and will answer you calmly."

"My dear lady," said Lintott, who intended to draw his conclusions without her help, "enough has been demanded of you already." Still, he pitied the dark hollows of her eyes. "I shall not trouble you more than I need to, ma'am."

"You do not wish to speak to me at all?" Laura asked, turning her amethyst ring, set like a flower in its gold oval.

Was she relieved or disappointed? He could not tell.

"It may be necessary later, ma'am. There are certain statements to check and corroborate. But, at the moment, your servants if you please."

He nodded at the bell by the fireplace, and she rang it, disquieted.

Kate escorted him to the kitchen, where the staff was oily with buttered muffins. And this was a different man who smiled on them all and accepted a cup of strong tea from Mrs. Hill's own hands: sharp-eyed, self-assured, and dangerously genial.

"The beverage that cheers but does not inebriate, ma'am," he observed. "A warm welcome on a cold afternoon. Very raw outside, Mrs. Hill. Very inclement weather we're having."

"Ah!" sighed the cook, refilling her own cup. "You may well say so. We feels it all the more, I can tell you, with the master gone."

[133]

And she looked up at the ceiling and lifted the corner of her apron to two dry black eyes.

"A sad business, Mrs. Hill. I can see you know what you're about in this establishment," and he admired the battery of iron and copper saucepans on the wall. "And somebody is clever with their fingers," tapping one of the rag rugs softly with his buttoned boot.

"That's Miss Nagle, Miss Blanche's nurse. She sets of an evening with me and makes them."

"I should like a word with her too, by and by. Yes, I *will* have a muffin, I thank you kindly."

"Five is the best time," said the cook, glancing at the eight-day clock, whose hands stood at twenty minutes to the hour. "Miss Blanche goes into her mama's parlor until six. Have a morsel of plum jam with that, Inspector. Harriet, cut the inspector a slice o' seed cake."

Red-cheeked, Harriet severed the giant cake.

"Thankee, my dear. I see you have an eye for art, Mrs. Hill," nodding at the Pear's calendar. "A very fetching study, that one."

"He looks the image of Master Lindsey," said the cook, striving to bring the conversation around to the family. "Poor little fatherless dear. Ah, yes!"

"Your husband's a lucky man, Mrs. Hill, having a wife that can bake as well as this."

"Husband?" cried the cook, bridling with delight. "Lor' bless you, sir, I ain't got a husband. They calls me Mrs. Hill out o' respect. And respect I will have."

"Then you've disappointed somebody," said the inspector coolly, wiping jam from his fingers. "You've sent some poor fellow off to war with a broken heart!" and he jerked his chin at the scraps of military red in the rag rug.

Harriet Stutchbury giggled, Kate smiled, and Mrs. Hill threw her apron over her head and laughed aloud. Lintott looked amiably on.

"That's Miss Nagle's intended, sir. They've been a-courting these ten year."

"Then she don't intend to have him, I'd say!"

"Oh yes, she do!" they chorused, enchanted with him.

He was so friendly, sitting there taking his tea with them. They had expected, somehow, to be bullied. Mrs. Hill poured him another cup and sugared it liberally.

"Try a scone," she urged. "Do!"

"It's beyond me," said Lintott idly, as if talking to himself, "why a gentleman of Mr. Crozier's standing should have made away with himself. Why, bless you, I haven't a half nor a quarter of what he had—and I'm as happy as larks in a pie. Particularly if it was one of *your* pies, Mrs. Hill! Is that a mutton pie on the dresser?"

Shining with pleasure, she cut him a wedge.

"I've had nothing since Mrs. Lintott grilled me a dish of kidneys for my breakfast. She's a fine cook, too, Mrs. Hill—but she don't make pastry like this. Never tell her I said that, mind! Yes, your master had a deal on his conscience, to be sure, but *I* wouldn't have made away with myself under the circumstances."

"He never did," said Mrs. Hill sturdily, "not the master."

The inspector dusted crumbs of pastry from his knees, and raised his eyebrows.

"Not the master," Mrs. Hill repeated with honest conviction. "He was a Christian gentleman."

"He wasn't afraid of nothink," Harriet offered. "He would have fetched a constable and sent that huzzy packing, not killed hisself."

"An upright and charitable gentleman," said Henry Hann, who so far had sat in nervous silence. "The only one he feared was God."

"Well, well, well," Lintott ruminated. "And what do you think, my dear?" to Kate Kipping.

She replied deliberately, "It's hardly my place, sir, to set myself up for the law. If the law decides that the master made away with himself that's good enough for me."

"Ah, you're a clever girl, I can see. And who's this little wench, then?" as the kitchenmaid appeared, gaping, from one of her sojourns in the scullery.

"That's only Annie Cox. She don't know nothink and thinks less."

"I've a daughter much the same age as you, Annie. How are you, Annie?"

"Pretty well, I thank you, sir," bobbing a curtsy.

"That's good, Annie." He signaled Mrs. Hill with a lift of his fingers.

"Annie!" said the cook, interpreting. "You've finished your tea. You can light the fires upstairs. Off with you."

"So you don't think your master committed suicide?" said Lintott, looking around. The cook, Harriet, and Henry shook their heads. "Then what did happen?" he asked in quite a different tone. "Remember, if it wasn't suicide it must have been murder. No one takes a bottle of sleeping capsules by mistake. Are you saying Mr. Crozier was murdered?"

His eyes threatened them. They did not speak, suddenly afraid: pleating an apron, fingering a cuff, twisting a button.

"Someone wrote those letters," said Lintott quietly. "I wonder who that was?"

The kettle boiled away on the kitchen range, unnoticed.

"All that was said," Mrs. Hill began timidly, "was that it didn't seem in the master's nature to do away with hisself. We don't know nothink more."

The door opened behind the inspector, and Miss Nagle walked in: tall, spare, starched.

"Come in, come in, my dear," cried Lintott cheerfully. "We've been waiting for you to join us. I know all about *you,* my dear!" And he smiled into her startled face. "There's one of Her Majesty's gallant redcoats a-pining for a kind word from you. Sit, do. I know Mrs. Hill won't mind me asking you to take a chair. I'm an admirer of hers. Now where can I go that'd be nice and quiet?" Lintott asked, hard and friendly together. "Because I want to speak to each of you privately in turn. Would your mistress let me have some small room, do you think, my dear?" To Kate Kipping, who alone among them eyed him steadily.

"I'll ask her, sir, if you like."

"That's right, Kate. It is Kate, isn't it? I thought so. Tell her I shall be a little longer than I thought. Say I'm on the track of an anonymous letter writer, Kate. That will set her mind at rest. At any rate, we hope it will. A good mistress won't suspect her own servants, I should hope. Eh, Mrs. Hill?"

The cook's answer was inaudible.

"We mustn't fret your mistress, must we, Kate?" Lintott asked, turning to her.

"No sir. Mrs. Crozier has had more than enough of grief."

"And you'd do anything to spare her grief, wouldn't you, Kate?"

"If it was in my power, and according to my conscience, sir."

"Oh, you're a quick one, Kate. I shall have to watch you, I can see."

"Will that be all, sir?"

"Yes, Kate, for now. So, mizzle!" He stared around, smiling. "That's a criminal's way of saying *cut along*," he explained. "But, then, none of you would know that, would you? Not unless you'd done something wrong and got yourselves in prison. Then you'd learn it fast enough, and the hard way. You see that?"

He opened his hand wide. Blunt-fingered, square-palmed, it lay on the scrubbed table like menace.

"That's a policeman's hand. The hand of the law, you might say. It's as safe with honest folk as a newborn babe, and as gentle. Do you know what it does with the wrong 'uns?"

He balled it into a fist.

[137]

"So mind you tell me the truth, the whole truth, and nothing but the truth," Lintott said, amicable again. "I *will* have the truth, you know. I'm a stickler for it."

No one spoke, staring at the strong fingers which closed viselike over the thumb.

12

*"I speak as I find, Mr. Sweedlepipes," said Mrs. Gamp.
"Forbid it should be otherways! But we never knows
wot's hidden in each other's hearts; and if we had
glass winders there, we'd need keep the shetters up,
some on us, I do assure you!"*

Charles Dickens
Martin Chuzzlewit

"I've taken quite a fancy to you, Miss Nagle," Lintott said, sitting in Theodore's study chair. "I can tell a pair of keen bright eyes when I see them. What's more, I wager there's a certain soldier in Her Majesty's Service that likes 'em too. Is he a private, my dear?"

"A sergeant, sir," said the nanny, wary after his confrontation in the kitchen. "Sergeant Malone, sir."

"Ardent men, the Irish. Quick-tempered. Big man, is he?"

"Not so very tall, sir, but stout and well made."

"A strong arm and a warm heart, eh? What are you keeping him waiting for, my dear?"

"Well sir, I'm a-saving up. My wages is twenty-five pound a year and all found."

"Oho! The sergeant's a bit of a free spender, is he? Likes his friends about him?"

"He enjoys his glass," Alice Nagle admitted, "but it will be different when he's a married man, sir."

"You'll see to that, won't you, Miss Nagle?" Shrewdly.

She looked up, wondering whether he implied criticism, but his face was bland.

"A pair of sparkling eyes. A cozy fireside," Lintott mused. "Why should he stray? And, speaking of eyes, nothing gets past those bonny blue ones, does it?"

Alice Nagle's orbs were neither blue nor bonny, being small and gray, but she tossed her head with pleasure, and admitted he was right.

"That's what I thought. While we're sitting together so comfortably, Miss Nagle, would you mind copying out these words?"

She read the paper he handed to her, and reddened.

"Not very nice, is it?" he asked. "That's not the real anonymous letter, my dear. It's a copy of number three—which says just about everything it shouldn't. Print out what's written there, will you?"

Tongue between teeth she did so, and handed it to him. He barely glanced at it, laying it to one side.

"Now what you tell me, and what I'm going to ask you, are both in confidence, so you needn't fear—and you mustn't say. I shall find out if you've been gossiping behind my back!"

She wormed her hands together on the white apron.

"There's been enough of gossip to set London afire," Lintott continued. "I'm not concerned with that. But conjecture is another pigeon. Do you know the difference between truth and conjecture?"

"I think so, sir."

"I hope so. The truth is what you know, and conjecture is what you think may be the truth. We'll have a go at the conjecture, seeing you miss nothing. Did your late master commit suicide, in your opinion? I shall want good reasons, mind, for what you say."

"No, sir, he did not."

"Do you think he was murdered, then?" She hesitated. "Come now, *you* don't know, and *I* don't know. Do you think he might have been?"

"Yes, sir."

"Who did it, then? And how?"

"The mistress, or Mr. Titus, or both together. They were a deal too familiar. I've been in service here since Master Edmund was born, and I've seen a thing or two. I'd be surprised if all the children was my late master's—"

"That's gossip," said Lintott coolly. "Keep to the point. Why should they do away with Mr. Crozier?"

"Well sir, it's plain enough. *He* was short of money, and *she* wanted her freedom to carry on as she pleased."

"I see. How do you suppose they administered a bottleful of capsules?"

She had been hoping he would ask her so that she could confound him.

"They quarreled that evening somethink awful, and the master was took poorly and went to bed."

At the end of their road and tether, whispering together in the drawing room, Laura calculating in white composure; Titus easily influenced and impulsive. The port decanter, suddenly glowing with terrible promise, taken upstairs and used as both palliative and deadly carrier. The pills crushed and administered, glass by glass . . .

"Have you any idea, Miss Nagle," said Lintott idly, "what a gritty drink that might have been?"

"There's ways and means," she cried, brushing away the suggestion. "They could have said they was medicine. The master would take anythink that was medicine."

"What made you think of port wine, I wonder?"

"Why, Harriet heard them talking of it, and she said that the mistress sent her away as if she didn't want her by. And the decanter and glass was there the very morning he died, by the bed."

Lintott's eyes were pinpoints.

"Did you keep it as evidence?"

She cried, frustrated. "Nobody thought at the time. Harriet never said nothink until it was all over. The decanter had been took back, and the glass washed by then, but that was when I thought of foul play, sir. That's when."

"I see. Well, that's the conjecture part. Now for the truth. Have you ever seen Mrs. Crozier and Mr. Titus together in a compromising situation? In her room? No. Exchanging a kiss, perhaps—ah! You know all about that, my dear! Under that parasol of yours with the brave sergeant, eh?" Wagging his forefinger at her in pretended rebuke.

She smiled uncomfortably, and admitted she had seen nothing of the sort. "But you can tell when people are over-fond of one another. I've been in that drawing room, when they was waiting for Mr. Theodore, and the air was full of it."

"The only trouble is, my dear, that a judge don't accept air as evidence. A lovely lady, Mrs. Crozier, very much admired, I believe?"

"She was always spoiled and ailing!" Miss Nagle's color was high. An old grievance and an old envy beset her. "Who watched over the master, well or ill, might I ask? It was me, sir, from the beginning. He asked for me whenever he was took poorly. 'Send for Nanny!' he used to say. 'She's a *good* nurse!' "

"Then he got what he wanted, didn't he?" said Lintott, unimpressed. "And he was ill often enough, Lord knows, to tire any wife out."

"She could never be bothered with him, sir. Dr. Padgett was taken in by her, too," said Miss Nagle, who had never taken in any man at all. "Giving her tablets and powders and sending her to Brighton for a month at a time, and Cheltenham Spa and that. I've no patience."

"Who looked after Mr. Crozier then, while she was away? You, Miss Nagle?"

Queening the household, chastising the children, indulging every sneeze from that miniature deity, undermining what little influence Laura still had.

"You don't like your mistress, do you, my dear? You don't think much of Mr. Titus, come to that. But it's your mistress that you don't like."

She was still, knowing she had said too much.

"It's not my place to like or dislike. I know my place, sir. I do my duty."

He returned to worry the main issue.

"Well, we'll say that Mrs. Crozier and Mr. Titus felt warmly toward each other—since I trust a woman's instinct in such matters. But there's no harm in that, is there?"

She twisted her hands and pondered.

Finally she said, "I found a letter in her wastepaper basket, a few months since, torn to pieces. A love letter. From him."

"I didn't know that a nanny was called upon to empty wastepaper baskets?"

"I happened to notice her tearing it across and across, when I come in, and I know his hand. Well, I should do, after fourteen year. So I took a look afore Kate got in."

His voice was lazy, his eyes alert.

"If it was torn to pieces how did you manage to read it?"

Her hands were a rough knot.

"I—put it together again."

"And then threw it away, I'll be bound. Well, that's not evidence either, my dear. I'll take your word for it, but a court wouldn't." She did not answer. "Or did you keep it, after you'd pasted it onto a sheet of paper, perhaps? Put it in a safe place?"

She justified herself with anger.

"The master was good to me, and I respected him. He

knew my worth—she never did. If he suspected somethink between her and Mr. Titus, and wanted proof, I had it for him. If he wanted to send her packing, I had that letter."

"Send her packing where?"

Miss Nagle gestured somewhere vague and far off.

"She's got an uncle in Bristol. She could have gone there, couldn't she?"

"Which would have left you in charge of his children, and nursing himself? And Mr. Crozier, separated from one wife and unable to take another, would have relied on you. You have a taste for power, my dear, haven't you? Quite a taste for backstairs politics. Does anyone else know about this letter? The other servants?"

She shook her head firmly.

"Not even the courageous sergeant—and *he's* a braver man than he knows!—not even the admirable Malone?"

"I believe I may have mentioned it to him once, casual like," she whispered. "But he promised not to say."

He smiled at the cornice over her bowed head, and smoothed his chin.

"Fetch it for me, will you, my love?" he asked gently.

Titus had been indiscreet. Little could surprise Lintott, but his eyebrows testified to the aptness of the phrases.

"Very warm indeed," he said at last, "but not conclusive. She tore it up. A love letter from her husband's brother. Hardly her fault? And she got rid of it, would have got rid of it but for a pair of sparkling eyes. Not conclusive. Have you anything else for me?—I'll keep this, my dear, it's safer with me."

"She's always a-writing in her diary, but she keeps it locked up and hides the key."

"Then this is all we have. Very well, my dear. You've done right by your master if not by your mistress, at any rate. I think that will be all, for now. Oh, Miss Nagle," regarding her closely, "if you *do* come across anything, let me know. Keys get mislaid. Drawers are unlocked. Diaries left lying about. I think you understand my meaning. Mind!" he cautioned her, as she nodded and curtsied, "I'll have no prying. But as long as you help me, my dear, I'll help you. You never know, you might be glad of a bit of help from me someday."

"Yes, sir. Thank you, sir."

His eyes returned from the closing door to Titus's letter. As a postscript the lover had drawn on the greater resources of the late Robert Browning. His writing drove across the paper: passion clouding judgment.

See the creature stalking while we speak! Hush and hide the talking. Cheek on cheek!

"That's a pretty way of putting it," said Inspector Lintott to himself. "Uncommon pretty!"

The tussle for power had begun fourteen years before.

"I should like the baby with me, Nanny," said Laura, as Miss Nagle seized and swaddled him.

The new nurse, engaged by Theodore, though only two or three years older than her mistress, already brandished the qualities for which she had been chosen. Begin as you mean to go on, she always said to herself. She had started from the first day.

"He'll only disturb you, ma'am, and the doctor says you must have your rest. Besides, as you're feeding him . . ."

The feeding was another tug-of-war. Nanny wanted the baby to herself, and on a bottle.

"But you are in the adjoining room, Nanny, and can hear him if he cries."

Laura's voice was fretful. The linen corset beneath her breasts stretched down to her thighs, and its four linen straps were tightened daily to restore her figure. She could move very little, dependent on those about her for every need, and the sensation of being merely a helpless body increased her wretchedness.

"Now, ma'am, we can't have you worriting yourself into

a fever. If you do that," Miss Nagle threatened, "you'll lose your milk."

"I want my baby where I can see him," said Laura, and as the nanny waited implacably she cried, "I *will* have him! I will, I will."

Two tears rolled down her cheeks.

"What did I say, ma'am? You'll fret yourself into a temperature if you go on so."

Miss Nagle laid Edmund in the crook of Laura's arm and sought an ally.

"Hysterical?" said Theodore. "Well, what do you propose?"

They had recognized each other as dictators, and himself as lord of the ascendant. She thought him a proper man.

"Mrs. Crozier takes too much upon herself, sir, instead of letting me do my duty. And the poor lady is too weak to know what's best for her and Master Edmund. Spoiling," said Miss Nagle, with a glint, "never formed character."

The baby was shunted through an obstacle race of artificial foods until, fortunately for himself and Laura, he found one which suited. By the time his mother crept downstairs to lie on the sofa he had been irrevocably cloistered behind the nursery walls.

Lindsey, less hardy than his brother, suffered more, and Laura suffered for him. Only with Blanche did she find a little freedom, for Blanche, being a girl, seemed of less account to both Theodore and Miss Nagle. Once, Laura spoke to her husband about the nanny's dominance.

"Her qualifications were excellent," he pronounced, "otherwise I should not have engaged her. I am satisfied that she knows her business. My sons require firmness and discipline—and you appear to hold small regard for either. Besides, you have them to yourself for an hour after tea. They go for rides in the carriage with you. They wriggle and chatter at breakfast, and that is another point—Laura, you really must control them better. I must not be disturbed. I will not be disturbed over my newspaper."

"If you'll excuse me saying so, sir, you seem on the poorly side this morning."

"It is nothing, Nanny, and I have too many responsibilities to care for myself as much as, perhaps, I should."

"I think you've got somethink of a heavy cold coming on, sir, myself. The Honorable Mr. Prout, as I was nursemaid to his children, was a martyr to heavy colds. Could you not rest yourself, sir, this morning?"

"Impossible!" Looking at her sideways for contradiction.

"Well, sir, I hope you don't think as I'm speaking out of my place, but I believe you should. A stitch in time saves nine."

His dark face intent on business appointments that must not be broken.

"At the very least, sir, you should come home early and I'll make you a black-currant cordial."

"I was to have taken Mrs. Crozier to the theater this evening."

"Why, sir, Mrs. Crozier would be the quickest to say as you must care for yourself first. If you caught a chill atop of that cold, in the night air . . ."

"Where did you expect that my sons would find an education, madam? At home in the parlor?"

"Fräulein Walther is most competent. I feel that Edmund has changed so since he left home, and Lindsey cries every time he thinks of it, Theodore."

"No boy was ever taught by a governess beyond his early years, Laura. And you should not indulge Lindsey's tears. He is too much inclined to weep. He must be a man. If it were not for Miss Nagle's training I should have been presented with *three* daughters."

[147]

Children locked in a cupboard. Perched on a table which leered below the short legs in a long fall. Favorite books, cherished toys, placed too high to reach. Lying in bed with the blinds drawn for punishment, while outside the sun shone. Weeping in the compulsory dark of night. Sitting down to bread and water, while the kitchen feasted on roast mutton and college pudding.

Between five and six o'clock they entered a forbidden Eden: all the dearer because of its brevity, already retreating from them as they grew older.

"Do not shout so, Edmund dearest. You must not be so noisy. Show me what you have painted."

Blood and rifles, soldiers slain by the dozen, misery and destitution.

"It is the battle of Waterloo, Mama."

All the violence that he could not wreak.

"Are you not going to sit by me, Edmund?"

Torn between the need for proximity, and the male pride which forbade it, the boy perched a foot away from her on the edge of the sofa. But Lindsey burrowed a fair head on her shoulder, and Blanche climbed on her knee, still.

"What shall I read to you?" Laura asked.

"Not *Struwwelpeter,* Mama," begged Lindsey, who dreamed dreadfully of having his thumbs severed by scissors.

"No, indeed, that is not one of my favorites." Nanny Nagle read it, and quoted constantly. Theodore approved of retribution, of great vengeance for little sins.

"*Alice in Wonderland,* Mama, if you please," Blanche whispered.

"That's a girl's book!" cried Edmund accusingly.

"We will read *Alice* another day, my love. What then? Quickly, or it will be six o'clock and we shall have read nothing."

"*Gulliver's Travels,* Mama?" Lindsey suggested.

Edmund did not disapprove. Blanche loved the Lilliputians. Laura reached for the book.

"Why did they not torture him, I wonder?" said Edmund curiously. "He was tied down."

"They were not cruel people," Laura replied, disquieted. "They were merely curious because they had never seen a giant. They must have been afraid of him."

The two fair heads, one on each shoulder, were very still. Dark as his father, inscrutable, deprived, Edmund thought of men buried to the neck in anthills, lidless eyes shriveled by the sun. He loved Lindsey, because the younger boy was dependent on him, and therefore he must punish him. Lindsey lived in Edmund's world of imaginary nightmare, and clung to the tyrant who might protect him from all others.

"How happy we are together in this pretty room," said Laura, momentarily content.

Lindsey's gray eyes met Edmund's opaque brown beseechingly. Mollified by this tribute to his power, the elder boy winked reassurance. Much she knew about life, they thought. Much she knew, who could throw up no mightier shield than soft arms and gentle heart.

Blanche closed her eyes, and two fingers wandered toward her mouth.

"No, dearest," said Laura. "Nanny will be cross with you."

13

It is remarkable that as there was, in the oldest
family of which we have any record, a murderer and
a vagabond, so we never fail to meet, in the records
of all old families, with innumerable repetitions
of the same phase of character.

Charles Dickens
Martin Chuzzlewit

Mrs. Hill copied the anonymous letter more slowly, received her warning against gossip with a heightened color, and sought to placate Lintott from the outset. Her small black eyes fixed on the curtains, she recited her particulars.

"Beatrice Hill. Fifty-one year of age come March. Seventy pound a year as cook-housekeeper and all found. Been with the family fifteen year and never a wrong word. The master give me a dress-length for Christmas—a nice blue it was. I respected the master, he was good to me. Yes, Mrs. Crozier is a kind mistress."

"You don't hold a grudge against her, then?"

"Why should I?" said Mrs. Hill roundly. "We've never interfered with one another. She was only a slip of a girl when she come here first. She didn't know a kettle from a quart pot. Not that that didn't suit me better," the cook added honestly. "I could do my own way—though I treated her with respect. And when she learned how to manage alongside, as you might say, she didn't come the high and mighty. No, I'll say that for the mistress. Always a thank you when I've done somethink extra, and her compliments. Very easy and proper."

"What about Mr. Titus? Is he well liked on the whole?"

Her mouth screwed up. She pondered between discretion and the inspector's flat gaze, and decided for the latter.

"Not by me he isn't and wasn't, sir. I'm quite a judge of character. I may say I'm known for it."

"Now that's lucky," said Lintott. "I'm something of a judge of character myself. Shall I tell you what I've thought and then you can tell me? Mr. Titus is an amiable gentleman with a weakness for the ladies. Free with money, whether his own or others'. Civil until his temper's roused. A good talker and makes it sound right. Women spoil him, and what he can't get from one he gets from another. A fine figure of a man until you need him, and then he turns into a suit of clothes. Lean on him, and he's not there. Am I right, Mrs. Hill?"

She nodded, lips compressed.

"What sort of man was your late master?"

"Why sir, I think I may say I knew him better than the other servants did—though Miss Nagle worshiped the ground he walked on. He was a Christian gentleman. He can't speak up for hisself now, God rest him, and I know as they're making out he was a hard gentleman, but I know different."

Interested, doodling with his pencil, Lintott asked, "How do you know, Mrs. Hill?"

She paused, embarrassed, and then replied. "I'd been ill, sir, for quite a time afore I came into his service. I hadn't got no job and my last mistress give me no reference."

"Why was that, I wonder? You were—how old?— thirty-four or -five? How long had you been in *her* service?"

"Five year, sir. But I had to leave sudden, on account of my complaint, and she took agin me in consequence."

"What was the nature of your complaint, Mrs. Hill?"

The cook said delicately, "Female trouble, sir."

"You cast yourself on Mr. Crozier's mercy?"

"Yes, sir. I saw he was a-advertising and I went along. I was pretty near desperate, sir, and I spoke out honest and begged him to give me a chance. It's a serious thing, sir, to be given no reference. She could as well have snatched the bread from my mouth and let me starve. And I'd had enough of worriting and sickness without that!"

"Quite, Mrs. Hill. But your late master took you on trust?"

"He did, sir. He said as we was all here to help one another, and he'd give me six month on trial. We started off together, so's to speak, and I thought as we should end off together—the more's the pity."

"Were your master and mistress happy together, my dear?"

She hesitated, and then said, "No, sir, they wasn't. They was civil enough in public, only—living in the same house—you can't help noticing what goes on in private."

"Did he treat her harshly, would you say?"

"Well, sir, he did, and he didn't, in a manner of speaking. Mr. Crozier and me knew where we was with one another. He'd say, 'I don't like this or that, Mrs. Hill!' Outright. 'Very well, sir,' I'd say, 'you shan't be troubled by it no more.' Or else, if it was somethink as he'd overlooked, I could say, 'Excuse me, sir, but have you noticed such and such?' And he'd say, 'No, Mrs. Hill, I had not, but now you mention it we'll say no more.' Straight out, sir. But the mistress—I'm not a-blaming her for it, it was the way she was brought up—she'd never come right out with anythink. Always coaxing him, or hiding things from him, and that he could never abide. So they never understood each other, in a way, sir."

"Ah!" said Lintott. "An upright man. How do you account for this mistress of his, then? That wasn't very Christian behavior, was it?"

"Well, sir, if you don't get nothink but coldness at home you look for it outside. But it may not have been him, sir, it may have been Mr. Titus. He's been in many a corner, what with women and money troubles, and Mr. Crozier got him out. Besides, I've a niece as works for Mr. Titus. She goes in every day and cleans his rooms. Though I warned her, and she keeps herself pure. Not that he'd fancy her, anyway. She's a good girl, but she's got a strawberry mark all down one side of her face. But what she's told me about him'd make your hair curl!"

"Do you think he and your mistress were overwarm toward each other?"

"Not to be truthful, sir. Oh, we all gets round the kitchen table of an evening and has a chat and a laugh and that. But, no. I was here at the beginning, and they was always jolly together, like a sister with a favorite brother. There's no more to it than that, and she looks to be admired."

"I never seen such a pair o' babies in all my born days!" said Mrs. Hill to her stockpot, but the comment was not unkind.

This new household, a fortnight old, already rolled sedately under her management. A new and awkward housemaid promised to do well enough, but must be snapped to perfection. Fortunately, May's quiet prettiness enabled her to act as parlormaid too. And when Mrs. Hill could find no fault in May there was always the new kitchenmaid, whose background and competence left most things to be desired. Then the mistress, eighteen and already sickly with her first, had been grateful for guidance.

"I'll just take the menu upstairs, May," said the cook, "and see if Mrs. Crozier approves."

"They're a-playing with a jigsaw, Auntie."

"*Auntie?*" Outraged.

"I mean, *Mrs. Hill,* Auntie. I keep forgetting."

"Well, just you remember in future. *Auntie,* indeed. What's this about a jigsaw, then?"

"Mr. Titus found one of them big old jigsaws in his boxes

in the lumber room, and he's spread it all out on the parlor floor and the mistress is a-directing of him with the pieces."

"I must see this," said Mrs. Hill, mounting the stairs. "They'll have to clear it away afore the master comes home!"

Laura was in her old element: cosseted because of her condition, and even presented with a playmate to while along the hours.

"I have not done a puzzle for years," Titus said, concentrating on finding straight-edged pieces. "And this is a confounded difficult one, Laura, there is so much sky."

"Is it a pastoral scene? There is the head of a crook."

"Pastoral in the extreme, with a moral in the shape of a lurking wolf."

"I do not care for the wolf, Titus."

"He shall be kept out, if you so command, madam."

"But there will be a hole in the jigsaw, then."

"Better an unfinished picture than that you should be disturbed. I have been given orders only to amuse you, and all fearful things are to be kept from your mind, Laura."

The knowledge of the coming child, unmentionable, lay delicately between them.

She considered his russet head and absorbed face, the elegance of his attitude: a graceful dandy sprawling at her feet, paying compliments.

"You are so unlike Theodore in every way," she observed. "Did you, perhaps, take after one parent and not the other?"

"I am a changeling," said Titus with satisfaction. "All our family are, or were, honest and upright and sober. I am none of those things, Laura. My late mother named me Titus Alexander, no doubt expecting me to conquer new worlds. I assure you I shall do no such conquering. The present world is good enough for me."

"Do you not desire to rise in it, Titus?"

"Not particularly. In fact not at all. But no doubt

[154]

Theodore will see that I acquit myself in some aspect. I owe that to him, at least."

"I think he is fonder of you than of anyone."

You seem the only person of whom he is genuinely fond.

"His heart has been captured by another, and I do not blame him for that!"

I had not thought his taste was so excellent.

"I fear that you must find it very dull to stay at home during your vacation, and entertain me. I beg you will not deprive yourself of gayer company."

Do not leave me, for you are all I understand in this strange new life.

"I wish for no more charming lady, and for no other occupation than to fashion her a wooden scene upon her parlor floor."

I shall, in any case, be going out this evening to find less spiritual companions.

"When I am better we must have a musical evening, Titus. And as a good sister-in-law I shall endeavor to amuse you with a circle of pretty young ladies who are unattached. I must matchmake, now I am married! I shall be an assiduous matchmaker!"

I am not jealous.

"I shall reject a thousand beautiful young ladies, since there will be none among them to compare with you, Laura."

I have no intention of settling down with one when there are so many.

"You are a tease, Titus. Let me help you with the jigsaw, pray."

"You are not allowed to stir from your sofa, my dear sister-in-law, and I am doing uncommonly well by myself."

"Indeed, you are not. That piece does not go there, but elsewhere. Besides, I wish to set the flowers in."

Titus gave the offending squiggle a smart slap with the palm of one hand, and it shot into Laura's lap.

"You see?" she cried, delighted. "You are quite hopeless

at such an intricate occupation. I demand to be allowed to help. Pray assist me."

Carefully he settled her on the floor beside him, and watched the ballet of her fingers. Knowing, without looking, that he was admiring her, she smiled around at him.

"Is it not pleasant that we agree so well? Relatives do not always do so."

"You do not know me yet, Laura. I get into fearful scrapes, and often annoy Theodore—though he comes to, in the end. You will become a respectable matron in a few years, and order me from the house!"

She laughed, and cried, "I shall never change toward you, Titus!"

"Promise me that, Laura. Here," prising a small gold coin from his watch chain, "here is your pledge. Heaven knows what will befall you if you break your word! I tremble to think!"

"I shall put it in my jewel box," said Laura, enchanted.

"And do not tell Theodore," said Titus ruefully. "He will think me a perfect fool, and so I am."

"Then let us be foolish together. That will be our secret."

"Ours is a big family, and very close," said Mrs. Hill, smiling. "I know what it's like to be overfond of somebody, but no harm in it. My nephew, George, is going for a drummer, sir. The day as I see him in the queen's uniform'll be the proudest day of my life."

Her face shone. Inspector Lintott considered her, but without the acid speculation he had bestowed upon Miss Nagle.

"You're ruining my case for me, my dear," he said in a jocular manner. "I can't see who should do away with your master, or for what! You make it all sound so fair and reasonable. Come now, admit that these pleasant evenings over the kitchen table spoiled your judgment! You think a great deal of your late master, and don't want to say that he made a fool of himself with a trollop—and took his life out of remorse, perhaps?"

Her face changed.

"Mr. Crozier never died by his own hand, sir. What do you *want* me to say?"

"I want you to be as honest with me as you were with your master. You must think *someone* murdered him. So who, and why, and how?"

"Mr. Titus, sir. My niece told me he nearly had the bailiffs in. They're holding off now, seeing as he can get at the firm's money. Mr. Titus was training for a doctor when I first started here, but they sent him down in his second year. I don't know why, but I can guess, sir. So he'd know all about poisoning."

She had worked it out: rolling her light pastry, mixing her rich cakes, stirring her savory sauces, ruminating.

"He was the one that took the port decanter upstairs, and give Mr. Crozier a glass or two. He put them pills in the port wine."

"Oh, we're back to that gritty decanter, are we?" said Lintott, amused, good-natured. "And you call yourself a judge of character, my dear. I'm surprised at you! Have you ever met a poisoner? No, I thought not. I have. They work in the dark, as you might say. Cool sort of folk. Secretive, calculating, clever, and capable of lying you blue in the face. Is that your Mr. Titus?"

"Yes," she cried passionately, "that's his very image, sir!"

"May?" Mrs. Hill called, and then to herself, "Drat that girl! She's never where she's wanted. May!" walking through to the scullery.

The girl was doubled over, arms clasped around her belly,

in the cold twilight of the storeroom. As the cook approached uncertainly, face concerned, May whimpered "I'm very sorry, Auntie, I can't help it!"

Apologizing for the life that was seeping out on the stone floor.

"Oh, my God Almighty," whispered Mrs. Hill. "Almighty God, May, why ever didn't you tell me, girl? Let me get you up the backstairs to your bed."

"It come on sudden. She said as it would. I'm sorry for the mess."

"Oh, May, you've never been to one of them women? How did you find *her* out?"

"Mr. Titus told me. He paid. He said as I wasn't to tell, so don't you, will you?"

Confronting the august majesty of Theodore, accusing the charm of Titus. And being told what? That May lied? That the word of a gentleman should be sufficient? That she and her niece might leave the house for good?

"I can't say nothink, May, you know that. Here, let me get you upstairs. Where's Miss Nagle? She'll know what to do for the best. Did he force you?"

"Oh no," May whispered, heavy in her arms. "I fancied him, you see. He was always such a gentleman."

"You didn't throw yourself at him, I hope?" But without the vigor of her usual questioning.

The heavy head moving slowly from side to side in moaning dissent.

"Oh, Miss Nagle!" cried Mrs. Hill, as the nanny appeared, scandalized, in the doorway. "It's poor May, and I know as she's been a bad girl but she needs help."

In the end they had to fetch Dr. Padgett, who could no more than ease her out of this world and into the next, with a prayer that God would forgive this sinner. May kept faith: refusing to inform on anyone, sparing the Croziers the embarrassment of exposure and a police inquiry.

Sternly dignified, Mrs. Hill sought a private interview

with Titus. He denied everything, as she had expected he would. His head was held a little more arrogantly than usual, his hazel eyes looked slightly beyond her, his manner was easy but wary. When he had dismissed the subject he dismissed her, too.

"I'll never forgive him, sir, never," said the cook. "You never saw anythink like poor May's condition in all your born days. Makes me sick to think on it, even yet."

Lintott said drily, "I've seen it all, Mrs. Hill. I walk St. Giles."

"Anythink as Mr. Titus wants, sir, he gets. By fair means or foul. And he talks hisself out of everythink. You see, sir, he gets folk on his side. Like Mrs. Crozier. She could be shielding him for all we know. And the master would never hear a word against him. Pay out and cover up, that's how it was, sir. For fifteen year."

"You're a handsome figure of a woman, Mrs. Hill," said Lintott, partly from kindness. "You never married?"

She came out of an old sorrow, smoothed her apron, and replied, "I had my way to make, sir, and I was the eldest. They needed my wages. By the time the children was all set up in life, it was on the late side for me."

"A pity," said Lintott. "You would have made somebody a good wife and been a good mother."

14

If he knew her value right, he'd rather lose
his greatness and his fortune piece by piece
and beg his way in rags from door to door,
I say to some and all, he would! . . .
than bring the sorrow on her tender heart that
I have seen it suffer in this house!

Charles Dickens
Dombey and Son

"Now, Kate," said Lintott, indulging in a little fanciful
jocularity. "Good Kate, pretty Kate, and never—I'll bet on
it!—Kate the Shrew. That's Shakespeare, that is. My elder
daughter learned me that. Sit down, my dear. I'm very
interested in *you*, Kate. Just copy that out, will you, my
love? Nasty, ain't it?"

Her forehead crinkled in distaste as she obeyed.

"You've had more schooling than the others, Kate. In
fact"—he surveyed her with respectful admiration—"you're
quite the lady, Kate."

"I hope something like, sir," but she spoke softly,
mollified.

"You watch your mistress as well as watching over her,

eh? Model yourself on her? A very handsome woman, Mrs. Crozier, but paler than I like a lady to be. This business will have upset her a great deal."

"Not only that, sir," Kate confided, losing her wariness in the face of his paternal manner and the kindness with whch he spoke of Laura. "She was badly done by, sir."

"A hard man, your late master. Hard but just, I understand."

"He had his good qualities," Kate admitted. "I had no complaint over the way he treated *me.*"

"What wages did he pay you, Kate?"

"Twenty-five pound a year, sir, and my keep. Very fair. And, of course, Mrs. Crozier gives me her clothes, so I don't waste my money on finery like Harriet does."

"Is Harriet fond of the feathers, then, my dear?"

Kate giggled before she could stop herself, and Lintott grinned at her.

"Harriet don't—doesn't—know any better, sir. You should see her on her day off! But everyone likes her."

"Just so. A good-natured wench. How old might you be, Kate? You don't look above twenty."

"I'm twenty-six, sir," and to his raised eyebrows she replied proudly, "and I've had many a chance of marriage, but I don't want to settle down just yet."

"Flying higher than sparrows, eh, my love? Well, to my knowledge, ladies' maids usually marry butlers. Now I'll wager there's some gentleman's gentleman walks you on the Common of a Sunday afternoon, isn't there?"

Kate looked down, and colored.

"Your mistress won't care to lose you, Kate. You're very close to her, ain't you? How close, Kate?"

His tone hardened and her flush deepened, but she met his eyes resolutely.

"You'll excuse me, sir, meaning no disrespect, but I've

[161]

done nothing to be ashamed of. I'll answer your questions truthful as you please, but I won't be bullied, sir. If you'll excuse me saying so."

His smile returned in all its benevolence.

"Bully you, Kate? I never bully anybody." A dimple showed in her cheek. "Who do I bully, now, Kate?" he asked genially.

"Oh, you know well enough what I mean, sir. They was—were—all frightened to death of you in the kitchen. *And* you meant them to be."

Lintott pointed a finger at her smile.

"I said you were a sharp one, Kate. Come now, my dear, I know I can't frighten you. You know what they're all saying about your mistress, don't you? Well, we don't believe it, and we want to help her, don't we? Put them all to shame and let her rest easy in her mind again. Eh, my dear?"

"I never saw her behave with Mr. Titus except as a lady should. It was all him, sir. He's too fond of my mistress, but that isn't her fault. She has a deal of admiration from the gentlemen, in the proper way. But him, sir. I've seen a many like him. Girls of my sort can get in trouble with a gentleman of his sort. He knows better than to pinch *my* cheek, sir, or chuck *me* under the chin!"

"Ah, he's a lucky man, that butler! Tell me, Kate, how was your master unkind to your mistress? He didn't ill treat her, surely?"

"He would never lay a finger on her, sir, if that's what you mean. But there's more ways than one of being cruel, and he knew them. I've seen her cry many a time. I've heard them quarrel—not to know what they said, just their voices raised. And the last months, since the summer, she couldn't sleep at all except she took one of her capsules. And she was always ailing in little ways."

Lintott was quiet, doodling, waiting.

"She needs a deal of kindness and attention," said Kate,

"and he never cared for her. No, sir, he didn't. She was no more to him than his china collection. Oh, he liked to hear people say how handsome she was, but he never cared himself. The night after he died, sir, she slept like a child."

"Without a sleeping capsule, even?" Lintott observed. "Because they had all gone and she was afraid to say so. And still she slept like a child—after all the upset?"

Kate looked frightened, but he did not appear to notice.

"Why did you take that package of letters to your mistress, Kate? Instead of directly to your master, as you were told. Don't tell me he was resting. That's all gammon, my dear."

"I knew what that woman was, sir. A common street-walker, for all her dress. It was only right that my mistress should know what was going on."

"That's the reply I should expect of Harriet, not you. Harriet would think that Mrs. Crozier should know what was going on. I'd have said that you might have taken care not to hurt Mrs. Crozier's feelings, and keep it from her. What good did you hope to do?"

Kate repeated obstinately, "She *had* a right to know, sir. Why should he get away with it?"

always do so, as long as Mrs. Crozier needed a roof over her head and a pretty gown to wear. So whatever you or she might feel about him, he always would get away with it. Wouldn't he?"

"Yes, sir," very low.

"Do you know what *I* wondered, Kate? I wondered if you didn't let her know out of a mistaken sense of delicacy."

"I don't rightly understand you, sir."

"Didn't you think that your mistress was in love with Mr. Titus, and perhaps guilty of unfaithfulness to her husband? Didn't you suspect that she tormented herself over it? Didn't you think that what was hell for the goose should be hell for the gander? Excuse me using strong language, my

[163]

dear, I associate with a very low class of person in my profession! And didn't you think that if you took her that very accurate description of a trollop, and the package that felt like letters, possibly love letters, she might feel a bit better?"

Stricken, Kate persisted, "There was nothing between them but family fondness. And not a policeman in the land'll ever make me say anythink different in court!"

Her vehemence had destroyed her gentility for the moment. She sat, all defenses down, endeavoring to gather the rags of her ladyhood about her.

"I know you would never *say* so, Kate. I just wanted to find out whether you *thought* so. And I have found out, Kate."

She was mute.

"You're a good girl, Kate, and a clever girl," said Lintott kindly, "but you'll have to get up a deal earlier in the morning to get past *me,* my dear. Having settled that question we can go on to a few others, that are more important. I believe that you were the only member of the staff to accept the idea of Mr. Crozier's taking his own life. Was that because it seemed the best way out for your mistress, or had you a *good* reason? The truth, mind!"

She had recovered herself, and met the challenge with some spirit.

"No, sir. I thought at first that he'd had a stroke, like the doctor said. Then, when it come—came—out, that didn't surprise me neither. Mr. Crozier was a brooding sort of gentleman. Very inward-looking. Very close."

"You don't think that Mr. Titus might have poisoned him, then?"

She said scornfully, "He's not clever enough for that, sir."

"Well, well. Not even with a decanter full of port to hide the pills, my dear?"

"Oh, that, sir! They don't half talk! Mr. Titus was just smoothing him down because they'd had a set-to. How would anybody grind up all them—those—pills without being noticed? Besides, there was nearly twenty of them."

"Someone suggested they might have been disguised as medicine, Kate."

"A whole bottleful, sir? They must be off their heads!"

"I tell you what occurred to me," said Lintott idly. "Someone might be laying the blame on your mistress by means of that bottle. There's nothing to prevent a person dosing a man with three grains of morphine and throwing away a bottleful of capsules, so it looks as though *they* were the culprits!"

She was startled, questioning him with her eyes.

"Only a theory, my love," said Lintott comfortably. "I've developed a very nasty mind, along of dealing with the wrong sort for so many years."

He saw he had puzzled her, but not disturbed her.

"Why should he commit suicide, my love?" Lintott asked.

"Laura! Laura! You have not, I hope, read this copy of the *Pall Mall Gazette?*"

"I have not had time, Theodore. I have been out to tea."

"Then observe that this is what I consider it to be worth!" And he tore it across and across, and tossed it on the drawing-room fire, as though she were personally responsible.

"Why, what has Mr. Stead done to offend you?" she asked, for the magazine had become yet another means to explore the world outside, and she cherished it.

"He has turned to the gutters for his information, in order to sell this scurrilous rag. I will not have my household corrupted, made filthy even by sight or contact. If I wished to wallow in man's depravity I should study the criminal reports. I thought him a person of some integrity, though his views are not always mine. Still, one must keep an open mind. Now I know him to be a scoundrel who would sell his birthright for a mess of pottage."

Kate, setting out her evening tray of wines and spirits, was noiseless: effacing herself.

"But, Mr. Crozier," said Laura quietly, addressing his most majestic self with due respect, "if what Mr. Stead has discovered is the truth, surely we should give him a hearing?"

"I have observed in you, madam, a tendency to romanticism and indulgence. There is right and there is wrong. One strives for the one and denounces and abhors the other."

"Are human beings so perfect, Mr. Crozier? You yourself contribute to many charities, giving money—for which I honor you—to those who have in some way fallen from grace."

"But I do not mingle with them, madam. I would rather see you dead at my feet than dishonored. I would rather my sons were taken in the flower of their youth than that they should explore the sewers of this wicked world. I uphold the sanctity of the home, the virtue of women, the innocence of children. And I say this to you, madam—if thy right hand offend thee, cut it off! Kate! What are you doing?"

"Your glass of Madeira, sir," withdrawing as quietly as she had come.

"You are saying that your master was a hypocrite, my dear?" Lintott asked.

"Oh no, sir. He meant every word of it. You could always tell when the master was on his hobbyhorse. He got quite passionate, and forgot that murmur at his heart. If he was just angry with the mistress he'd shout and rave, and then clutch his chest like and have to lay down. And we was—were—all running after him in consequence. I'm saying he truly meant it. But folks are human. He held himself very tight, sir. They're the sort that fall hardest and regret it most."

[166]

"You're an observant lass," said Lintott, regarding her.

"He stayed out late at nights, sir, as long as I remember—and I've been with the mistress since Miss Blanche was a baby. Mrs. Crozier didn't seem to mind or to notice until recently, and then she began to fret herself. But I saw a difference in him the last year. Once or twice he forgot his key, and I went down to let him in. I sleep light, sir, unless I'm poorly."

The dark brooding face on the doorstep, the apology that was mere outward good manners. The heavy body shrugged from its greatcoat, turning away.

"Before last year, when he'd been out late, he'd march straight into the drawing room and pour himself a glass of spirits. He never wanted any attendance—just used to say, 'That will be all, Kate!'—but the next morning I'd notice how much he'd had. He never looked any different. He could carry his drink like a gentleman, but he drank heavy, as if he wanted to drown hisself."

She was losing her gentility as the remembrance wrapped her about, and Lintott smiled slightly and listened attentively.

"Then what happened last year, Kate, my love?"

"He changed, sir. Oh, he was still carrying the sins of the world on his shoulders, as my poor mother used to say, but he was different. Used to smile to hisself. It must have been that woman as did it. Though what he seen in her I'll never know! But he cared somethink for somebody, that was certain. You can tell, sir. He seemed like weighted down and lighted up all at once. You see, sir," cried Kate, at last finding an intelligence to which she could unburden herself, "they're all a-sniggering behind their hands, and saying as he had a loose woman, but what does it matter what she was if he saw her different?"

"I'm with you, Kate. You're saying he was in love with her?"

"Yes, sir, and pulled down with the influenza and his

own ailments—and whatever Dr. Padgett said would make no difference, Mr. Crozier looked on hisself as a sick man. Gentleman, I mean," recollecting her status and his. "So supposing he really cared somethink for this—woman—and she'd got all she wanted out of him, and then blackmailed him atop of it? And him already a religious man that knew he'd done wrong. Isn't that enough, sir, to drive him to it? Besides . . ."

But she had run her course, and was sorry she had said so much.

"Besides what, Kate, my dear? You've given me change for a gold guinea already—another few coppers won't harm us!"

"It was what you said about somebody trying to blame Mrs. Crozier by throwing her pills out, and taking morphine so as it looked like she'd done it. May God forgive me if I wrong him," cried Kate, perplexed, "but he fair hated Mrs. Crozier. He might have thought as there was nothink left to live for, and he'd see she didn't live to enjoy herself neither!"

15

A smattering of everything, and a knowledge of nothing.
Charles Dickens
Sketches by Boz

Lintott wasted no subtlety on Harriet, who was anxious only to oblige him without implicating herself. Twenty years of age, in service with the Croziers since she was fourteen, wages twenty pounds, no talent for cookery, and too clumsy to wait at table or on her mistress.

"Would you like to be a cook then, Harriet?" Lintott asked amiably.

"Not really, sir. But I'd like to do what Kate Kipping do."

"And what does Kate do? I'm very ignorant about these matters, my dear."

"Well, sir," Harriet's mild brown eyes fixed on a distant and enchanting prospect, "she don't do no rough work, on account of her hands. She has to keep them nice for sewing, and brushing of Mrs. Crozier's hair and that. And she has a nicer uniform than me, with frills on it, and a little cap, and a better-quality gown. And she answers the front door, and speaks very soft, and Mrs. Crozier talks to her—and I'd like that, sir."

"Of course you would, my love. You'd be very good at it, too, given time."

She was pink with pleasure, and then faded with recollection.

"I made a proper mess of it, the night as Kate had the influenza, and I feel as I started the master off on one of his tantrums like. I might," said Harriet, eyes rounding, "have been the cause of it all!"

Lintott tutted and shook his head, smiling.

"Cook told me off, proper," said Harriet, abased. "I dropped the tureen on the carpet, and knocked his pudding over."

Lintott gave a snort of amusement. She glanced at him timidly, and smiled.

"Now I want you to help me, Harriet," said Lintott casually. "I know you're a quick girl, and a noticing one." Harriet concentrated, in an effort to be all that he desired in the way of a witness. "I understand you made one or two mistakes at table—that's beside the point, and don't matter—but can you tell me how each of them reacted? I want that evening in front of me like a picture. Just keep talking. I'll follow."

And through the labyrinth of an untrained mind, particular as to detail and hopeless as to construction, he did follow: holding the thread firmly as Harriet digressed and repeated herself and corrected first impressions. He saw Theodore: cat-cruel, unreasonable, tyrannical. He saw Laura: baited, desperate, full of suppressed anger. He saw Titus: provoked at last into some chivalry of consequence. He drained the decanter of port to its last bitter dregs.

"I've become quite attached to that decanter," said Lintott mildly. "It's quite a favorite of mine! I wish somebody had thought to keep it and put my mind at rest. Now why didn't Mrs. Crozier go to bed if her husband was comfortable? And how long did she stay up, or don't you know?"

Excited, Harriet cried, "Until midnight, sir, or a bit past. She come to the attic and woke me up because she wanted—"

"A lady's maid?" Lintott suggested chivalrously, since Harriet's face had "stays" written all over it.

"Yes, sir. Thank you, sir. And I heard the clock strike twelve after I got back in bed."

"And why did the lady stay up so late, do you think, my dear?"

"She liked a bit of P and Q, as Mrs. Hill says. She liked being by herself, and they'd had ever such a to-do, sir."

"Well, everybody's very good at doing my job for me," said Lintott cheerfully, knowing he could get nothing more from her, "so what's your opinion of this sad affair, Harriet? Throw a bit of light on it, for me!"

"Well sir, it's plain to me as that Woman did it. Mr. Titus and the mistress, sir, are too much the lady and gentleman to do a thing of that sort. Besides," leaning forward, "they don't see nothink beyond Each Other. It's a Passion, sir, like in the novelettes."

"Now this is a new line," Lintott purred. "How did the Woman do it, do you suppose, Harriet? Crept into the house at midnight, crushed up a mort of pills into the port, just in case Mr. Crozier felt like a glass sometime, and then waited to see what would happen?"

"She Poisoned the Letters, sir. In *The Duchess of Tramura*, sir, the Duchess got a Eyetalian Poisoner to Poison a Letter, and wrote it to her Husband. And he Writhed, sir, on the ground, and cried, 'My God, my God, I am Undone!' "

Lintott strove to find one corner of this wild narrative that could be pinned down, and failed.

"I suppose it's no use asking you *why* she did that, Harriet, is it?"

"Because All was Over, sir, don't you see?"

"I'm a bit fogged at the moment, my love, but I'm doing my best. While I'm just working it all out you'd better go back to the kitchen, I think."

"Yes, sir. Thank you." She hovered, obviously in great doubt and confusion. "I think there's somethink else I ought to tell you, sir—only it might upset Mrs. Crozier if ever she got to hear about it. *And* Mrs. Hill."

"You can trust me, Harriet. Cross my heart and hope to die! Split, girl!"

"That evening as I was waiting on," said poor Harriet, "I dropped the saddle of mutton on the kitchen stairs."

"Yes, Harriet?"

"That's it, sir. I thought, with you being an inspector, as you might find out and then tell the mistress. So I'm a-telling of you first, so as you won't."

Lintott's face was a study in amazement. He recovered sufficiently to ask a final question.

"What did you do when you dropped it, Harriet?"

"Wiped it on my apron, sir, and served it up. But don't tell, sir."

Lintott looked down at the desk sternly.

"You did well to confess, Harriet," he said at last. "You were quite right. We'll say no more about it. Off with you, my dear."

She dropped a curtsy, relieved, delighted. Lintott sat staring at the door for a full minute after she had closed it. Then he shook his head from side to side and laughed out loud.

"The dimmest of the lot!" he said to himself, admonishing the hound who had followed a wrong scent. "The dimmest of the lot of them, John Joseph—and she had you hanging on to every word! Lor' bless my soul for a Dutchman, if she didn't fool me for a moment!" He laughed again, even more heartily this time, and wiped his eyes on a colored handkerchief, which he replaced in a side pocket. "You've smelled so many rats," he told himself, "that you can smell 'em when they're nothing but one mouse as drops the mutton on the kitchen stairs!"

"And whose side are you on, Mr. Hann?" Lintott asked drily.

"I don't rightly understand you, sir."

"Your master's, I suppose, since he was good to you. We'll just run through the details and then we can get down to the particulars. You're Henry Hann. Sixty years of age. Wages, twenty shillings a week and board, and a room over the stables. Fond of your glass. Well, ain't we all? The late Mr. Crozier took you on because you couldn't get a situation. Made a condition that you didn't drink before you drove the family, but undertook not to notice if you drank in your own time. Am I right?"

The coachman nodded, stout and crimson-faced, though the crimson owed more to alcohol than to confusion.

"You thought a great deal of your late master, and rightly so, Mr. Hann. What do you think about your mistress?"

"A gracious lady, sir."

"She has her enemies, even in her own household, Mr. Hann."

"Not me, sir."

"And yet you spread scurrilous tales about her, without foundation?"

"Did Miss Nagle tell you that, sir?"

"No one in this house told me, Mr. Hann. That's how far the tales have spread. Why, I could double and redouble the information I've got this afternoon—just with what I hear from outside! Tongues—aye, and pens, too—are busy around this neighborhood."

The coachman rubbed his hands on his knees, discomforted.

"It's that Mr. Titus, sir. He's a right bad lot. He tells stories about me to make folks laugh. That's slander, sir, isn't it?"

"Not if they're true, Mr. Hann."

Henry turned over the muddled contents of his skull and could find no answer.

"So you don't mind slurring the reputation of a gracious mistress provided you can cast a clod of mud at Mr. Titus?"

"I didn't think on it that way, sir."

"Then do so, Mr. Hann. Do so in future, if you please. Will you copy this for me?"

The coachman sat bemused, turning the paper around and around in his hands.

"I don't know my letters, sir. I can't neither read nor write."

"Then give it back here, man. Now, what's *your* version of this matter? Let me guess! Mr. Titus poisoned his late brother with his sister-in-law's sleeping capsules, which he crushed into a decanter of port wine, so that he could pay his debts. The fact that the late Mr. Crozier kept a mistress, who was blackmailing him by means of love letters, is beside the point. Correct?"

"Sir," said Henry slowly, but with some dignity, "it wasn't the master's fancy woman. It was Mr. Titus's."

"Well, well, well," said Lintott softly. "You can be too clever for your own good, John Joseph. If you get much sharper you'll cut yourself! Tell me what you know, Mr. Hann, if you'll be so good."

"It was like this, sir. When my master recovered from the influenza he was pretty well knocked up for a week or two after, and instead of riding into the City on his horse I took him in the carriage. Now I never knew about that woman coming with the letters, sir, because Kate is very close and said nothink. None of us knew anythink about that until the inquest. So when this woman run up to the carriage I didn't know as it was her."

"When was this, Mr. Hann?"

"A day or so after he went back to work. She run up, and the master was fair put about. She said somethink like, 'I've been waiting to see you!' And he called me to stop, very sharp, and held up his hand as if to tell her to shut her mouth—excusing the expression, sir. Then they was whispering together, and then she went off, and he told me to drive on."

"How do you know she was Mr. Titus's flight of fancy?"

"He just said to me, as we was driving off, Mr. Crozier

[174]

said, 'That brother of mine will get into one scrape too many!' Then he sunk his chin in his hand, like this, and never spoke another word until we reached Crozier's."

Lintott tapped the desk with his pencil, thinking.

"How do you account for the fact that Mr. Titus reported her as his brother's mistress, Mr. Hann? Or don't you believe that?"

"It could be lies, sir. Mr. Titus don't know the difference between truth and falsehood. He takes whichever serves him best at the time. But it could even have been, sir, that Mr. Crozier was a-trying to protect Mr. Titus from somethink serious and passed it off to him as somethink else."

"Far-fetched," said Lintott, "far-fetched. But worth bearing in mind, of course. Truth's a funny thing and can take a corner or two that nobody expects. There's nothing more than that, then?"

"Well, sir, that's what I know. But there is somethink else. Mrs. Hill is a great one for her family. Harriet's a cousin's daughter, and Mrs. Hill's niece cleans for Mr. Titus. So we get like a view of both sides, with them seeing each other on their day off."

"You're a lovely lot!" said Lintott, in admiration. "So what does Mrs. Hill's niece say?"

"Mr. Titus was taken up with a young woman in the theater line, as sounds just like the Woman in Question. Put two and two together, sir, and what do you get?"

It was plain that Mr. Hann would get nothing at all, so Lintott helped him out.

"I'd make it four, myself. But having met everyone here I'd say it was ninety-nine at least. Thank you, Mr. Hann. Is there anybody in the kitchen that I haven't seen yet?"

"Only Annie Cox, the kitchenmaid, sir. She can't tell you nothink."

"I'll be the judge of that. Be off with you and send her in—and keep your observations to yourself, Mr. Hann."

"Annie Cox, sir. I think as I'm thirteen, sir, but I don't

rightly know. There's a many of us at home, and my mam don't remember. Wages is ten pound a year and keep."

"And what do you do with a fortune like that, Annie?" Lintott asked, rattling the change in his pocket, and smiling.

"I shall take it home on my day off, sir, and give it my mam—else my dad'll have it for the drink."

"I don't suppose, Annie, that you can read or write, can you?"

"No, sir."

"It's of no consequence, Annie. Don't trouble yourself. Are they kind to you in the kitchen?"

"Sort of, sir. Mrs. Hill, she don't half tell me off. But then she gives me a piece o' pie, sir."

"Ah! That pastry is worth the end of her tongue, isn't it, Annie?"

"I 'spect so, sir. Yes."

"And the mistress, is she kind to you?"

"I'm not allowed in the house, sir, while the family's about, except for prayers."

"I see. Well, Annie, do as Mrs. Hill tells you and say your prayers every night as well as every morning. Then I shouldn't be surprised if you were a housemaid in a few years' time. You'd like that rarely, wouldn't you? Yes, of course you would. Here, Annie, here's a ha'penny for you. And, wait a minute, Annie. Here's a humbug. Cut away, and be a good girl, mind!"

16

Lord Ellingworth: *"The Book of Life begins
with a man and a woman in a garden."*
Mrs. Allonby: *"It ends with Revelations."*
Oscar Wilde
A Woman of No Importance

"Now let's take another look at her," said Lintott to himself, and found his way back to a subdued kitchen, busy for once only with the details of dinner.

"I'll just have a word with Mrs. Crozier, before I go. If that's convenient to her."

They hastened to send word up to Kate, who was performing her evening duties. They accommodated him at a corner of the table and were careful to say nothing. Amused, aware, he made himself comfortable until summoned to the drawing room.

Laura had decided on her attitude toward him: courteous, remote, without attempt to charm.

That's better, Lintott thought. Now we can get somewhere.

"I can see how gossip starts, ma'am," he said cheerfully. "Envy is at the bottom of all of it. A compliment here, a smile there, and they've got a regular love affair going—if you'll excuse me mentioning the matter."

She inclined her head and said nothing.

"A heap of talk and no evidence, ma'am. So you can rest your mind on that score. Of course, with Mr. Titus Crozier being what you might call a ladies' man, and you being a close friend of his, talk was likely. You *are* close to the gentleman, aren't you, ma'am?"

A quiver of the black-feathered fan betrayed her, but her voice was composed.

"We are much of an age, Inspector, and have known each other for many years. If I had had a brother with similar tastes, and grown up with him, we should have been as close. And there would have been no gossip," she added bitterly.

"Your late husband apparently saw no wrong in your association, at any rate, ma'am." The statement lulled her, and he spoke casually. "Were you happy in your marriage, Mrs. Crozier?"

She opened her mouth, hesitated, and glanced rapidly at him. Imperturbable, Lintott raised his eyebrows to encourage her to the truth.

"Not particularly," she replied, and, as he seemed neither surprised nor shocked, "no, Inspector."

"It's not uncommon, ma'am. I wish it was. I'm a happily married man, myself, and grateful for it. This unfortunate association of his must have caused a deal of trouble between you. Very wounding and hurtful to any lady to be passed over for a woman of this sort."

Her bent head was so rigid that Lintott guessed she withheld tears.

"But I believe your brother-in-law acted in good heart on this occasion, and reconciled you both. Acted out of kindness and affection. He admires you, naturally," Lintott continued mildly, giving her time, paying out the rope. "I'd even say he was in love with you. What would you say?"

She wanted to cry that he was impertinent, that he lied, that he must leave the house immediately. But he sat opposite her in his solid, humorous, commonsense way that dared her to do any such stupid thing.

"Come now, ma'am, let's have no humbug. I can't abide humbug. He was in love with you, wasn't he? That's not your fault, is it? He must have made no end of a nuisance of himself, and worried you into the bargain. Why, bless you, a gentleman of that kind can't help courting a woman, now can he?"

She shook her head, soothed and riven at once.

"But you saw through him straightaway, I know. It must have been a temptation—not a real temptation, I don't mean that. I'm thinking that you needed a bit of comfort with your late husband ignoring you, and for someone you wouldn't care to wipe your shoes on. I daresay you didn't know where to turn." She whisked a handkerchief from her sleeve and dabbed at her eyes, under cover of fanning herself.

"I'm not sitting in judgment," said Lintott. "I'm not such a saint—and I don't come across any, in my line of work—as to judge a person's feelings. Feelings aren't actions, you know, ma'am. How long had you and the late Mr. Crozier been at odds with one another?"

"I never knew him," she cried at random. "He was a stranger to me. He led his own life and told me nothing. Anything I ever knew I had to find out for myself, secretly, and keep to myself. I could not please him. I tried, and I could not please him."

Tears were running down her face now, but she made no effort to wipe them away or to conceal them, staring proudly at Lintott: daring him to probe further.

"Would you like me to go away, ma'am? I will, you know. I'm just a policeman doing my duty, not a member of the Spanish Inquisition. I can come back another day."

"No, no. Give me a moment. A moment only. Would you be kind enough to pour me a glass of sherry wine—and join me, of course, if you wish."

Quieter, eyes reddened, she sipped. He had had the effect of a priest hearing confession: cathartic, cleansing, healing.

Now for the next fence, thought Lintott.

"Of course these things happen, ma'am. Men are inclined to say a great deal before marriage, and then forget after. Mrs. Lintott keeps me up to the mark—not that I need keeping, for I know my luck. I daresay your late husband wrote you letters that you've still got by you, tied with a ribbon. My wife keeps mine—and they were poor enough rubbish, though well meant. Still, you know, happy memories. Think of that time in your life, ma'am, and forget the rest. Men do and say unkind things to their wives that they don't mean. Take it from me. God forgive us all."

His strength lay in his sincerity, and in the fact that he never once lost sight of his objective.

"You are exceedingly kind," said Laura, thankful for any kindness.

She felt she owed him something, and repaid with honesty.

"My late husband never wrote me any letter more intimate than a distant acquaintance would write. I have no pleasant foolishness to tie with ribbon."

My dear Laura, I shall be in Bristol during the coming weekend. This is a note to prepare you for what should be no surprise, since you know my mind. I purpose to ask your father for the honor of your hand in marriage. I assure you that I shall do my utmost to make you happy. Your servant, Theodore Crozier.

And out of this she had made a little god of *your servant,* thinking that he meant it truly.

"Men are not always good at expressing their feelings," said Lintott, sorry and alert. "I know I wasn't, but it came through somehow."

Dearest Miss Mouse, I looked in on you while you were asleep last night, and thought a little leopard cub had crept into your bed. But as no leopard ever born had golden hair I knew it must be you, under all those spots. Poor Mousie, I shall buy you a musical box to charm them all away. When you are well again, my love, we must take a long ride in the carriage, and find you a place which sells strawberries and cream. And I shall order two tons of strawberries and twenty gallons of cream, and make you eat every bit. Will you like that, or shall I just ask for a mouse-bowl full? Your loving Papa.

Into her bruised recollection Lintott said, "You found those letters that your husband wrote to his mistress, didn't you, Mrs. Crozier?"

"Yes," said Laura. "It took me a long time, but I found them. He had hidden them in a secret drawer in his desk, but I knew where the spring was."

"Did you burn them? You said you thought they had been burned."

A sleepwalker, she replied, "I did not burn them then, of course, because he would have discovered the loss. There were six altogether. I began to burn them in the bedroom grate, after his death. I kept two, though, in the end. They were the sort of letters I wanted him to write to me, a long time ago."

"Might I see them, my dear?"

The lapse of courtesy passed unnoticed by either of them. Submissive, uncaring, she rang the bell for Kate.

"My jewel box, Kate, if you please—and the key."

The letters lay at the bottom, and she rummaged heedlessly through a little fortune of stones to find them.

My loved, forbidden love, I am laid up again with a wretched chill that my doctor says is the result of the weather we have been suffering. But I could tell him that the fastest cure would be to have you with me. Perhaps I was ill because I had not seen you for a week? I expect so. We speak so lightly of time, and it hangs so heavily upon me in your absence. He tells me that a mere five days will see me on my feet again. If he said five years it would seem as long. I looked into my glass this morning to catch a glimpse of your eyes, and they were not there. I must see you soon, or I shall be ill in earnest. I live to see you. Smile for me. All mine are gone. Theo.

"What color were your husband's eyes, Mrs. Crozier?" Lintott asked gently.

"Dark. Oh, I see what you mean. Her eyes were dark also. I had thought he quoted from John Donne. *Your face in mine eyes, thine in mine, appears.*"

"I thought I'd find a gold mine with these letters," said Lintott, "but now I hardly know what to look for! Unless he saw something that was never there. That's likely enough. We look for someone who fits what we want, and then hang the notion on them like a suit of clothes."

She sat, mute and spent, looking for help in whatever guise.

"Don't you fret yourself," said Lintott, patting her hand. "Eat your dinner up. Food's a great restorer."

Eat your dinner up, like a good girl, Miss Mouse, or you will fade quite away. And then what shall I do without a mouse to buy presents for?

"I should like to thank you, Inspector Lintott. You have been most kind."

Thank you for having me. It was most kind of you.

"And get a good night's sleep, ma'am, if I may be so bold as to say so. Dr. Padgett should be able to help in that direction."

Good night, sleep tight, sweet dreams. God bless, see you in the morning.

"I'll have to take these letters, you know," said Lintott.

No, my love, these are Papa's papers.

"It is of no account to me," said Laura. "They were never mine."

"No," said Lintott.

But they should have been. Why not, I wonder? he thought.

Gauging his expression at the front door, Kate cried, "Mrs. Crozier has had a deal of trouble, sir. I did say so, sir."

"Kate, my dear, *what* was that woman like who brought the letters?"

"A baggage!" said Kate roundly.

Her matter-of-fact response brought himself to himself again. He pinched her cheek.

"So are you, in the nicest possible way, Miss Kate!" said Lintott.

Laura was sitting over her jewel box, a small gold coin clasped in her hand: severed from Titus's watch chain, fifteen years earlier.

We look for someone who fits what we want, and then hang the notion on them like a suit of clothes.

17

"Contrariwise," continued Tweedledee,
"if it was so, it might be; and if it
were so, it would be; but as it isn't,
it ain't. That's logic."
Lewis Carroll
Through the Looking-Glass

Inspector Lintott was always honest with himself, particularly as the nature of his calling demanded that he be sometimes dishonest with others.

But set a thief to catch a thief, Lintott thought, and you never hook a fish but with bait or a crooked pin.

So he partly deceived Mrs. Hill's niece by reporting himself and her aunt as being on especially close and friendly terms.

"Now what a fortunate occurrence," the inspector beamed, "to find you here. I was looking for Mr. Titus Crozier. But I know you, my love, by very good report. I tell you this much—if you can cook a half or a quarter as good as your aunt you'll make some chap a fine wife!"

Lily Day was a plain girl, and his compliment brought up a blush almost fit to match the cruel stain on her left cheek. To which she lifted one hand as if she would blot it out.

"Yes, Lily—it is Lily, isn't it? And as pretty a name as

ever I heard! I'm a police inspector, my dear, but don't be frightened. Lintott's my name. I can see you're a good girl, and I ain't after them, of course. Is your master at home?"

"Please to step inside, sir, if you will. But Mr. Crozier's always at business this time of day."

"Is he now?" cried Lintott, smiting his thigh with his Bollinger. "That's a pity. I thought he kept easier hours."

"No, sir. He's always off afore nine and not back afore six, most days."

"Let's sit down, my dear, I won't keep you above ten minutes."

She crept into a chair and attended him closely.

"I don't expect you've seen any young ladies visit your master, have you, my dear?" Lintott began directly.

She shook her head.

"I gets his breakfast, and then he goes to work, and I've finished here by midday. But I've found hairpins afore now," she said, and lest she had failed him she added, "and I know the name of his regular young lady, because she come here in a proper wax when he was out, and left a message with me."

"I knew," said Lintott, to some invisible deity, "that this young woman had her eyes and ears in the right place, and her head screwed on. What's the lady's name, my dear?"

"Miss Eliza Tucker, sir, and she ain't no lady—she dances at the Alhambra."

"Ah! That means an evening visit, and Mrs. Lintott keeping my supper warm again! A policeman's lot is not a happy one, Lily, eh?" He regarded her with some ruefulness. "What does the lady—we'll call her a lady for form's sake, Lily—what does she look like, now?"

"Showy," said Lily, in a tone reminiscent of her aunt.

"Medium height, a bit on the buxom side, darkish, refined way of speaking? Might wear a veil, a thickish veil?"

"How did you know, sir?"

He laid one finger to the side of his nose, and winked.

"Well, I never did. That's her, sir. Lor' bless me."

"I suppose you haven't seen any other ladies, while he was out?"

"I seen Mrs. Crozier, but then she's family. No, sir. I've gone home long afore he starts amusing of hisself." Mrs. Hill's warnings had taken effect. The girl's voice was tart. "But the hairpins is all different colors."

"I don't suppose you've kept them?" asked Lintott wistfully.

"Well, now you mention it—I have. I don't know why I should, I'm sure," she added ingenuously.

He knew, picturing her on the fringe of Titus's private life. The hairpins were the nearest she was likely to get to romance. But he commended her foresight and prudence, and looked through the little scatter of pins.

"These are a delicate color," he observed, picking out three golden ones.

"Yes, sor, For a fair-complexioned person."

"A lady with light-colored hair?"

"Yes, sir. And this is for brown, and that for auburn, and for black. That Miss Eliza Tucker must've dropped *them*. I tell you, sir, when I took this post my aunt told me what to expect, and I thank my stars she did. I'm 'orrified, sir. I really am."

He patted her arm and set his hard felt hat squarely on his head.

"Mrs. Hill is a remarkable woman, my dear. And so's her niece. Now then, Lily, since you and I understand one another, you needn't mention to Mr. Titus that I called. I'd rather tell him myself, And, Lily, if you happen to see your dear aunt and get to talking about me—I'm a great favorite of hers, you know—tell her the same. If it was anyone but her and you," he said thoughtfully, staring at her, "I'd say that I always find out if someone's been gossiping when they shouldn't." She understood him, and her lips moved as if to repeat the message. "But I don't need to say so, do I?"

She shook her head violently, mesmerized by the slate-colored eyes.

"So, God bless you, Lily. And remember to invite me to your wedding, won't you?"

She was still giggling when he left: one hand lifted to conceal the discolored cheek.

Miss Eliza Tucker was not as young as she would have liked to be and, judging from her manner, bore no deep affection for the police force. Nevertheless, the habit of charming the male animal dies hard, and she allowed the inspector to see more than a ladylike expanse of black net stocking. Otherwise, she pretended to ignore him, bending forward to repair her makeup in the cracked mirror.

She shared a dressing room at the Alhambra with a quantity of other young ladies, and the inspector sat in a pleasant state of siege. They could tell from his serviceable boots, his old Inverness greatcoat, his speech, his hard sensible face, that he was of no use to them. Still, they brushed past him, crying "'Scuse *me*, duckie!" and smiling: leaving a cheap fragrance behind them, a reminder of small armored waists and rustling skirts, a trace of whitening on his sleeve.

"I'll be in trouble with my wife over this," Lintott said good-humoredly, rubbing away at the clinging powder, nodding amiably at each damsel.

He surveyed Miss Tucker's strong calf muscles and over-blown flesh, and reckoned that she had passed her meridian.

"I believe you're acquainted with one Mr. Titus Crozier, my dear," he began in his mild way.

She rouged her mouth, staring at his distorted reflection in the mirror.

"I might be. What of it? I can't remember all their names, I suppose?"

"Ah! You'll have a deal of admirers, my dear, won't you? Thinking of marrying one of them, are you?"

She pulled down her red satin bodice to a more seductive level, and inspected her teeth.

"I might, and then again I might not. That's not what you've come about. I know crushers! Get on with it, will you? I'm not bloody well paid to talk to *you*."

The colloquialism for "policemen" had not escaped him. He became blander.

"Now, my dear, that's an ugly sort of talk. Are you on friendly terms with Mr. Crozier?"

"Friendly? With that bastard? Not on your dear sweet life, I ain't."

"You know very well what I mean, my dear," said Lintott softly. "I know you visit him in his rooms, if you want me to talk plainer. Did you visit his brother, Mr. Theodore, too? There, or elsewhere?"

"You ought to wash your mouth out, you ought," she cried forcibly. "I'm not that sort of a girl."

Lintott sighed, and lifted his eyes to the smoked ceiling.

"We're wasting your time and mine, my dear. Did you or did you not?"

"Never knew he had a brother. He's one of them as says a lot and don't tell you nothing."

"Ah! He's fly."

"Rotten bastard," said Miss Tucker emphatically.

"So you never visited his brother, Mr. Theodore Crozier, or stopped his carriage in the street, or delivered a packet to his house?"

"I told you. How could I if I didn't know him?"

He looked directly at her, for fully a minute. But she glared back: sure of herself on this point at least.

"All right," said Lintott, disappointed. "I believe you. Thousands wouldn't—but, then, I've got a trusting nature. What was Mr. Titus like as a spender? Pretty free?"

"Mind your own ———business."

Lintott tutted. "Now lookee here, my dear, if you don't speak civil to me I'll have a word with Mr. Henderson here and make it hot for you. You want to keep your job, don't you? This job, at any rate?"

She attempted to stare him out, and failed.

"What do you want to know, then?" she asked sullenly.

"I want to know how he paid you," said Lintott bluntly. "Rent? Money? Jewelry? Suppers?"

"He used to give me supper. Sometimes he give me money. But he did the dirty on me with that bloody bracelet."

"Oh, he held out a bracelet, did he? What was dirty about that? Did you take it to the jorryshop and find the diamonds were glass?"

"No. He took it back. Said he wanted to match it with a ring. I'd lent him some cash. Not much, but what I had."

Lintott shook his head slowly in disbelief.

"You don't look like a flat to me, my dear. Whatever came over you to do a thing like that?"

She shrugged thickening shoulders, then looked up with a little hope.

"You can't do anythink for me, can you?"

"No, my dear. There's a many in this world that should be in the stir, by rights. He's one of them, and *I* can't nab him. You'll know better next time. So you got little enough out of him?"

She nodded.

"I should find yourself a decent fellow and get out of this," said Lintott, "before you're coopered."

"One of our girls married a member of the aristocracy," she said defiantly.

"Forget it," Lintott advised. "Take what you can get, and scarper. That's good advice, that is. They won't have room for you here, in another year or two, and then it's the streets or starve."

He rose, nodded at her.

"I'm only twenty-five," she said, challenging him to deny it.

"They come up younger every year, and two a penny. And watch your language. The sort of chap that'll be any use to you won't like it."

"Filthy pig!" she said to herself, when he had gone. "Bloody jack!"

Then danced on stage with the other girls: smiling, glittering, hungry.

18

A child should always say what's true,
And speak when he is spoken to,
And behave mannerly at table:
At least as far as he is able.
        Robert Louis Stevenson
        A Child's Garden of Verses

"Now this is what I like to see," cried Inspector Lintott heartily. "A fine strong child a-tucking into good food," though Blanche was making a poor attempt at tea, in spite of constant dosing with Liebeg's Extract.

"Eight of bread and butter afore she has a slice of sponge cake," said Nanny firmly. "Was you wanting to see me, sir?"

"I can wait," Lintott replied comfortably, accepting a deal chair. "A pleasant room, Miss Nagle."

The nursery overlooked the garden at the back of the house, and Laura's hand was evident in its decoration. The lower portion of the walls was pasted and varnished with scenes from the Christmas books of Mr. Walter Crane and Miss Kate Greenaway: the upper portion distempered for the sake of health and cleanliness. Miss Nagle had made the rag rug on the linoleum. The brass-railed fireguard gleamed and flickered in reflection. Window boxes promised spring flowers.

"And do you keep your toys in that cupboard, my dear?" Inspector Lintott asked the child, seeing not a single Dutch doll, not a golliwog in sight.

Blanche, already in difficulties with her bread and butter, laid the slice down and nodded.

"Speak when you're spoken to, Miss Blanche!" Nanny warned.

"Yes, sir, if you please," said the little girl obediently.

She had inherited her mother's pallor, though it was now flushed with anxiety.

"You needn't mind me, my love," said Lintott, smiling. "I ain't an ogre, you know."

"This gentleman is an important policeman," Nanny threatened, "come to see you eat all your tea like a good girl!"

"Not a bit of it," said Lintott cheerfully. "I've come to see you have your sponge cake. Do you like sponge cake, missie?"

Head bent, speechless, Blanche stared at her plate. Nanny's mouth opened, but he waved at her peremptorily, sternly.

"I like cake," said Lintott, sitting four-square. "Miss Nagle, as you're a friend of mine, you wouldn't like to offer me a cup, would you? Yes, of course you would. I can see it in your face."

Nanny rang the bell with some asperity.

"It's a half after four by my watch," Lintott observed, consulting its plain dial. "Suppose we let poor Nanny have her tea in peace downstairs, and you and I have ours together? Would you like that, missie?" The child, in dread of them both, looked uncertainly from one to the other. "Yes, of course you would."

Harriet Stutchbury appeared at the door with an injured air.

"Ain't you got everythink, Miss Nagle?"

"The inspector'd like a cup of tea," said Nanny reluctantly.

"And give my best compliments to Mrs. Hill, Harriet," said Lintott, "and just mention that I've been on my feet all day, will you, my dear? She'll know what I mean, I'm sure."

"Fetch a tray up, then, and hurry yourself, Harriet!"

"Yes, Miss Nagle. Yes, sir."

She returned with a little banquet that made her arms ache.

"Buttered crumpets," said Lintott, lifting a metal cover. "Piping hot! Three kinds of cake! Cherry conserve! Huntley and Palmer's biscuits! I must be a favorite. Now, my handsome lass," to the bridling nanny, "off with you and enjoy a chat in the kitchen. I'll take care of your young lady here. Lor' bless you, you needn't worry about us. I've got two girls of my own. *I* know all about children."

"Very well, sir. Miss Blanche, mind you eat all your bread and butter!"

"Oh, she will," said Lintott blandly. "I'll see to that."

A straggle of sun crept across the table, and Lintott poured his tea in relaxed silence. The child sat, pink with terror, small hands knotted in her lap, glass of milk untouched.

"Have a piece of crumpet," Lintott offered, holding out the plate.

She shook her head and bit her bottom lip.

"Why ever not, my dear? Don't you like it?"

She swallowed, and said, "Nanny thinks it's too rich."

"I don't," said Lintott. "I think it's capital!"

He threw a bit in the air and caught it in his mouth like a dog. A quiver of lips told him that this was appreciated, so he repeated the performance. She glanced at him quickly, and smiled.

"That's better, my love. Come on. We shan't let Nanny know."

Her fingers sidled to the plate and secured a delicacy. Then she paused.

"What about the bread and butter, sir?"

He stared at the eight triangles in amazement.

"Do you ever get through it all, my love?"

She shook her head, the crumpet clutched in one palm.

"So you never have any cake?"

Another shake.

"I tell you what I'll do," said Lintott, "I'll eat it for you. What about that? Here, you've got your hand all over melted butter. Let me wipe it on my handkerchief." And this he did most carefully. "Now you tuck into whatever catches your fancy, and I'll have a go at this mountain. Do you know something?" Spreading cherry conserve thickly on the bread, and cutting it into strips. "I'll wager you could eat one or two of these as well. Yes, I thought so."

They ate together amiably.

"Sometimes my Uncle Titus eats my bread and butter for me," Blanche confided.

"Does he now? He's a kind uncle, isn't he?"

She nodded several times. "He's funny, too, like you. He makes us laugh. He snored at Christmas, for the man on the lantern slide."

"That's good, my love. Does Nanny make you laugh? And Mama?"

"Oh no. Nanny says not to do things. Mama reads to me. But Uncle Titus is funny all the time."

"What about your two brothers, missie?"

The gray eyes were surprised.

"Edmund and Lindsey are boys. They would not play with a girl. Besides, they are not at home now, except in the holidays."

"Who do you play with, then? Other little girls?"

"Sometimes. Fräulein Walther is my governess, but she is not my very own governess. She teaches at three houses and we all share her. One week she comes to our house. Then next week she comes to Julia's house. Then next week she comes to Frances's house. Then next week to our house. She teaches Julia's sister and Frances's sister, too."

"And what do you learn, my love?"

"Deportment and French and music and drawing and arithmetic and history and general knowledge. And when I am older, I shall learn German and watercolor painting as well."

"I daresay you're a clever girl, aren't you?"

"Not very, because I think of something else instead of listening. But Nanny says better to be good than clever. But Fräulein Walther says to pay attention."

The state of her fingers dismayed her.

"Wipe them on my handkerchief again, and destroy the evidence, missie. Poor Papa must have been proud of you. *I* should have been."

"Papa has gone to heaven because he was a good man."

"That's right, my love."

"He would like me to speak the truth, since he watches over us." She was troubled, remembering. "Papa could not love me very much because I made so many mistakes, you see."

"We all do, missie."

"I make more mistakes than anybody else. All the time. The pennies fall off the back of my hands when I am playing the piano, and Nanny has to wash my sewing before I can show it."

"But Mama doesn't mind mistakes, does she?"

"Mama does not notice. She has so many headaches."

"And is there nobody in the house that makes much of you, my love?"

"Only Uncle Titus. I love him best—except for Papa and Mama, of course. May I get down now, sir? I have had sufficient."

"Yes, my love. Did you know that rag rugs told stories? Come and look at this one. Here's a bit of bright blue that might have been one of Mama's gowns. And a bit of dark gray that might have been Papa's suit. Do you see?"

[195]

"That red is Sergeant Malone's old jacket. If I am a bad girl, Nanny says, the sergeant will fetch me and put me in prison."

Lintott's plain face was expressionless.

"A soldier can't do that, missie. That's *my* job. You see this here key?" He brought out the humble instrument that locked his garden shed at Richmond. "You see the size of it?" She nodded, impressed. "That's the prison key," said Lintott deeply. "Now if I've got this key how can anybody else open the door?"

She stood by his side, hands clasped behind her back, white-stockinged legs together, low-heeled strap shoes shining. He looked at the pale pretty face, the pale tongue of hair, the submissive head and gentle mouth.

"Is Nanny telling—fibs, sir?" she dared to ask, and was appalled.

Lintott considered the question gravely.

"She's made a mistake, that's all. She thought it was true, but it isn't. So next time she mentions the sergeant fetching you, you tell her that Inspector Lintott said she had made a mistake. Say it politely, mind. And tell her, by the bye, that I've spoken with Sergeant Malone, will you?"

"Was there any message, sir?"

"No message, my love. Just tell Nanny I've spoken to him."

The sound of Nanny's footsteps on the stairs took the ease from the child's body, and brought anxiety back.

"Well now," Lintott said blithely, "Miss Blanche is a credit to you, Miss Nagle. All that bread and butter's eaten right up!"

Miss Nagle did not return from the parlor immediately, and when she came into the nursery she was concealing something in her apron.

"I've got somethink for you, sir," the nanny whispered, though no one could have overheard.

"Indeed, Miss Nagle? And what might that be?"

"You know what you said, sir, about keys being left in desk drawers and that?"

"I can't remember every blessed thing I say, my lass. You may have misunderstood my meaning, for all I know."

"I've got her diary."

"Be careful, now," he warned her with an uplifted finger. "Be very particular as to your words, Miss Nagle."

"Oh, I've done nothink wrong, sir. It all turned out as you said."

"I said nothing."

She was impatient, wanting to impress and soothe him, to rid herself of him since he had the power to make her uneasy.

"Very well then, sir, you said nothink. I happened to notice this diary lying about and I brought it to you while Mrs. Crozier and Miss Blanche are in the parlor. Only I must be quick to put it back, sir."

"Lying about, eh? Harmless enough, I should think," turning the pages swiftly, snapping up items.

Nanny stood tall and thin, twisting her hands in her apron, trying to read his expression.

"A lady writes down her daily sorrows and blessings, Miss Nagle. Our dear queen, God bless her, keeps a diary. Nothing that can't be read by anyone. But precious, Miss Nagle, very precious to the lady concerned." He stopped, noted, passed on. "Something to look back on in one's old age." Turning, memorizing, calculating. "Something to pick up and think, 'Ah! That was the time!' Eh, Miss Nagle?"

"Yes, sir. To be sure."

"A carriage ride here. A theater there. A gift. A letter. What does it mean to the outsider? Paltry stuff, one might say. And yet, to the writer, a whole world. Yes, as I thought, nothing here, Miss Nagle." He closed the book, held it out, and said sharply, "When did you find the key?"

"On Tuesday, sir."

"Two days ago. Have you read this?"

"Oh no, sir. No, sir."

"Where did you find the key, Miss Nagle?"

Ferreting among silk and velvet and serge and linen. Searching closets and drawers. Feeling beneath pillows and mattresses. One ear cocked for footsteps. Finally, closing the fingers around it at the bottom of a bowl of potpourri. Sly cat! So that's where she hides it?

"I must take it back, sir. I'm sorry it's of no use to you."

"Not a bit of use," said Lintott airily, examining his fingernails. "But then I didn't expect it would be."

"I hope I did right, sir," holding the green leather volume to her starched front.

Lintott looked at her heavily from beneath his brows.

"I hope you did, too, Miss Nagle. Private property is private property. If you were so tempted as to commit a little breaking and entering, or anything of that sort, it would be a serious matter."

"Oh no, sir," she sought to protect herself, falling between one lie and the next, contradicting herself. "The key was in the lock and the drawer half open."

He regarded his nails with interest.

"And if you were to talk to anyone—I hope you haven't done so, my dear—even to that dashing sergeant that worships the ground you tread on ... Well, I couldn't answer for the consequences. That would be slander atop of theft, to my mind. But then, you've done nothing of that kind, have you, my dear?"

"No, sir. Indeed I haven't."

He became genial and patted her shoulder.

"Then pop it back and let's forget it, shall we?"

"Oh yes, sir, if you please."

He donned the hat from which even Kate had been unable to part him, and nodded amiably.

She watched the inspector descend the stairs in slow

dignity, and then hurried to Laura's bedroom. Fearful that Kate might come in on her early evening duties, she thrust the diary back, locked the drawer, and buried the key beneath the dried confetti of potpourri. Then she smoothed the surface, so that no one should notice.

19

As a general rule, a modest woman seldom desires
any sexual gratification for herself. She submits
to her husband only to please him . . . . No nervous
or feeble young man need, therefore, be deterred
from marriage by an exaggerated notion of the duties
required from him.

William Acton, M.R.C.S., 1857

London at dusk was poignant enough to stir even Lintott's stolidity. The evening light on the river, the long exquisite shadows, the dark alleys, the tall chimneys on the skyline, softened him. Clicking his tongue in contentment, he walked more slowly and looked all about him. A lamp-lighter trod his nightly rounds, leaving behind a train of shimmering gas globes. At the street corner an old man roasted chestnuts on a brazier, and shoveled them into paper cones. A hurdy-gurdy ground its plaintive tune, and the monkey whisked off his military pillbox hat. Lintott, finding the animal's eyes distressingly human, dropped a farthing into its braided cap.

The steamed windows of food shops shone against the dark, cajoling customers with warmth and odors. For one penny you could buy a meaty saveloy, two faggots, a paper of fish and chips, a fried or boiled egg, a bloater, sardines on toast, a slab of Nelson cake (sweet with icing sugar), two large oranges, two thick slices of bread and butter, a pair of kippers, or a big cup of tea, coffee, or cocoa. Twopence brought you into the realms of ham sandwiches, sausages, bacon, and fresh cream horns. For threepence you could dine on a helping of Harry Champion (boiled beef and carrots), Baby's Head (steak and kidney pudding), or Side View (half a baked sheep's head). Butchers, clad in blue and white striped aprons and straw boaters, offered fresh rump steak at one shilling a pound; or the same quantity of any boiled joint at the same price with a pint of gravy; wing rib and sirloin at eightpence; small chops and stew cuttings for fourpence to sixpence. The walls of the general stores were studded with cheeses, and a shaving of any was given on request, for tasting. The dairies—brass scales gleaming, deal counter scrubbed white—sold eggs in wicker baskets at ninepence the dozen, full-cream milk at twopence a pint. All the shops had opened before eight that morning, and would not close until ten or eleven o'clock that night.

By the bookstalls, men with more learning than substance browsed endlessly and sometimes bought a battered volume for a penny or so. In the great workshops of the West End the seamstresses and milliners stitched twelve hours a day, and would work through the night on a special order.

A cavalcade of horse-drawn buses bore an army of clerks home from offices: lit inside by oil lamps, rich outside with advertisements. *Holloway's Pills & Ointment, Oakey's Wellington Knife Polish, Paysanda Tongue, Vinolia Soap, Pink's Jam, Borwick's Baking Powder.* On top, muffled in scarves and greatcoats, topped by oilskin capes and an old hat pulled well down, rode the kings of the highway: the omnibus drivers. Their bellies were warmed by frequent draughts of Disher's Barley Wine (a potent ale); their faces crimsoned by all weathers. They carried their whips like wands of office. Their horses, also supported by an inward application of a Burton beer, hauled their loads fifteen hours a day. These Victorian knights bore the burden of envy and impudence with stalwart indifference: taunted by boys who could not afford the fare. "Garn whiskers!" they would shout, running alongside, "Who strapped you in? Muvver?" Sometimes to be dispatched with a light flick of the whip, like flies. And there were conventions among the passengers, too. Ladies and children rode inside, young bloods rode outside; and no young man would be seen boarding a bus in the usual style—they either leaped on when it was moving or jumped down before it had stopped. Furthermore, the Dumb Friends' League insisted on printed pleas bearing the message "Stop the Bus as Seldom as Possible as the Restarting is a Great Strain upon the Horses." But the drivers stopped anywhere, when signaled from the pavement.

Now, as the light waned, and the muffin man took home his bell and tray, the other life of London came awake. Fortunate children were at home or abed. The unfortunate scurried into shops to buy fragments of cheese or ham for the family supper; begged from the shadows; waited outside public houses; or huddled together for warmth in doorways and arches and along the embankment, homeless and destitute.

The majority of chophouses and coffeehouses would be closed by eleven, but taverns and supper rooms and night coffeehouses were coming into their own. The earlier entertainments—from the glitter of Covent Garden to the tawdry threepenny show at the Royal Victoria Theatre—were done. As lonely men finished dining or applauding, the darkest face of London turned from its looking glass and sought the streets.

In the West End, the great courtesans distributed fleshly largesse to an exclusive and well-heeled clientele. In Brompton or Chelsea, in St. John's Wood or Fulham, clever ladies, securely established, gave their favors exclusively to one admirer who settled the rent. In the night resorts their more available sisters, gaudily dressed, coquetted for money among the gentlemen present. Along the Ratcliffe Highway, and in every dock, sailors' tarts strolled arm in arm and hoarsely cried their wares to any passing seaman: lifting beribboned gowns to show a plump pink-stockinged calf, flourishing bright brass heels which could dance or stamp. Against the damp walls of alleys, love and cash made rapid exchange. A man could be robbed and coshed if the lady had a waiting accomplice, but on the whole the trade of buying and selling was straightforward enough. Lower down still, the worn vendors of pleasure walked the city pavements, soliciting. They promised paradise for a few pence, in a voice husky with gin; though the pocked face beneath the veil and the ravaged body beneath the frippery were visions out of hell. And deepest in the pit, lying or squatting on bare boards, racked by disease and wasted by poverty, the remnants of the oldest profession in the world died in rags and squalor.

Expensive but obtainable, virgins of thirteen were lured, drugged, and raped by particularly fastidious connoisseurs—some of whom thought to cure themselves in this way from venereal disease. A little court of necessary accomplices ministered to this gourmet's market, from the procuress to the woman who first pronounced the girls pure and then made good the subsequent despoliation.

Less prolific, because less easily traced, the other side of sexuality catered mainly for members of the services who had acquired a taste for the male body. Open solicitations were infrequent, but behind the respectable skirts of many a madam, boys sat up late at night "waiting for Jack," and older she-shirts were available at every port. The Amendment Act of 1885—the Blackmailer's Charter, as it was dubbed—pronounced any public or private sexual act between males a criminal offense, thereby arousing an interest among members of the underworld which had formerly been absent. Threats of giving information to the police now drew gold from the pockets of citizens who could not afford to be known as homosexuals. This simmering cauldron was to boil over England in 1895, dimming the brilliance of Oscar Wilde and marking "Bosie" Douglas's failure to be either a normal man or a loyal friend. They had made the cardinal mistake of being found out: a sin Victorian society was unable to forgive.

From these various caterers incarnate, the brothel-keepers, the fancy men, and the pug-uglies collected a lion's share of earnings. The honeycombed lodging houses of Bluegate Fields rented out rooms for a few shillings a week, or a shilling a night, to any wretched whore who would pay. But elegant establishments charged a couple of guineas per client. Allied to the accommodation houses were the introducers, who found ladies to suit all tastes and contacted potential customers at their clubs or offices, by letter.

Last and most vulnerable of all, the unwanted offspring of a desperate girl could find a market. For the sum of five pounds a baby-farmer would undertake to adopt and raise the infant, promising a comfortable home and a parent's care if the child was sickly. Bastards, being the result of vice, naturally succumbed more quickly. The death rate among illegitimate children was eight times higher than among the legitimate.

All this Inspector Lintott carried in a shrewd head, and regretted in a private heart. So much misery, acquisitiveness, and degradation must have set his face against humanity had it not been for the Richmond sanctuary. Here, in his slippers and old jacket, he could listen to lighter voices and enjoy a sweeter world. Twenty years of marriage had fleshed Mrs. Lintott handsomely, turned a vivacious girl into a mettlesome woman, and transformed a tendency to giggle into sound good humor. She thought her husband the cleverest and best man on earth, and he concealed nothing from her but the noisome details of his profession. So she darned and sewed and knitted, and passed on the news of the neighborhood while he smoked and thought. He listened because he loved her and the sound was pleasing, but the policeman in him never rested: sifting, docketing, remembering. As he often said, all information could be useful. So Richmond, too, was under his vigilant eye. He picked up knowledge from his children in the same manner, and was proud that John thought of entering the police force, and Joseph the queen's army. He tended—as his wife told him—to be overindulgent with his two daughters, though he insisted on good schoolwork so that they might attain posts in offices. This consideration apart, they took gross advantage of his affection. And he, knowing how hard life was for a woman, rendered their girlhood easy.

This tenderness in him could temporarily bemuse his judgment, and he had clung to a belief in Laura's innocence of adultery until the evidence was paramount. Now, treading his corrupt city, he turned over the pages of her diary in his mind and searched for excuse. She had taken him into deeper feminine waters than those to which he had been accustomed, and he brought all his seamanship to negotiating them. Titus's love letter might have been merely an expression of his feeling for Laura; and no woman could be blamed for arousing love, only for wrongly gratifying it. She had torn his letter into pieces, and could have appeared to dismiss his suit.

Foolish, Lintott thought. She should have burned it. But then she is careless with pen and ink. The diary.

The name of Woman, to him as to all members of his sex, even though they might desecrate it, was synonymous with Virtue.

When lovely woman stoops to folly, and finds too late that men betray. She should have thought of that. And she should never, never have written it. Anyone might have found it. Her husband even.

He wondered for a moment whether Theodore had

indeed unearthed the diary and doubly betrayed, sought a violent way out. Then sent the idea packing as romantic nonsense.

"Fiddlesticks!" said Lintott aloud, and startled a beggar in a doorway.

He had formed a pretty accurate picture of Theodore Crozier, and his strength of purpose was too powerful to be dismissed.

No, you would never find a man like that shirking his duty, Lintott thought. A great one for duty. He would have confronted both wife and brother and demanded an explanation. Then what? Dissolve the partnership with the brother, probably, and turn the wife onto her relative. And he himself, brooding over the household and children, would face life alone. Alone but right. That was what mattered to Theodore: the rightness. A righteous man, a correct man, a man, who insisted on all the rules and kept them strictly.

Then why the mistress? And, taking it further, why the letters? A man's physical needs were not the same as those of a woman, but even there a code existed, rules existed. It was laid down in heaven, where marriages were made, that one loved one's wife. So it followed that one did not love one's mistress, only found relief or amusement with her. This mistress, according to Kate—whose opinion he respected—had been one such as a fastidious man would not be expected to love.

But you never get to the bottom of the human heart, and that's a fact, Lintott mused. Anything might be so.

That diary!

Laura's hand etched the night with words and phrases which caused him softly to click his tongue in rebuke.

It wouldn't be half so bad, he thought, if the Titus fellow was worth it. But he ain't.

He stopped in his tracks, appalled, and shook his head as if to clear it. No, it would be bad whichever way you looked at it, he admonished himself. What more could such a woman want than a rich husband, three fine children, and a nice house? Theodore Crozier wasn't mean with her. Those dresses of hers cost a pretty penny, let alone the jewels. Money of her own, of course. Five hundred a year was not to be sniffed at.

I'll never smell that much, and that's another fact, he thought. But *he* didn't keep up such a front on four times that amount, I'll wager. That firm must be worth—what? And she's inclined to whim money away, I'll be bound. Reckless, though you'd never think it to look at her. Reckless with money as long as there's nobody to stop her. I wonder if that fellow has coaxed his debts out of her, yet? Got her to sign something. Reckless with her reputation, and that's a thing a woman should value above all else. Everybody talking, sniggering, speculating. Reckless in feeling, more heart than judgment. Reckless enough to . . . Well, women are fickle cattle. Even the good ones can surprise you. The desperate ones usually do.

If only he would allow me a room of my own I could endure him a little better. But to him appearance is everything and, though he cares no more for my presence than I for his, we must seem to be man and wife. I thank God that is all over. What misery men can inflict upon us! And yet, not misery when it is the man one needs.

I don't like "needs," Lintott thought, walking faster. "Loves" would be more delicate. Women don't need. Do they? Not her sort of woman, at any rate. Of course, there are society women who—one hears tales. She don't appear forward, not in any way forward. My Bessie, now, I would call—cozy. A warm woman, a womanly woman, a happy one I should say. But not "needs." Never "needs" surely? That's not right, somehow.

Do I really love Titus? I do not know. Is that not a strange thing to wonder when he disturbs me so deeply? At eighteen I should have said with confidence that I did love him, and say so from blind ignorance. He could have made me happy in this way, but not in others. Could I ever have tired of him? I love him when he is loving. At times I have hated him. If we had been married for fifteen years, and I had been constantly hurt by his weakness with women and with money, with his gambling, should I still have loved him? Should I still have needed him as a lover, or would that have been over by now as it is with Theodore? Yet, with Theodore, that never began.

Well, your late husband was no more pleased with you than you were with him, madam, Lintott chided the phantom in the dusk. He had to discover love outside his own home, and make a scandal of himself. Yes, ma'am, love. There must have been "need" as you so immodestly call it, but there was love too—of a sort. I'd like to meet that woman he made a fool of himself over, and see what he cared so much about. I should find a clue to all the rest in her.

I was told by Mama to expect something that I should not, as a woman of delicacy, find agreeable. But she assured me that this was a necessary part of marriage. She informed me that a lady accepted a man's ardor with forbearance. I believe that my mother even used the words "with fortitude." She said this must be so if I was to fulfill myself and my duty by bearing children. I had assumed my parents enjoyed a loving marriage. I think of them both, and I wonder what years of wretchedness they shared between them. For my father was an ardent and tender man—I know what ardor and tenderness are!—and she was not a passionate woman.

And very proper, Lintott reflected. Why should they not have had a loving marriage? Very likely they did.

Theodore wasted no time on words of passion, of loving protestation, as Mama had said he would. He spoke of duty and submissiveness. I did not understand him. I looked for some token of consideration or solicitude. There was nothing. Cold, cold, cold, and then chaos.

Lintott strode his London more firmly, resolving on his next course of action.

My Mama told me that my father had recited to her from the Song of Solomon and that she had found this even more shameful than what followed. She said she could not wait for him to be done, but that this was the lot of women. After Titus and I had been together in his rooms I locked myself up at the house for an hour, and wept. I was not weeping for myself or for shame—that came later when I feared he had made love to me lightly. I wept then for my father, and felt close to him. I wished that he were still alive so that I might see him, sit with him, and say nothing. We could always share silences, he and I. We should have shared that loss which must never be mentioned, in that particular silence. I wonder if he ever thought of me?

Ah, you're a strange one, Lintott admonished her. Let well alone, ma'am. Men are as different from women as chalk from cheese. Don't you go setting your bonnet on your father's head. It won't fit. What am I to do about you, I wonder? For you've enough evidence around you—though I shouldn't like to use it—to make that coroner change his mind in five minutes flat. Crime of passion, he'd call it. But what could you have gained by it? Deceased man's widow can't marry his brother. Or did you think it would leave room for another game or so on the side? Surely not. Surely not. I can't fathom you, madam. Perhaps you just thought, as women are inclined to do, that the best way to deal with a knot is to cut it!

I strive daily to separate from my husband, in my mind. Given time I shall do so. Then I may be at peace, and he will have what he most wants—an obedient stranger. Our lives will not be any worse than others I know. I have watched and listened to friends and acquaintances, and many of

[209]

them are as dead as ourselves. If I were all mother, as most women are, I could be content. But I am not. There is something else within me which must and shall be answered. I wish I could go far away. I wish I had never been born at all. I wish I could die.

He halted, and his face cleared. I'd forgotten the significance of that bit, he thought. I wonder—she'd never dare say so—whether she tried to make away with herself? She's quite a possible suicide, not probable but possible. Perhaps she crushed up those capsules in a glass of water or wine for herself, and he took it by mistake? And then she told that tale of the one pill she gave him as a sort of half truth. Perhaps not. Perhaps it's that fellow Titus. I can't see how he did it, but he's hard enough to clear folks out of his path if they stand in his way. Not murder as a matter of course. He's no common murderer. But given the opportunity, once in a lifetime, he's weak enough and strong enough to take it. Much more likely. Much more likely. The only other that I can see, that had some sort of grudge against the deceased, is our pretty Kate. And she wouldn't commit herself. Our Kate won't budge an inch unless the country's mapped out first. She'd like to be her mistress, but she never will be. Not in a thousand years. Kate has a head on her, and she's cautious. The other one, in the same position as Kate, would have ruined herself by now with an underfootman! Aye, and called it love and need and whatever word best suits her. Ah, reckless, reckless! And yet—poor creature.

But I must let them know what I've found out, and put a stop to it. Why, Lord above, what might happen to her else? She can no more deal with that sort of fellow than a baby can. We don't want another scandal atop of this one. If she got herself in trouble we'd never fetch that piece of fat out of the fire! And it brings everybody else in, too, children and all. No, no, no. She must get through her widowhood as best she can, without Master Titus's attentions. She could marry again later—some steady chap who would look after her, fuss over her a bit. Women only need a little management. A kind word here and there, a kiss before you go in the morning and another at night, an arm about them when they're feeling down, and just to say what you think about them now and again. Like my Bessie. A cozy woman, my Bess, a warm woman, a woman that loves me. But all that about "needs." I'd set it down to sheer badness!

They were wary of receiving him, but had no choice. Lintott thought them a handsome couple, an elegant couple, as he permitted Kate to take his hat. Titus stood in his favorite attitude by the fire, one arm on the draped mantelshelf, one foot on the brass fender. Laura sat resplendent in black velvet; her amethysts about her neck, and pendant from her ears, and sparkling on arms and bosom and fingers. Mourning suited her, lent her an added dignity above which her pale beauty seemed more moving and more fragile than usual.

Her dressmaker does well out of her, Lintott reflected. What an air she has of giving a fresh picture of herself—like my Bessie with a new hat. And his tailor knows his business. I hope he gets paid!

"Good evening, Mrs. Crozier, Mr. Crozier. My regrets for asking an interview of you both, but it is a matter of some importance. Of grave importance, I may say. Thankee, yes, I'll take a chair." And he sat stolidly upon the balloon-backed ornament, his thick boots planted between its gilt legs. "Cold again, this evening?"

Something in his manner alerted Laura, and she looked at him quickly. He looked back, remote and implacable.

"Cold indeed, Inspector," said Titus amiably. "Now, perhaps, if you would state your business?"

"Certainly, sir. Straight to the point. That's what I prefer—if it suits the lady?"

Again she raised her head, sensing withdrawal. Then nodded slightly, in agreement, and fanned herself.

"Evidence has come my way—I shan't say what or how unless it's necessary—but conclusive evidence as to one aspect of this inquiry."

"You have discovered something in connection with my late brother's death?"

"No, sir. In connection with yourself and this lady."

"More gossip, no doubt," said Titus angrily, shifting his position as though the fire were too hot.

Laura became very still, the fan drooping from her hand.

"I said *evidence,* sir." And, as Titus prepared to brave him out, he added persuasively, "Surely you won't cause the lady further distress by asking me to produce it? I will, if you insist. I can, you know."

You made a fool of me, ma'am, with that lost air about you. But I found you out. Not what I thought, ma'am. Not what I thought at all.

Titus flung himself into Theodore's easy chair, crossed his legs, set the palms of his hands together, and regarded Lintott steadily.

"I will accept that you have evidence, Inspector. Pray go on."

"There's little enough to say, sir—and ma'am. I can prove that a certain relationship existed—I don't say that it does so now—between you. I can prove that it was a strong one. I venture to say, strong on *both* sides."

He didn't take you lightly. At least, he may have done so in the beginning, but not in the end.

Laura spread out her fan slowly, and did not see a silk flight of hummingbirds winging across it. A little warmth comforted the supreme chill of exposure. He had said, *on both sides.*

"Now before we go any further," said Lintott carefully, "and I shall go no further than I must, I assure you of that, do you admit the said evidence?"

Titus replied coolly, "If it is evidence then we need no admission, surely?"

"It's just that I never did like talking in the dark," said Lintott bluntly.

Titus hesitated, wondering if it were possible to outfox him. But Laura spoke softly and definitely, staring at her painted aviary, trying to set everything right again.

"The relationship did exist, and now does not, Inspector Lintott."

If he does not take care of me, then I shall come home to you.

"Very well, ma'am. You've spoken out fair and open. I'll do the same. A man that was inclined to jump to conclusions would say that he had a case here that could stand up in court."

Let us have no nonsense on that score, Laura. You understand me?

"You consider," said Titus quietly, "that my sister-in-law and I, being guilty of the one offense, are also guilty of the other and greater?"

"It is a possibility to be explored, sir, but it is not yet the answer."

Laura, wounded and drooping, communed with her fan. Lintott glanced anxiously at her.

"If my word is of any value to you," said Titus slowly. "I can assure you that neither of us is guilty of murder, at any rate."

Lintott nodded, short and sharp, as if to say *I hear you.* But no more.

"I believe we are not above halfway through this case yet, sir. I have to trace the lady who delivered the letters, and in her will lie other answers. I don't say all the answers. I don't know. I must find her first."

He glanced again at Laura, but she had been rebuffed once too often.

"Perhaps you and I could have a word alone somewhere, sir? Mrs. Crozier need not be disturbed any more this evening."

Run along, now, Laura.

"Pray do not trouble yourselves," she said quickly, and with great dignity. "I have household matters which require my attention. I beg you to excuse me." She confronted Lintott without defiance, without hope. "Good night, Inspector. Please do not hesitate to call again if that is necessary."

Still he had one more duty to perform, that of cautioning her.

He bowed awkwardly.

"Good night, ma'am. And, if I might mention it, I should leave any personal papers in the house exactly as they are. I have witnesses as well as evidence. If you was inclined to tear or burn anything, say, I should take it as an admission of guilt and act accordingly."

Alarmed, Titus surveyed them both, trying to gauge the gravity of the situation. Laura held herself proudly, tried to meet Lintott's flat gaze, and trailed gracefully from the room.

"Now, sir, we may speak a bit freer. I've had a word with an old friend of yours, Miss Eliza Tucker of the Alhambra, thinking she might be the lady involved with your brother. I am satisfied that she was not."

Titus's disgust stopped him for a moment.

"Did you imagine that my brother and I would share a mistress, Inspector?"

"I've heard of it before," Lintott replied frankly. "Why should it be any worse to share Miss Tucker with your own brother than with half a dozen strange men?"

Titus flushed.

"If that were so I should have known, should I not?"

"Oh, I don't know about that," said Lintott, very easy, very light. "The lady might be robbing Peter to pay Paul. It has been done, sir."

"I find your suggestion both vile and dishonorable."

"Ah well! Our notions of honor are different, sir," said Lintott drily. "I had observed that."

Titus was silent, lighting a cigar.

"Now do you know of anything at all, sir, that might help to trace the lady concerned?"

Titus shook his head, and blew out the spill.

"Very well, sir. I must go about it the long way then."

"Will that be all, Inspector?"

"For now, sir, yes. Oh, by the by, none of those anonymous letters was written by any of Mrs. Crozier's servants—or by your servant, Lily Day. Perhaps you'd be good enough to tell Mrs. Crozier of that? She may be worrying."

"I shall inform her, of course," said Titus coldly, and rang the bell for Kate.

"And, sir, I trust that Mrs. Crozier's reputation will not be further blemished. It would look very bad in court, sir, and we may come to court yet, if I was to be forced to give evidence on that as well! And I shall find out, sir, make no mistake. I have eyes and ears all over the place. You'd be surprised. I probably know more about Mrs. Crozier than even you suspect."

Ah! You're a handsome villain, Lintott thought, regarding the well-set head and hazel eyes.

"Nothing about you would surprise me, Inspector," said Titus lazily. "Do you not find police work a rather dirty business?"

"Yes, sir," Lintott replied. "But then, it's the people I deal with that makes it dirty—not me. Good night to you, sir."

In the hall he pinched Kate's cheek: an outrage which she condoned with one toss of the head. Lintott shook a finger at her and winked joyfully.

"Tell me, my love, you did say that the veiled lady came in a hansom cab?"

"Yes, sir. It was waiting for her."

"I don't suppose that you noticed what the cab driver looked like, did you, my love?" Lintott asked wistfully.

"You're a sharp girl, but I don't expect many people to be as sharp as that."

She thought carefully, and he waited.

"He was a stout man, with a red face, and spoke very husky telling the horse not to move about so."

"They're all stout with red faces and hoarse voices, my dear. It's the beer inside and the weather out that does it."

She thought again, drawing her brows together, and he saw what she would look like when she was older: shrewd and highly competent.

"But I remember thinking he must have been stout, even without two greatcoats, sir."

"Two of 'em, eh? Any particular style or color?"

"A dirty green one atop of a dirty gray. Very old-fashioned, sir, with a double cape, the green coat. Oh, and he wore a hat that had once been white. A dirty white velveteen. It must have belonged to a gentleman when it was new."

"That's good, Kate. Well, the two coats and the hat might find him—though he ain't the only cabbie as wears old-fashioned greatcoats that once belonged to a gentleman. They gets them from the dunnage shops."

"There was somethink else, sir," said Kate, losing her gentility with mental concentration. "His left arm was stiff, as if he'd been wounded and it didn't mend right. I remember with him reining in the horse—along of the cat running across the road, and right under its feet—and his arm being nearest to me."

She stopped, eyes shining. There was something about Lintott that made people want either to please or to placate him.

"A stiff arm, eh? A stiff left arm. Been in the Crimea, belike. Now I'd have you in the force along of me, Kate—if they allowed the ladies. Except that you'd be a distraction to my men! Kate, I take off my hat to you," and he raised it in admiration.

She did not demur when he took her by the chin and

smiled at her.

"That butler!" said Lintott sincerely. "He's a lucky chap! Ain't he, my love?"

Laura sent down an excuse to Titus in the form of a headache, and felt in the potpourri bowl for her key. The diary, too, was still there. But she knew that he had read it, that someone in the house had betrayed her to him. She sensed the chill beneath his courtesy, the accusation behind his eyes.

Thou shalt not.

Her fingers gripped a handful of pages, and paused. She meditated on the book and then on the fire which burned in the hearth. Two things stayed her: Lintott's warning, and the preciousness of this possession. The diary had been breath in a room without air, and all that remained of love.

For several minutes she struggled this way and that with the problem. Then, clutching the book to her bodice, she bowed her head and wept.

PART THREE

CONCLUSIONS

20

The prostitute is the most efficient guardian of virtue. But for her, the unchallenged purity of countless happy homes would be polluted.

W. E. H. Lecky
History of European Morals

"Mrs. Molly Flynn? My name is Inspector Lintott of Scotland Yard. Is it convenient to come in, my dear, or shall I come back?"

"I was expecting a friend in about an hour," said Mrs. Flynn delicately, "but come in, pray. Always delighted to assist the police in their duties."

She pinched her vowels and held on to the consonants as though they were intimate friends, but Lintott detected a native Cockney striving to get out. Furthermore, though her dark red dress was of good quality and fitted well, it fell short of elegance. Mrs. Flynn's fondness for pleated frills rose from hem to bodice, and the bodice was something lower than a lady would have worn in the afternoon. Her waistline had been achieved at the cost of extremely tight lacing, and combined with a volatile nature it tended to render her slightly breathless. She rouged a little, powdered more, used patchouli lavishly, but set her fancy free on jewelry.

"You'd be worth knocking down and robbing, Mrs. Flynn," said Lintott waggishly, placing his hard hat on one of the several little tables scattered about the room. It rocked gently.

"I'd like to see anybody try!" cried his hostess, forgetting herself. "Take a look at that!"

Whereupon she flexed a plump white arm. The muscles stood out ripely.

"Now I do like a woman of spirit. Shall I sit here, my dear? You make yourself very comfortable, don't you?"

The chair was overstuffed, like all the furniture, and bore a curious resemblance to its owner. She had been making up her mind about him. Now she smiled frankly and good-naturedly, and he grinned back.

"I've done nothink wrong, dear," she said, doffing the acquired accent. "And you know I haven't. This is a private house. I pay my rates and taxes. I don't have no trouble with the police nor my neighbors. Nobody's ever complained about me."

"Well, they won't, will they, Molly? I can call you Molly, can't I? They're on the same dodge as yourself."

"Have a lush, do!" she coaxed, ignoring the remark.

"Not while I'm on duty, Molly. But don't let me stop you having your drop, my dear."

She threw back her head and laughed, showing a fine strong throat. Given another twenty years and her present prosperity, she could retire to some respectable place and set herself up as a respectable citizen, and probably would.

"Shall I read your mind, Molly?" Lintott asked. "So that we understand one another? I'm not here to beef or blow."

"I'm with you, dear."

"I know you keep a nice house, and I'll wager you could show me your marriage lines, too."

She poured herself half a tumbler of gin and nodded in the direction of her walnut bureau.

"I thought so, Molly. Very good, my dear. I'll lay another little bet. There's even a Mr. Flynn round. Not quick-tempered as a rule, but a well-set-up chap that could turn nasty if anyone made trouble while they were here. You're not Irish, though, Molly."

"Whitechapel, born and bred. Have a cigar? They're good ones. Havanas."

"Not just now, my dear, thankee. But you light up, if you've a fancy for them. I'll give you a glim," and he struck the match for her cigar, which she inhaled with considerable enjoyment. "Is your husband at home, Molly?"

"Down in the kitchen, reading his paper. He'll come up if you want him," and she indicated the bell rope at her elbow.

"I'd rather have you to myself, if he makes no objection, my dear."

She shrugged her magnificent shoulders.

"He don't mind."

"No, I don't suppose he does. A clever wife, popular among her friends, plenty of finnies to spend, and nothing to do but throw the lushingtons out. Am I right?"

She smiled broadly and nodded, drinking her gin, drawing on the cigar, eyes half closed and glinting beneath shaded lids.

"And Mr. Flynn is quite the family man. Having no kynchin of his own he fetches his nieces over from Ireland to give them a holiday. Some of 'em like it so much here that they stay years. Lovely girls, eh? I'll bet you're better than a mother to those girls, aren't you, Molly?"

"A lot better," she said, shrewd and amiable and hard-headed as himself. "Their mothers'd have to watch them starve, wouldn't they? Virtue never filled any woman's belly. They come here to find husbands."

"I was just coming to that," said Lintott, thoroughly enjoying himself with someone of his own caliber. "Plenty of courting going on, eh, Molly? But they can't find anyone to suit their fancy, until they're too old for the dodge. Then off they go, I daresay?"

"Some of them get comfortably settled. Some of them aren't so smart. I settle them when I can."

"Ah! You're a kindhearted lass. I'll lay that there are one or two city gentlemen that think so, too. Only one or two, mind. The sort that like the best of everything. And you're particular, aren't you, my dear?"

She watched and drank and smoked: as cool as himself.

"Does the name of Mr. Theodore Crozier mean anything to you, Molly?"

"I've never entertained a gentleman of that name."

"Tall, dark, quite a toff. Newgate knockers," sketching invisible side whiskers. "Going gray. Square-rigged," well-dressed. "Plenty of soft," rubbing invisible money between his fingers. "*You* know, Molly."

She shook her head, but a wariness in her manner alerted him.

"I like you, Molly. Even though you do keep a ken full of judies, and a cash carrier to look out for the lot of you. And I think you can help me so I'm going to be nice to you. I'll give you the lie of the land."

He had begun to see what Theodore was looking for, and though he thought him a fool he could not wholly condemn him. A mature man with an appetite for red meat might well find Laura and domesticity an insipid diet.

It wasn't her fault, Lintott thought with pity. She couldn't be a Molly if she tried for a lifetime. Not that she'd want to try. She's got a good enough opinion of herself. But she's not Molly.

For here was a man's woman, not subtle, not complex, not hampered by good manners or delicate health or an ingrained regard for propriety. Molly knew that life was for living, and she enjoyed it. She could help others to enjoy it, too. A hard day in the city, the knowledge that at home your wife was suffering from migraine behind drawn blinds, could make a man turn toward South Pimlico and a hearty welcome. Molly would be there, with a laugh that warmed you like a bowl of hot soup on a cold day. No fine needlework, no chilly silences. A bottle of excellent wine, a first-class cigar, a joke rich enough to tell at the club. No pale beauty, no soft-voiced charm. A high color, robust health, and loud good temper.

A man could be as easy with Molly as with another man, and then delight in her as a woman. She could smoke and drink with him, laugh with him. She held no illusions that might be shattered. She had no heart to be broken. She took her pleasures lightly, like a man, and gave pleasure in return. So long as you were prepared to pay through the nose, Molly would make up for any number of estranged wives.

You aren't my cup of tea, Lintott reflected, but I can see you might well have been his.

"I'm going to describe Mr. Theodore Crozier and the sort of life I think he led, Molly. I want you to listen, and if you recollect such a gentleman let me know. It's very important, Molly, because he died a short time ago."

Her face changed. She was hearing something she did not want to hear, something that might affect her.

"I must find out how he died. Whether he took his own life, or whether some member of his family did away with him. Are you attending to me carefully, my dear?"

"Yes," she replied stoutly, "I am. I've nothink on my conscience. I shouldn't be such a fool, I hope. Go on, then!"

"Mr. Crozier came of a good family. Went to a public school. Never knew what it was to go short of anything—not like your early days, I'll lay!" She raised her eyebrows, but did not contradict him. "Mr. Crozier was only twenty-two when his father died, leaving him with the responsibility of the family firm—that big toyshop in the City—his widowed mother, and a brother nine years old. Being of a serious turn of mind he took his responsibilities seriously. Instead of sowing a few wild oats, taking a look round at the world, he put himself in bondage. And in bondage he stayed for the next eleven years, until he had enough time and money to find a wife and set up housekeeping on his own account. His mother had died. His young brother was studying medicine. Mr. Crozier chose well. He was accepted by a young lady whose beauty and virtue—and dowry, let's not forget that little item!—were beyond reproach."

Molly made a face, laughed, and puffed at her Havana.

"I'll tell you what I think about good women, one day," she said. "It'd surprise you, the tales I hear in this room—or that one," nodding at the adjoining chamber, which was dominated by an overstuffed four-poster. "Good women are mean."

"Not all of them aren't," Lintott chided, pained for his Bessie.

"Mean," said Molly, "and *having*. I never did like a *having* woman. I work for my living—oh, you might turn your nose up at me, but I earn my keep, dear! I pay my way, and everybody's satisfied all round. Ask any of my gentleman friends what they think of Molly Flynn. They'll tell you."

"I'm sure they would," replied Lintott, mildly amused. "Anyway, you follow what I'm saying, do you?"

"Yes. He got tired of her having a headache, and looked round for a bit of fun. I cost them less, too," Molly went on, aggrieved. "Good women must have an establishment and fancy gowns. They breed good children, too, that have to be educated at good schools and have good dowries. Don't tell me! And then the bitches have a headache. Give me an honest tail anytime! A clean, good-hearted judy. They're worth half a dozen ladies!"

"You're quite the orator, Molly. Well, well. So he looked round for a bit of fun, as you say, at last. And by this time he was in his late forties. A dangerous age, Molly, for a man to meet a bonny lass like you, after a lifetime of cold respectability. And he went head over heels, didn't he?"

She was puzzled, sipping her gin, stubbing out the cigar.

"You've come to the wrong drum, dear. You have really."

"Wait a bit, Molly. Wait a bit, and listen. He fell in love—it does happen. Don't tell me nobody's fallen in love with you. I shan't believe it."

"Boys," said Molly, laughing. "Boys, dear. A very young man might take me a bit too serious, being his first. But none of them ever died of it!"

"He wrote letters," Lintott persisted, obdurate now. "And you kept them. You knew he had plenty of the soft, and you wanted to part him from a bit more. So you put the finger on him. You stopped his carriage one day, and spoke to him. The coachman can identify you. But Mr. Crozier wasn't going to pay if he could help it. It's bad enough for a man to be scorched, without being robbed atop of it! You went to the house, and took a few letters to frighten him—and the parlormaid can identify you, too."

Her color was higher than the rouge, her eyes guarded.

"Molly, I'm surprised at you!" said Lintott, still with the same obdurate patience, but friendly. "I shouldn't have thought you'd stoop to blackmail."

"I wouldn't put the finger on anybody! she cried. "Not because it's beneath me—there ain't many things as is beneath me—but because I don't want the crushers on my back. You can't find anythink wrong here. You'll never put me in the stir. That's the truth—and you *know* it!"

Lintott's face was expressionless, his disappointment bitter.

"Molly, it's taken me days to track you down, my girl. I've found the driver of the hansom cab that took you to Wimbledon. I've checked and double-checked. You're my quarry—and *you* know it!"

"Oh, I took the letters to him," Molly admitted. "I didn't know what the package was, but it could have been letters. I wasn't bothered, either way. When you're well paid to drive out and deliver a message, and then driven back as easy as you please, you don't ask rude questions."

"Ah!" Lintott breathed.

He could have slept, out of relief, out of weariness.

"Here," said Molly. "You're tired out, dear. Have a drop of brandy. I'll not peach on you at the Yard!"

And she laughed most splendidly.

"Just another minute, my dear. I've got a job to do. Did you know Mr. Theodore Crozier personally?"

"Never. He's never been here. That's what you want to know, isn't it? He's never fallen in love with me. And he's never written me no letters. There's the truth again!"

"I believe you. Who used you as messenger, then?"

"It was a favor for a friend, and I'm not saying who."

"Oh yes, you are, my dear. Because if you don't I'll have you arrested and charged for blackmail. And then we'll be making a few inquiries about this house of yours, and Mr. Flynn ain't half as clever as his wife! Savvy? Now blab!"

She poured another gin and her hand was steady. She pondered.

"All right," she said. "I'm no nose, but I shan't take the knock for anybody else. His name is Mr. Rice. I'll give you his address."

"Another cash carrier?" Prostitute's manager.

She smiled suddenly.

"No, he's a charitable gentleman. Very well liked. Very respected."

"A client of yours?"

"No, not that, neither."

"Give me the address, Molly. This case is a blessed honeycomb. I keep a-popping out of one place and into another, and they all look alike to me!"

"You're sure you won't take a drop of somethink to keep the cold out?"

"No, thankee, my dear. I'll say good day to you."

She said, "I don't want no trouble, you know. And I'm looking for none."

"You needn't fret," Lintott replied, ironic. "It's the fools and the unfortunates that get caught. The clever ones, like you, will be living in clover while I'm still plodding the streets!"

21

*I am not ashamed of taking a thing that is given
in love and affection: I am proud of it.*

Oscar Wilde
De Profundis

Mr. Rice seemed to exist in a world of lubrication. Macassar upon his hair, to conceal the gray and coax a sleek curl on either side of his forehead; wax on the upward-turned mustaches; and a gloss of skin bestowed only by nature. His hands moved slowly and restlessly together as though a modicum of oil lay perpetually in his palms. His voice and manner were exceptionally smooth, and he even favored the softer fabrics—being very emerald and magnificent in a velvet jacket, at six o'clock of an evening.

Lintott disliked him at sight, concealing his reaction as always behind a plain good-natured countenance and opaque eyes. The drawing room was as hushed and voluptuous as Mr. Rice, and the inspector's vibrant tones were muffled in plush curtains and hangings. On the walls hung portraits of innocent, nubile girls in Greek draperies, bending over doves and flowers and seashells. And Lintott's heavy boots drowned in thick carpet.

Something too—soft—here, altogether, he thought. Something nasty. Something I don't care for at all.

Beating down the atmosphere, like a man beating off a suffocation of feathers, Lintott came to the point.

"I understand that you paid a Mrs. Molly Flynn to deliver a packet of letters to the late Mr. Theodore Crozier."

Mr. Rice fiddled with his rings, smile set and eyes careful, and did not answer.

"I want to know about it," said Lintott. "I shall know about it, make no mistake."

"Difficult, my dear sir," Rice replied, watching him. "A matter of considerable delicacy."

"I'm delicate," said Lintott doggedly, "as delicate as anyone could wish. I've got secrets locked up here," pointing to his knobbed forehead, "as wild horses wouldn't drag out. I'm making no trouble unless I have to, and then I'll show you what trouble is, my friend."

"Do sit down," Rice murmured. "My dear sir, sit down, pray. This will take some explanation and some time."

"I have a mort of time," said Lintott, selecting a high-backed chair, less upholstered than the rest.

Mr. Rice found the truth an unsavory morsel in any event. As a meal it became an ordeal of torturous proportions. But he began circuitously, creeping further and a little further toward the purpose of the inspector's visit.

"I am fortunate, sir, in having some private means. I am not rich," he added quickly, spreading out his arms to show Lintott how empty they were though clad in fine velvet. "Not rich at all, my dear sir. But I have means, and I have—I say this with due modesty—I have a *heart*."

Lintott's nostrils lifted. It might have been the man's scent, it might have been instinct. It might have been both.

"I look around me," purred Mr. Rice, "at the distressing conditions in this Glorious Age. The queen, my dear sir—"

"God bless her," said Lintott reverently. "God bless her."

"—indeed. I go on these knees every night, my good sir—I am a religious man—and I pray that she be spared to us for many, many years."

"So you're well lined, religious, and warm-hearted," Lintott summed up briskly. "A philanthropist, in fact. You are telling me you are a philanthropist?"

"You put it so well, Inspector. In my humble way, sir, I do what I can."

"Fetch little children in off the street, perhaps? Girls?"

Mr. Rice flung up his hands in outrage.

"You mistake me, I can see. If you will forgive me, Inspector, you deal with the saddest and darkest side of Human Nature. And, oh, how sad and dark our Natures can be! Dear, dear! No, no. Let those who will—and they *do,* you know and I know—let *them* take advantage of a child's purity. None of that here, Inspector. None of that. I swear upon my mother's Holy Memory and this"—and he laid his fingers upon a very large Bible—"the Holy Book. I swear it. I should take it as quite a favor if I was struck down for telling a lie!"

"All right, all right," said Lintott, sick of him, "then let's get down to what you *don't* want to swear to. That's what I'm after."

"I have nothing to be ashamed of," said Rice, after a pause. "I go about the highways and byways, as did Our Lord. I walk the Embankment and look under the Arches of a nighttime, and I console and relieve the Dregs of Human Nature."

"Something for nothing?" Lintott asked, knowing.

Mr. Rice's face was as mild and open as that of an honest clergyman.

"I take in delinquent boys, my good sir, and offer them a

home. It's not all like this," he said, indicating the overfurnished room. "This is my part of the house. But they are very comfortable, and they join me here of an evening—"

"When the visitors come?"

"Well, I do try to introduce my boys to people of substance who can help them make their way in the world. They move on, you know, as they get into their twenties. I can only take a dozen at a time, and when a boy reaches maturity he naturally wants to make his own way. I give them a Bible when they leave me, Inspector, and a little present of money." Lost in the image he had created, Mr. Rice became rapt. "I've seen a boy stand here with the tears pouring down his cheeks, thanking me. I do give them a Bible," he said anxiously. "I've got a cupboard full of them that I can show you."

"Don't trouble yourself to open it," said Lintott. "I know the truth when I hear it. I've had such a lot of practice, you see. So you take these delinquent lads, as nobody cares about . . ."

"And nobody does," Rice interrupted, with a glint of his black eyes. "If I didn't take them in, who would?"

"There are benevolent institutions," said Lintott stoutly, knowing there were not enough.

"My dear sir, a Drop in the Ocean of Want! Why, they die—not just the boys, but men and women and babies too—die not a stone's throw from restaurants where a gentleman thinks nothing of spending a couple of sovereigns on his dinner. They die unwanted and ragged with their stomachs empty—my boys don't!"

"You needn't offer to show me your kitchen, neither," said Lintott drily. "I believe you feed them, too. And clothe them. They wouldn't catch any benefactor's eye if they was dirty and ragged, would they?"

Mr. Rice pondered over this remark, subdued.

"So Mr. Theodore Crozier was a benefactor, was he? Where did you dig him up?"

"Oh, we've been good friends—I think I could call the gentleman a friend—for years and years."

"Don't tell me you were at Rugby together. I shan't believe that!"

A curious dignity possessed the small man.

"I was a foundling, my dear sir," he said.

Then he lapsed back again. "Any schooling I had was in the School of Life, and with His Divine Light ever upon me!"

And he cast both moist eyes to the ornamented ceiling.

Lintott gave a snort of disgust.

"So you reckoned to be friendly with Mr. Crozier. A strange sort of friend, Mr. Rice, to foment a scandal and threaten to ruin him."

"Scandal? I was trying to *prevent* scandal, my dear. I have the reputation of this charitable house to uphold! And I did ask Mrs. Flynn to be particularly discreet."

"She did her best, but I was after her, you see. Now you must have read about the coroner's case, and you never came forward with the information, though I understand that some letters are still in your possession. What were you hoping for? To wait until the scandal died down and then put a bit more pressure on Mr. Crozier's wife or brother, for instance? Hush money?"

Mr. Rice pursed his lips and shrugged expressively.

"Best let sleeping dogs lie, my dear sir. Best let them lie, believe me."

Lintott considered him thoughtfully.

"Very well, Mr. Rice, I think we understand one another. So you are a philanthropist, and the late Mr. Crozier was a philanthropist. He visited you, or visited this establishment, for several years—no doubt introduced by other philanthropists?"

Mr. Rice nodded, and breathed on rosy fingernails.

"There are a number of gentlemen very high in the City, and in the professions, who patronize my boys and seek to alleviate their unfortunate lots. I never mention names. Love vaunteth not itself, you know. They prefer their benevolence to be of the anonymous variety."

"I'm sure they do. Now when did he part from the usual conditions of philanthropy, in a manner of speaking?"

"Well, it was this way—I hope I express myself with sufficient delicacy, and that you don't misunderstand my meaning—"

"Get on with it!"

Mr. Rice traced a pattern on the carpet with the toe of his moroccan slipper.

"Mr. Crozier always took a *general* interest in my boys, until I found Billie Mott. He took what you might call a *particular* interest in him. 'Billie, mark my words,' I said to him many a time, 'Mr. Crozier will see you right!' Billie's a very bright boy indeed, quite a cut above the usual. Nicely spoken and knows his letters. Mr. Crozier had it in mind to make him a clerk, and Billie was very fond of him. But then there was the suggestion, in a most underhand way, of removing him from my protection and setting him up in his own rooms. And then I found the letters that Mr. Crozier was writing to Billie, and I realized that all was not well." He paused. "Would you like a word with Billie while you're here? It's of no consequence if he's eating his dinner. My boys dine early. Mott don't mind, bless you."

"Fetch him up."

An uncertain smile sidled across Mr. Rice's mouth as he interpreted Lintott's tone. The inspector sat there, solid and expressionless; his boots planted on Mr. Rice's carpet, hat set squarely on his knees, hands set squarely about the hat. Much had been said, more lay unspoken between them, the greater part was yet to come.

"Billie, my dear," cried his benefactor, as the door

opened, "this gentleman is an inspector from Scotland Yard. He wants a private word with you. It's all right, you know," as the lad hesitated. "It's absolutely confidential, my dear." Then he tried to ingratiate himself with Lintott and the boy at once. "They ain't all as handsome as Mott, but they're every bit as well fed and well clothed. *I* bought him that octagon tie—they're all the rage. Yes, yes, a credit to the establishment. Sit down, Billie my dear, and talk to the inspector nicely. He wants to know about your late friend Mr. Crozier. Oh, Billie was *prostrated* when Mr. Crozier died, weren't you, Billie? Well, it was a friend and patron lost in one go—"

"Sit down, lad," said Lintott crisply. "I don't know if you're as good at speechifying as your master here, but I'd rather you wasn't. I'm more in the direct line myself."

The boy could have been no more than sixteen, and in the epicene stage of young male beauty. For he was beautiful, not merely handsome as Mr. Rice had said. Later he would become handsome and thereby lose his present attraction. Now he appeared as vulnerable as a girl, and even his uncertainty was another grace.

"What sort of a delinquent were *you,* then?" Lintott asked, surprised by his evident gentility.

Mott looked to his benefactor for instruction.

"He lost his mother, Inspector. A very sad case. I endeavored to help her but she was too far gone in"—he tapped his chest and whispered—"consumption, you know. A widow for many years. Well born, too, I believe. But married beneath her. She asked me to watch over Billie here. He's very like her, aren't you, my dear? Show the inspector your Mama's portrait."

The lad felt obediently in his elegant breast pocket and handed over a little gold locket of some value. Imprisoned in paint and time, Mott's female counterpart smiled at Lintott: silver-gold of head, dark and soft of eyes, with the same air of delicate hope.

"Who was your father, lad?" asked Lintott, handing the locket back.

"Tell the inspector, my dear," Rice counseled, receiving another inquiring glance from the boy.

"He was a music teacher, sir. My Mama eloped with him against the wishes of her family. He caught cold and died when I was a small child. My Mama had a very little money of her own, which was set aside for my education. She took in sewing, and painted in watercolors, to keep us."

"Weak chests," Rice explained, shaking his head in regret. "Both parents. Dear, dear!"

Lintott remarked the transparency of the boy's complexion, and shook his own head.

"Couldn't you have helped your Mama out a bit?" he demanded, thinking of Bessie in the same situation: beleaguered and valiant.

"She wanted him to be a gentleman," Rice broke in. "So she insisted on his schooling. The family wanted nothing to do with him after she died, and her little nest egg was spent on her last illness. I was a friend to them both. I was a father to this boy. I was a brother in Christ to that dear dead lady. Wasn't I, Billie?"

"You were very good, sir, to us both," said Mott frankly.

Rice turned to the inspector and spread out his hands, as if to say, "Note this!"

But Lintott replied, "You would have done better to set yourself to some honest trade, lad. Aye, better to sell that locket—though you do value it—than accept help of this sort. Aye, a thousand times better. Not that it's my business. How long have you been here?"

"Nearly twelve months, sir."

"You won't remember your father, I expect? Just kept your mother company, eh? And loved her, of course, and she loved you and lived with the memory of him? Ah well! That's often the way of it. Mr. Crozier must have seemed an impressive sort of man to you, then? Stop looking to Mr.

Rice for your answers, lad! I'm not concerned with what goes on here, for the moment. When I'm tramping round after one case I don't trouble to make more work for myself. Though I do remember anything that might come in handy if people don't tell me the truth. Did you meet Mr. Crozier as soon as you got here?"

"Yes, sir."

Lintott regarded his hat as though the nob on top of it held a solution.

"I'm going to put this matter very nicely," he said, after some reflection, "so that nobody's sensibilities will be hurt. But I want proper replies, truthful replies, mind! Mr. Crozier took a great liking to you, I hear. More liking than to the other lads?"

Mott pondered, and said, "We were more of a kind, sir. The others," with an apologetic look at Mr. Rice, who was occupying some sorry world of his own, "are pretty rough sort of fellows, sir. Not"—he glanced at the inspector, who was also "not," and stopped.

"Not gentlemen," said Lintott bluntly. "I see what you mean. So you and he, in a way, were lonely here. Here and elsewhere, likely."

The boy flushed up, and closed his lips as if to forestall the truth.

"There was more to it than the usual relationship, then?" Lintott pursued.

The boy nodded and swallowed. Then stuck his hands in his trouser pockets and leaned back in his chair, legs outstretched, imitating ease.

"It was a *real* friendship, in short?" Lintott continued, banging each fact home like a dutiful nail. "You thought as much of him, perhaps, as you thought of your Mama?"

Mott bent a highly intelligent pair of eyes on the inspector, and hazarded the truth.

"I loved him," said Mott, quite simply.

Into the silence Mr. Rice cried, "As a father, Inspector, as a father, of course."

Neither the youth nor the policeman paid any attention to him.

"That's what I wanted to hear," said Lintott, satisfied. "Now give me a picture of him—your picture of him. Tell me what Mr. Crozier was like."

"Very lonely. Very sad. Very sensitive."

"He was married, you know, to a lady of great qualities and beauty. He was the father of three fine children. What was so special about you?"

The boy was searching his inexperience for the unraveling of a mystery. He no longer eyed his questioner, nor tried to translate Mr. Rice's intentions. He was speaking as he must have thought, night after night, of something most strange and precious to him.

"When I first saw Mr. Crozier I thought of him as the father I had lost. I knew what he wanted of me. I knew what this house was. But what choice had I between this and starvation?"

"Using your hands, perhaps?" Lintott suggested obstinately.

Mott's dark eyes beneath the silver-gold lock were unyouthfully ironic.

"I am a weak person, sir, in both mind and body, and not particularly disposed to hard labor." He lifted both long hands from his pockets and spread them for the inspector to see. "That does not serve as an excuse, sir, merely an explanation."

"Well, well. Go on, lad."

"It was not as though we were strangers at all, but as if we had met before and recognized each other, sir."

The bright head held a little to one side, the bright mouth inquiring. The dark face suddenly amazed.

"We needed each other, sir. I needed his strength of

[239]

character, the sense of protection he offered. He needed"—
the boy shrugged, unable to describe himself—"whatever I
am, whatever I have to give."

"He was going to find you a position in life, was he? A
clerkship in his firm?"

"Something fairly light, sir."

"And set you up in rooms, so that he could visit you? So
that no one else could visit you?"

Lintott saw a dream flare and vanish in the boy's eyes.

"How long could such a friendship have lasted?" Lintott
asked heavily.

"For as long as both of us lived," said Mott with utter
conviction.

"A nice thing, to lure him away from me," Mr. Rice
cried. "What sort of recompense was I going to get for the
feeding and clothing and improving of his mind? And don't
lean back so on the legs of that chair, Billie!" he added
petulantly.

"I beg your pardon, sir, I was not thinking."

"You keep quiet!" Lintott growled at Rice, never taking
his gaze from the boy, for he sought further truths. "Now
did you know that your philanthropic master here was
blackmailing Mr. Crozier?"

"Yes, sir, but I was helpless, I am afraid. Dependent
upon Mr. Rice for my living."

"How did he get hold of your letters? Intercepted them?
Stole them?"

"Inspector! Billie!" Rice beseeched, unheard.

"Nothing can be private in this house, sir. They were not
stolen so much as confiscated."

"Why should Mr. Crozier write to you, if he was able to
see you?"

Again the lad replied simply, "He loved me."

"It was a stupid thing to do," Lintott grumbled,
professionally annoyed.

The boy said nothing. The curve of his mouth was compassion itself.

"Rice!" Lintott shouted, and smiled a little as the man jumped. "What were your terms to Mr. Crozier? Speak up and speak fast!"

"I suggested that since the boy's reputation was tarnished he should pay some recompense. Five hundred pounds," said Mr. Rice, in answer to the inspector's eyebrows.

"How much did a visit cost him?"

"A guinea for any of the other boys. Two guineas for Billie."

"Vice comes high these days," Lintott observed. "And did you stop the visiting?"

"Oh yes, Inspector. Of course. Certainly. Stopped absolutely."

"Until he paid up?"

No answer.

"And you judged that he would pay up, mostly because there was no one else he wanted. You could have ruined him, privately in the eyes of his family, publicly in the eyes of society, finished his firm. But the real draw was this lad here, wasn't it? He'd pay up. Pay up and come back again. Probably pay you to let the lad go. So why didn't he, then? Why didn't he pay up and then never write another line? Never get copped again the same way?"

He stared at his little audience, and Mott leaned forward, clasping young hands between his knees.

"Theo was a good man, as I am not," said the boy. "He could never accept himself. I can, you know. Deuce take it!" said Mott, lightly, sadly, "I know myself pretty well, sir. I was closer to him than anyone, but there were times when I was no comfort to him. There were times when he hated himself, and then I was best out of the way, because I reminded him of what he was. If he had been ill and fretting over this trouble, and saw no end to it, he could have found himself alone once too often."

Rice was being pettish with the antimacassars.

"Is there anything else I can tell you, sir?" Mott asked.

"Not about Mr. Crozier, but about yourself in another minute or so. Rice!" And again the man's leap to attention elicited a wry grin. "Where are the rest of those letters? In your Bible cupboard? No? Well, fetch them for me. All of them, mind, and sharpish! Now, Billie," as Rice hurried out, "can't you stir yourself to do something better than this, lad?"

Mott's beauty shone in the stuffy room, but his eyes reminded Lintott of the monkey on the barrel organ: adult-sad. Still the inspector continued to proffer charitable inducement.

"There must be something you can do, lad."

Mott smiled.

"You are very kind, sir, but there is nothing. I have been trained for nothing except to make myself agreeable. I possess nothing except this locket, and in spite of your counsel I would not part with it if I were starving. The only two people I loved are dead. Don't trouble yourself over me, sir. I shall live somehow until I die, like everybody else."

Lintott contemplated the gold-framed pictures until the return of Mr. Rice, at whom he loosed the lash of his tongue.

"I hope I see you and others like you soundly judged on the Day of Judgment! Ah! You confounded hypocrite! I'll remember you. See if I don't. But for the moment you and I must make a bargain. Are these all the letters, now? That's right. I don't want any of Mr. Crozier's family held to ransom over this affair. Now mum's the word, or I'll have my lads on this establishment faster than you can wink."

The only audible words in Mr. Rice's incoherent prayer for mercy were "purely charitable concern."

[242]

"And so far as you can," said Lintott, "look out for this boy here."

He was silent, aware of inadequacy in the face of life.

"That'll be all," he said.

But Mott followed him to the door and laid a hand on his sleeve.

"The letters, sir, were written to me. Could I not keep even one of them?"

"You know as well as I do," Lintott replied steadfastly, not looking at him, "that he'd have it off of you. No, lad."

The boy stood watching him descend to the street: young hands in pockets, bright head held a little to one side.

22

There was things which he stretched,
but mainly he told the truth.

Mark Twain
The Adventures of Huckleberry Finn

Titus sat for a long time with the letters in his hand, and then roused himself to act the host.

"You are weary, Inspector. Pray join me in a glass of brandy. We shall both feel the better for it."

"I don't as a rule, but a rule may be relaxed now and again, sir. And we have more important matters with which to concern ourselves than the odd glass of brandy. Thankee, I will."

The skill of Titus's unpaid tailor was evident even in the braid on his smoking jacket. Lintott watched him lay the letters gently down, and reach for the decanter. Apart from an unusual pallor, Titus was taking his late brother's iniquity with admirable composure.

Then, suddenly gripped by a greater force than good manners, he cried, "I never knew him. Is it not strange that we should be so close, and so apart? He was my brother, and he and I were nearer than any other living soul—or so I thought—and I did not know him."

"Yet, in spite of the closeness and the affection, you didn't mind seducing his wife?"

Titus nursed his brandy, and brooded.

"He did not care for her," he said at length. "I have a code of morality. Had he cared for her I should never have approached Laura. Besides, I have a fondness for her, and she was always good to me."

"There's right and wrong," Lintott pronounced.

"Sometimes one can hardly tell the difference. They become strangely mixed to my mind."

"I can tell the difference," said Lintott.

"Then you are a wiser man than I. I do not doubt that you are. And a cleverer. So tell me what we are to do, for I am at a loss. Is it necessary to produce these?" And he touched the letters.

"Let me think a bit," said Lintott. "I must think very carefully about this."

They had dropped the usual small courtesies: at one with · each other for the first time.

"It is not only the question of social disgrace," Titus pursued. "We shall all be marked—Edmund and Lindsey most of all. Laura will have to leave London altogether, and change her name and theirs. They will live until they die under the monstrous shadow of this evidence. I am a bachelor and likely to remain so. This revelation of my brother's private life gives me great sorrow—and arouses some pity, I must confess—but I can live with it. Laura and the children cannot, should not."

"Let me think," Lintott repeated. "I must think."

They sat, warming their balloons of brandy, sipping.

"Besides," Titus mused, "it is a terrible thing for a wife to hear. I am sure Laura knows nothing of this blighted form of love, and cannot fail to be soiled, in consequence. You, with your inflexible knowledge of right and wrong, may look upon her as an erring wife, but Laura is pure in my eyes. I pray that your justice be tempered by some mercy."

Lintott said candidly, "I am not inflexible. I don't excuse the lady's conduct, but you were the one to blame for it. And, yes, Mrs. Crozier is pure—though that sounds a contradiction, don't it?"

Somewhere along the line he had made his peace with her: bent a law, admitted an exception.

"You no longer have any doubt that my late brother committed suicide?"

Lintott shifted and frowned.

"I should think it the most likely explanation. A man of strict morality, divided against himself, deeply depressed, threatened with blackmail—aye, and with further blackmail as a threat. No future, in fact, except the need for secrecy, and with the lad Mott to look out for as well. He would want to provide for him. Your late brother took all his responsibilities seriously."

"He trod, as he once said to me, a dark road."

"Ah, uncommon dark, and leading nowhere. So snuff out the candle, eh?"

"He was a religious man. A God-fearing man. The taking of one's own life is forbidden," Titus observed. "But even that deterrent may prove to be less strong than one supposes."

"Even that," said Lintott. "Why, bless you, we fetch them out of the river by the dozen. Girls mostly, in the family way. They'll have been taught their catechism at one time or another. It made no difference when they jumped. And he must have felt cast out, in any case, mustn't he? Set apart. He was set apart."

"If it is at all possible," Titus urged, and motioned at the letters lying beneath the lamp on the table.

"It's how to go about it that foxes me," said Lintott honestly. "I thought I'd found the answer in Molly Flynn, you know. Aye, Molly. I saw how he could have made a fool of himself over her. I wish he had."

"If my brother had felt as deeply about her as he felt about this boy, would he not have been as desperate at the thought of losing her?"

"It was the blackmail that set the cap on it, though. She wouldn't wear that."

"Nor is there any disguising that these letters were written to a boy."

"No, that villain Rice kept the best to the last. But I've got two that could have been written to a woman," said Lintott, quietly pleased. And, as Titus stared at him, "Mrs. Crozier found and read the letters that Molly brought. She burned four but kept the others. No specific names or descriptions. *My forbidden love,* that sort of thing."

"Laura never confided that to *me.*"

"Ah! Mrs. Crozier tends to be secretive. She didn't confide in *me,* come to that. I drew it out of her. Where were we up to? And put it so that it doesn't sound like conspiracy. I'm sensitive about conspiracy."

His humor tickled, Titus said, "Then let us put it this way. If my late brother had fallen in love with Mrs. Flynn, and you produced two letters of his to show the jury, which sounded as though they were written to a woman—that would be a happier conclusion than the one you have discovered."

Lintott pursed his lips and nodded.

"It would alter nothing," Titus continued. "It would not change the fact that my brother died by his own hand. But it would look better, and in the eyes of the world appearances are paramount."

Appearances can be very misleading, Lintott heard himself say to Dr. Padgett. *That's the difference between your work and mine. Appearances mean nothing to me, sir. I take no account of them.*

"Appearances," said Lintott, "can be very misleading. We have no *evidence* that Mr. Crozier was being black-mailed. It would *appear* that some tremendous pressure was brought to bear, but we can't prove it, only assume it, guess at it. I doubt the credibility, myself, of a man dying for love alone. So will the jury. But Molly Flynn won't admit to blackmail, and we can't make her, only everyone will smell it there. I'll promise to make it my personal concern to keep an eye on Molly, in case she tries it again! Until then, they can only suspect her of it, so's to speak. I'll have to persuade her to play the mistress, though. I *could* persuade her."

"She has a husband, you say? A husband takes his wife's infidelity very much to heart. He might have bullied her, threatened her."

"Ah! Found her out at it. Said he'd take her back if she returned the letters. Molly panics. Tries to see Mr. Crozier and finish it all off. He's mad about her and won't listen. It sounds," said Lintott, "like a farthing novelette. Perhaps they'll like that?"

"So long as they feel they know more than can be proven, and that their suspicions are correct."

"Mrs. Crozier won't be too pleased to have Molly Flynn set up as your brother's one great passion, you know. She's a proud lady, and she isn't stupid. We can temper it a bit for her, privately. But publicly she'll have to sit through a fair bit of humiliation, and she won't like that! Well, we can't have everything in this world."

"Better to have one's pride hurt than one's life ruined. Can Molly and Flynn stand up to questioning?"

"It's only a coroner's case, you know," Lintott reminded him. "They aren't being tried by queen's counsel."

"And you believe that the inquiry could stop with Molly Flynn, an undertone of blackmail that cannot be proven, and a verdict of suicide while the balance of the mind was disturbed? A kind of *crime passionelle* in reverse?"

"Yes, it'll stop with Molly. Rice daren't open his mouth. I'll nab him for everything on the books if he steps out of line. Blackmail, homosexuality, running a house of ill fame for she-shirts, concealing evidence. I daresay I could rummage up a few more if I looked about me."

Titus smiled and rolled the last drops of brandy.

"Does this not involve you in some risk?" he asked ironically.

"Not it," said Lintott sturdily, setting down his empty glass, swathing himself in his plaid Inverness. "I work on my own. Nobody knows what I do—except those that daren't talk."

"I meant," said Titus, with a pleasurable touch of malice, "in some risk of being unable to discern right from wrong?"

Lintott stared in amusement.

"I can discern it well enough," he replied. "As you remarked earlier, sir, I'm wiser and cleverer than you. So I'll tell you this. The truth is something we like *other* people to be particular about. And it's a good servant, but a bad master. This way, we're telling the truth, since your brother killed himself over a love affair as you might say. What we keep back is only what could hurt innocent folk and help nobody."

"And what of these?" Titus asked, one well-shaped hand on the letters.

"Those, sir, being your late brother's property and rightly bequeathed to you along with the rest of his effects, I leave to your discretion. You may consider them as purely private papers. Don't burn 'em before I go out of the door!" he warned, turning back. "I should be forced to prevent you, in my professional capacity, owing to them being evidence. But if you choose to destroy them when I'm gone I *can't* prevent you!"

"I have never liked you before this evening, I must confess," Titus said truthfully, "but I have always respected you. I respect you even more, now, and I thank you from the bottom of my heart."

"I'd rather have the respect, sir," Lintott replied with equal frankness. "Any fool can make himself liked!"

[249]

23

Man has his will—but woman has her way.
Oliver Wendell Holmes
The Autocrat of the Breakfast-Table

"I regret that I have something of a painful situation to put before you, ma'am," said Lintott, ill at ease in Laura's dark-blue drawing room, "but Mr. Titus Crozier and me have talked it over, and this will save a deal of unpleasantness."

He peered at the deep frieze around the walls, where a series of semi-Greek ladies disported themselves with vases and peacocks. He wished he had his hat between his hands, since it gave him something to hold and he had always been an awkward man.

Laura had been playing on the grand piano when he was shown in, and now sat, half turned toward him, on the gilt-legged stool. The seat had been worked in bright wools by her own hands, and he found further evidence of her industry in the profusion of footstools and embroidered cushions.

"You have discovered the lady in question, and the manner of my late husband's death, Inspector?"

"Yes, ma'am. I am of the opinion that Mr. Crozier took his own life, under the pressures of emotion and circumstance." He knotted his hands together, and took the first hurdle manfully. "Mrs. Crozier I must be frank with you, and not entirely frank, and both for your own good—and the good of your children. The woman who brought the letters was not your late husband's mistress. She was acting as a go-between for somebody else—it don't matter whom— and he *was* being blackmailed. And he could, and would, have been blackmailed again until they bled him white. That's rough speaking, ma'am, but I don't know how to put it any nicer."

Pale and attentive, she motioned him to go on.

"I have uncovered an aspect of the late Mr. Crozier's life that does not bear mentioning. I shouldn't like my own wife to know if it, nor any lady, come to that. We'll just say that it's best left alone. Taking a mistress is very small beer—if you'll excuse the expression—in comparison with what did happen. They had him in a cleft stick, ma'am, and he knew it."

"The love letters? What of the love letters?"

"He *was* in love, with someone else. That, too, pushed him over the edge as it were, because there could be no proper end to such an association. Now, ma'am, Mr. Titus and I are anxious to spare you shame and suffering—without, of course, being untruthful or impeding the course of justice. And I do assure you, that if it all came out, your life, and the lives of your children, would be under a shadow until you died. Are you with me, ma'am?"

She nodded.

"So we propose to tell the truth, and nothing but the truth, up to a point. Mrs. Flynn—the woman who carried the letters—is prepared to testify that they were written to *her*. The question of blackmail will come up, and of course, she'll deny it. Nor have we any evidence. We have only Mr. Titus's report of his brother's conversation, and no money passed hands. They must still have been arguing the toss between them. Your late husband was a gentleman of strong character. He wouldn't go under without a fight, even though it was a losing one."

"Why should *she* go free?" Laura cried.

"Look here, ma'am, Molly—Mrs. Flynn—is doing us a favor. We *want* her to go free. If she doesn't she'll blow the gaff, and then we're all in the soup. It could take a few lids off London that had best remain covered, as yet. Now, if you aren't prepared to go along with us, say so. I'll fetch the whole lot out in court, name names, state facts. It's your choice, ma'am, and nobody else's. I'd just say one thing to you. Make sure you have some good friends in the country that'll take you in for a few months. Put this here establishment up for sale. Take your sons away from Rugby, before you're *asked* to take them. And send a prayer up for Mr. Titus, because he'll have to face the music and try to keep his sales level. Do you understand me, ma'am?"

She made a gesture of resignation, or acceptance, and bowed her head.

"Now you'll have to sit through an awkward hour or so in the courtroom. Those letters will be read out. Molly Flynn will be acting like Lady Hamilton. And you'll have to bear it, ma'am. Nobody minds if you cry a bit, or faint, or anything of that sort. But if you stand up, halfway through, and start saying it's all lies, I may as well hand in my resignation now!"

"I shall not go back on my word," said Laura with dignity. "And that word I give you most wholeheartedly, Inspector."

He wondered what wild imaginings passed through that subdued head, and tried to set a few of them at rest.

"It wasn't forgery, ma'am, or anything like that. I should have had to bring that up. He was mostly a danger to himself, so's to speak."

She was attempting to rob the courtroom of its sharpest humiliation, preparing for what must come.

"I shall do as you suggest, Inspector," she said quietly. "After all, I need not look at Mrs. Flynn, and I shall be heavily veiled. Mourning has its uses."

She could say so with conviction, for it became her. This was the third ensemble Lintott had admired, and he wondered how long the money would last.

"I was about to drink coffee," she said, in a different tone. "I should be truly obliged if you would join me, Inspector. Perhaps Mrs. Hill has baked some biscuits. I understand you admire her skill, and with good reason."

He caught a demure and vanishing smile on her face, and was glad she took his news so calmly.

"Well, that's uncommonly kind of you, ma'am. I wouldn't object."

Kate appeared to have adopted her mistress's air of serenity, and though she did not respond to Lintott's covert wink she tossed her head as she passed him, and set down the silver tray with its complement of Theodore's fine china.

I've always been an interfering sort of fellow," said Lintott, friendly, "so will you forgive me if I ask—not out of curiosity, but interest—whether Mr. Titus has got himself any sort of a manager?"

She glanced at him quickly, and he was suddenly aware of her intelligence. It had never struck him before.

"I am only too pleased to discuss such a matter with a man of understanding," Laura replied simply, "because my brother-in-law is the head of the family, and as such his opinion is paramount. Rightly so. But I should be so much obliged if you could render me a small service. That is, if you approve my purpose."

Lintott blossomed over the hot coffee, with a biscuit in his square hand.

"Anything I can do, within reason, ma'am."

She looked at him a little shyly.

"I am afraid you do not think as well of me as I could

wish, Inspector. I fear you have cause for your opinion. Yet I should like to think that you do not entirely condemn me."

"Let's say," Lintott ventured, "that one deplores the sin but does not hate the sinner."

He felt rather pleased with the success of this remark, which brought radiance as well as relief to her.

"I should like to start afresh," Laura continued. "Just now you mentioned the necessity of a manager. My brother-in-law has a gift for all the artistic sides of Crozier's—indeed, his gift is, one might say, without parallel. But he had not the knowledge of practical matters and of finance that my late husband possessed. I fear that I am not very practical myself, as no doubt you have observed. I know that you observe much, Inspector Lintott."

He watched her keenly, unable to guess what she was after. She smiled at him, and sipped. He wondered how much her gown had cost: the little buttons covered in black velvet, the four flounces edged in the same material, the collar and bodice exquisitely braided and buttoned, the yards and yards of fine wool flowing from the trim bustle. It was mourning in the deepest sense: a nocturn of elegance and pathos. Kate had curled the small wisps of hair on neck and forehead, and gathered the long fair fall into a smooth chignon.

"You made me very much afraid, Inspector, when I first met you. And when Kate told me—for she confides everything of importance—with what grasp of situation and deployment of detail you had discovered our sad tale, I was even more afraid. But I learned much from you, and of you, because of this. Inspector Lintott, I have the utmost confidence in you. I am quite alone, as you know, and have no male relatives to speak for me—my uncle is close on eighty-four and almost blind. Could you not somehow suggest to my brother-in-law that we allow a good business-man to take shares in the firm? Or am I," and she hesitated, pale and pretty, "talking nonsense?"

Lintott set down his cup, suspicious and astonished.

"Far from it, ma'am. Far from it." He looked hard at her. "Had you someone in mind, then?"

"*I* had no one in mind. How should I? I know nothing of the firm. But one of my late husband's City acquaintances called upon me yesterday, to offer his condolences. I believe," said Laura, uncertain how much to confide, "that he might be interested. He asked me a great many questions, which I am afraid I was unable to answer as fully as he could have wished, but I did receive the impression that he was prepared to take on my late husband's work in return for a share in the firm."

"I am surprised," said Lintott gravely, "that he troubled a lady with such matters and did not approach your brother-in-law himself."

She sought help from the many pretty things scattered about the room, and did not find it. Lintott watched each thought pass across her face, and smiled to himself.

"You see, I do not know how Titus would feel about letting so much power pass out of the family. The firm would still be Crozier's, of course. Indeed, this gentleman has a considerable business of his own. He does not seek to alter Crozier's, only to make an investment of it."

"He talked to some purpose," said Lintott, grasping the situation. "But why to you?"

"He thought I might have some influence with Titus. You see, Inspector, my own money is tied up in the firm. That was my late husband's wish, and I have no reason to change matters even if I could. But I have no control, except that if this gentleman and Titus were to become partners my shares would be the deciding factor in any discussion. I mean," she endeavored to explain, "that if they disagreed on any matter, any disposition of money, for instance, my shares could weigh the balance on one side or the other."

Lintott grinned. He could not help it.

"I should not wish to be a bone of contention," Laura

cried, pink with distress and perhaps with a flavor of excitement, "but you do see that the position could be a delicate one? This gentleman is a stronger character than Titus—I do not say that with any criticism. You do see my difficulty? And yet, if Titus was to employ a manager, one with no power at all, I fear that we might well lose all the ground that Theodore so patiently gained over many years."

Lintott rubbed his head, amused.

"It sounds a good proposition, as far as I can judge, but I shouldn't advise *you* to raise it, ma'am."

She poured more coffee, relieved again, and nodded her head.

"Do you know this gentleman well enough to meet him socially, or was he merely a friendly stranger who had known your late husband?"

"Oh, he has visited us here many times."

"It wouldn't seem odd if you had a little evening with friends, and included him along with Mr. Titus so that they could get together?"

"Not at all."

"Then that would be my advice, ma'am. It's not a bit of use," Lintott said kindly, "expecting *me* to say a word to your brother-in-law. He wouldn't listen to me, bless you, why should he? I'm not a businessman, I'm a policeman."

"One is so helpless," Laura murmured. "I ask your pardon for any error of judgment on my part."

"No, no, no. I don't mind. If this gentleman is as clever as he seems to be he should be able to talk Mr. Titus into a partnership—even with your shares as a reckoned factor. But don't you, my dear"—he had so far forgotten himself as to talk to her in the way he would talk to Kate—"don't you go saying what a good idea you think it is. Quite the reverse. If I was you I'd tend to play it down a bit. Say you're not sure and beg Mr. Crozier to consider it carefully. Else he might smell a rat when none was there—when none was there. And I do," said Lintott, setting down his second cup empty, "I do think it's the best solution. In fact I think it's capital. Capital!" And he chuckled over the crumbs on the biscuit plate. "I must be on my way, but I wonder if you'd mind my having a final word or two with the servants, Mrs. Crozier?"

A shadow crossed her face, and again he saw the intelligence through the beauty.

"You are going to tell me that this is merely a formality, and then reveal another and more terrible skeleton, are you not, Inspector?"

"No, ma'am. Not me. But as you say, we want a fresh start after this tragic affair. You'll have enough to put up with, what with the reopening of the inquest and having Molly Flynn brassing away, and the slur of suicide. I'd like to see that you have nothing more. In short," said Lintott frankly, "I'm going to close a few clattering mouths for you. Is that all right?"

She was laughing and clasping his hands, thanking him. In his heart he wished her well, and translated the emotion to plain words.

"Best of luck, ma'am," said Inspector Lintott.

She sat there smiling, long after he had left the room, and then trailed gracefully to the mirror and touched the little curls on neck and forehead. She was no longer thinking of the inspector, and the sting of the inquest had softened considerably.

24

The Law is the true embodiment
Of everything that's excellent.
It has no kind of fault or flaw,
And I, my Lords, embody the Law.
    Sir William Schwenk Gilbert
    The Gondoliers

"Here I am again," said Lintott cheerfully. "You'll be glad to see the last of me, I shouldn't wonder. Well, so you shall when we've had a chat."

His presence arrested them in mid-motion. Mrs. Hill's wooden spoon dribbled sponge mixture into the big blue bowl. Henry Hann paused with a tankard of beer halfway to his open mouth. Harriet stood still, holding a pile of clean dinner plates. Annie Cox's scrubbing brush ceased its busy swish and scratch. Only Kate smiled as she waited.

"Where's the sergeant's sweetheart, then?" Lintott asked heartily. "Upstairs with Miss Blanche? Aren't you going to ask me to sit down, Mrs. Hill? I thought you were a friend of mine."

"Offer the inspector a chair, Harriet, and shape yourself, girl!"

"That's right," said Lintott. "That's comfortable, ain't it? I've got some very good news for you all. No, not good, but better than we hoped. You were all wrong except our sharp little Kate, here. This is in confidence, mind," threatening with a smile. "Your late master *did* make away with himself, that's the bad part. And consequently he wasn't murdered, and that's the good. What do you think of that?"

They were, apart from Kate, bitterly disappointed, but made a great show of pleasure and astonishment.

"That's not all," Lintott continued, enjoying himself. "Your mistress and Mr. Titus have been slandered and libeled. Libeled and slandered. Which means, in short, that people have been telling lies about them, and writing lies about them."

Mrs. Hill said it was a shocking shame and she didn't know what the world was coming to, and for her part she had never believed a word of it.

"That's a police matter," said Lintott very gravely. "We're just wondering how to prevent it in future. There is one way, of course, which is to make sure that everything said or done inside or outside this household is watched, and noted down. Because we can't have it, you know, we really can't. Why," said Lintott, "there's been public time and money wasted over this alone. Somebody might be on the cockchafer for this—that's the treadmill. Or picking oakum. Terrible what oakum does to your fingertips!" And he smiled around blandly.

"I ain't said nothink!" Annie cried in terror.

He became fatherly in an instant, feeling for a humbug in his pocket.

"Here! Shut that noise on this sweet, Annie. I'm not after you, my lass."

He looked at Henry Hann.

"I should finish that beer off if I were you," he observed. "There must be something for you to do at a half after eleven in the morning besides sitting in the kitchen. You won't get another position like this one. I'll say more. You won't get another position. See that you keep it, and keep your thoughts to yourself in future! And remember what your late master said about driving the lady and children about when under the influence. Savvy?"

"Yes, sir, thank you sir," said Henry, and was off after a last long swallow. "Thank you, Mrs. Hill," wiping his mouth.

"Now you, girl!" to Harriet. "You mind what Mrs. Hill says to you, because she only says what's right. And don't embroider it, neither, with *The Duchess of Tramura!* Hasn't she got anything else to do of a morning, ma'am, but in the kitchen?"

"Yes, o' course she has. Harriet, it's high time the attic rooms was cleared up. You sleep like pigs up there—*I* know!"

"But, Mrs. Hill, the ceilings are due for a whitewashing in April. I shall have everythink to do all over again then," Harriet protested, with some cause.

"Am I asking you to wash the walls, girl? Go and turn them flock mattresses over, and wipe the chairs down with soap and water—don't forget the legs, and scrub them washstands. Here, take Annie with you, then you'll be done afore I need you with the luncheon."

She glanced anxiously at Lintott to see that she had interpreted him aright, and he nodded and smiled.

"I shan't take up your morning, bless you, Mrs. Hill. I know you're a busy woman. We'll just have a word together, you and me."

"Mrs. Crozier did say to sort out the clothes, with her being in full mourning and them having to be put away for a year, Mrs. Hill," Kate offered.

"You know your own work best," said the cook. "I should do that then, Kate. We're all right here for a good hour yet, afore you need to lay the table and that."

"I shan't be long," Lintott reassured her.

The woman was perturbed, but the professional in her

continued to beat the cake, to grease tins, and to slide the mixture evenly into each and set them in the oven. Lintott watched her movements with contentment.

"I'd like to taste that sandwich cake, Mrs. Hill," he said kindly, "but I shall be off and away, and then it's goodbye to a very pleasant friendship between you and me."

"Well, sir, I can say the same—and I'm glad you've cleared everythink up to your satisfaction."

"It's not in the bag yet," said Lintott, "but I'll eat my hat if I don't put it there, and put it there for good."

He surveyed this prospect with amusement, and then became serious.

"Mrs. Hill, if you found that Harriet was tattling behind your back and saying injurious things about you—things that could set you wrong in the eyes of the world, things that wasn't true—what would you do?"

"Give her her notice, sir."

"I'd do the same, if it was one of my constables. There's been animosity in this household against Mrs. Crozier, and it must not go on. Your master was kind and fair to you, but he's dead. It's the living that count, and the lady has always spoken well of you."

Mrs. Hill wiped down the deal table with a damp cloth and rinsed it.

"I've been a bit on the tattling side now and again," she admitted, "but I never hated the mistress."

"We know who did, and does, though. Don't we?"

She shook a due quantity of salt into a pan of peeled potatoes, and slowly nodded.

"And you must never tattle about that, either, whatever happens. Good cook-housekeepers are hard to come by, and when they've been in a family for uppards of fifteen years they want to stay. Now we've all got things in our lives that we'd rather folk didn't know about. Things that we've sorrowed over and put behind us, and learned to live with."

He watched her closely. Her hands trembled as she

smoothed her apron and then attended to the soup, skimming it delicately.

"How's that young nephew of yours that's going for a drummer?" Lintott asked, very friendly, on another tack.

"Very well, sir, thank you."

"How old did you say he was? Fifteen, eh? A fine young chap by all accounts, and you'll have done all you could for him. I know a woman of your heart and sort. He must have been born about the time you had your illness, mustn't he?"

"Around then, sir," almost inaudibly.

"Your family would have had a deal of worry. Worry over you and over him. Well, these things happen, but when folk stick together and show each other a bit of love and affection it all comes right in the end, don't it?"

"Sir!" she cried, and then could not go on, stirring the soup with one hand and wiping the other across her eyes.

"You see what I mean, my dear? It's best forgotten, ain't it? No point being hurt over and over again. That's all I've got to say to you, and all that will be said. You stick by your mistress, and what you say in this here household goes. That's why I spoke to Harriet as I did. She looks up to you. You tell her that night's day and she'll believe you."

Mrs. Hill did not answer him, but brushed her hand more firmly across her eyes, sniffed twice, drew up, and stirred as though her life depended on it.

"Goodbye, my dear," said Lintott gently.

He rose, walked over to her and gave her a friendly pat on the shoulder. She attempted a smile and a nod.

"Wouldn't he marry you, my love?" Lintott asked.

She shook her head, wordless.

"Well, he *was* a fool," said Lintott grinning. "He left you to be an ornament and an example to a heap of people, instead of having you all to himself! *I* wouldn't have done!" said Lintott, and winked.

She burst out laughing, crimson with trouble and

pleasure. She was still roguish when he went out and closed the door quietly behind him.

Blanche was standing in one corner, with a heavy book on her head and her hands clasped behind her back, when Lintott knocked on the nursery door and entered without being asked.

"She's been a naughty girl!" cried Miss Nagle defensively. "And I won't have naughty girls in my charge."

"Take that book off her head," said Lintott quietly, "and ask her Mama to have her for half an hour or so. Say that I asked specially. Don't you drag her by the arm like that, neither. She's not the size of Sergeant Malone, and he'd fetch you one if you did that to him, and quite right too."

Very white, Miss Nagle escorted the child to the door. Lintott sat in one of the hard chairs and waited without kindness for her return.

"I ought to have you in the force," he observed drily, "you'd be a good one with the naughty lads—or don't you pick on anybody that can scratch back? Sit down. There, where I can see you. You're a fine one, aren't you?"

"I do my job, sir, and a-bringing up of children is my job."

"You're still answering back, too, I notice. Well, that'll be *my* job to correct. We'll start with Sergeant Malone, who's the man I'm after—and the man you're after, too, if I'm right. You should try a spoonful of sugar now and again, instead of all that vinegar! And don't give him orders, neither. A sergeant don't like having orders, especially when he's asked to do something in the criminal line. Ah! That's better. Now you look more like a woman and less like a shrew—I should practice that if I was you, it'll come in handy."

"I've done nothink wrong," Miss Nagle whimpered. "I tried to help you, sir, that was my only intention all along."

"Oh, I'm not talking about what happened once I'd arrived. I'm talking about what happened after your late master's funeral."

She was weeping into her apron, terrified.

"Now I want you to get two facts into that busy head of yours," said Lintott. "Your late master did away with himself—we've proved that. And all that about Mrs. Crozier and Mr. Titus was wicked, libelous lying. Do you believe me?"

She nodded fiercely into the apron.

"Good, because if you didn't believe me, and started a-gossiping again, that sergeant of yours could have a taste of prison—instead of a good home and a loving wife. I hope you'll be a loving wife, my dear, because if you ain't I think he'll be a bit of a tartar. I know his sort," Lintott mused, head on hand, watching her. "A simple man, good-hearted, and easily led. Don't cut his drink off altogether, he could get nasty. Oh, he's the one for you all right," with relish, "you couldn't have picked a better."

"But he don't want to settle down," Miss Nagle wept.

"You don't know the right way to go about him, then. Tell him how much money you've saved up, and stop telling him how to behave himself. I should bring him to the point," Lintott added, "because you can't stay here making trouble. I won't have it."

He judged her to be amenable, and altered his tone.

"An upright good-looking lass like yourself," said Lintott, jocular, "with a waist as any honest queen's soldier would like to embrace"—she had a neat waist, trim and compact beneath the deep starched band—"and can't get a man to pop the question? Nonsense. I don't believe it. You've been keeping him dangling, I know you ladies! You can make him do as you please. If I didn't know what a decent man he was I might think he'd been persuaded into printing those anonymous letters! But as long as you keep a quiet tongue I'll do the same."

She nodded, and tried to compose herself.

"So you fetch him up to scratch, give your mistress a month's notice, and treat Miss Blanche as if she was a new-laid egg until you leave. Those are *my* orders. There'll be no more gossip downstairs. Mrs. Hill'll see to that, and you see that you go along with her. All right, Miss Nagle?"

"Yes, sir."

"Ain't you going to ask me to the wedding?" Lintott inquired cheerfully.

"You'll be very welcome, sir."

"That's right, my dear. I'd like to pop my head round the church door and wish you well. There's nothing wrong with you," he added, "that a good husband won't cure. You should've got married before. I'll lay that you don't slap your own children about like you slap other folks's!"

"I'll come down with you, sir, if that's to your way of thinking, and fetch Miss Blanche. And," interpreting his raised eyebrows, "thank you, sir," grudgingly.

They descended the stairs together: he amicable, she subdued. But on the first floor he paused, seeing Kate's neat figure busy among a heap of silk and velvet.

"I'll just have a last word with Kate," he murmured, and knocked loudly on the half-open door.

"You can't come in, sir," said Kate firmly. "I'm sorting out Mrs. Crozier's wardrobe and it wouldn't be proper for a gentleman."

"Then you come out, will you, Kate?" wooed Lintott, grinning.

She appeared, closing the door smartly behind her, and looked steadily at him.

"Don't I get a smile this morning, after saying you was the only one that was right about your master? That's cruel, Kate."

"You don't want a smile from me, sir," she replied, but smiled nonetheless. "You want information of some sort. I know you."

They eyed each other with pleasure: friendly adversaries.

"And I've looked out for your mistress as well as you could have done yourself," Lintott mourned, leaning against the banisters. "Taken a load off her mind, shielded her reputation, and just given her some very good advice too. Has she had any callers recently, Kate?"

"Mr. Titus hasn't been, if that's what you're after, sir."

"No, I warned him off," said Lintott. "Who *has* been, then?"

"No one in particular. Just friends of Mrs. Crozier's to wish her well and offer condolences, sir."

"I love you, Kate," said Lintott. "You make me work for my living, don't you, my dear?"

She did not answer, smiling.

"No business acquaintances, then? No old friend who might think of helping the lady out with Crozier's? Because you may not have liked your late master, Kate, but he was the one who made the money. That affects every person in this household. No money, no household. Mr. Titus don't know what to do with money, apart from spending it, and your mistress has been at the dressmakers since she was widowed. That's a fetching gown she has on so early in the day, ain't it? You did her hair up nicely, too. I'm not such a stick that I don't notice refinements of that sort, Kate."

Still she regarded him, and smiled, hands clasped on the pretty apron. Lintott rubbed his head, and grinned, delighted and exasperated.

"Come, girl, somebody's got his eye on the firm and the lady too, now hasn't he? Else she wouldn't have told me, and confided in me, and asked my opinion. She don't want it to go amiss, does she, Kate?"

"I don't know what you mean, sir. Mrs. Crozier is in mourning for a full year. It wouldn't be proper for any gentleman to approach her so early."

"That butler's a brave man," Lintott observed. "I hope he's as brave as he needs be, that's all! Kate, if you won't tell me I'll tell you. I think it's the best way, all round, if there's a firm hand on the reins. Or you'll all be in Queer Street, between her extravagance and his."

"Well, if you know all that," said Kate saucily, "you don't need me to say anything, and I must get back to my work, sir."

"Wait a bit! Is he an elderly gentleman?"

"If you're talking about Mr. Edgeley, sir, he'll be about—your age, I should judge."

"My age?" Lintott said. "How do you know my age, miss?"

"I don't, sir. But then, I don't know his either!"

"This is very agreeable, Kate," said Lintott, grinning. "I wish all my inquiries was as agreeable, I can tell you. Mr. Edgeley, eh?"

"Yes, sir. He has known my late master and my mistress for a number of years. He and his wife came here very often at one time."

Lintott's face clouded.

"Until she died, just a year ago," Kate continued demurely, fingering the frill on her apron. "He took that very badly. His family is grown up, you see. His daughter, Miss Florence, is married and lives in Bath. His son, Mr. Hubert, is in the army."

"I could shake you, Kate. You had me thinking I was wrong, for a minute. What sort of a gentleman is he? Because a lady of her sort can make mistakes, can't she? She's made a couple of bad ones already!"

"I could leave her with Mr. Edgeley, sir, and feel easy in my mind."

Lintott took the liberty of pinching her cheek.

"And when are you leaving, Kate, eh?"

"Not until my mistress is settled. We've been together for seven years, sir, and that's a long time."

"You're going to keep him waiting for you, are you, Kate?"

"He'll wait, sir. He's that sort."

"Ah!" said Lintott, in genuine admiration. "If your mistress was as cool a customer as you, Kate, she'd have saved herself a deal of trouble. Goodbye to you, my dear. It's been a pleasure meeting you."

"Let me show you out, sir, if you please."

She preceded him gracefully, but turned at the foot of the staircase, for the first time asking help.

"It will be all right, sir, about the inquiry and Mr. Titus?"

"You needn't worry, Kate."

Still she wanted everything to be smoothed.

"And it'll be all right about Mr. Edgeley, sir, if everything is as we think?"

"So long as Mr. Titus don't smell a rat. But if she's clever enough he won't. And I needn't ask how close and clever *you're* going to be, need I?"

She shook her head. A little satisfied smile touched her mouth.

"Mr. Titus is a vain man, sir, if you'll excuse me mentioning it so open. A vain man doesn't notice quite so much, do you think?"

Lintott laughed aloud and shook his head, clapped the Bollinger hard down, and walked off still laughing.

The front door closed quietly behind him, and shielded the family again. Inside all was as it should be. The servants went briskly about the task of lunch. In the nursery Nanny Nagle allowed Blanche to thread herself a string of beads, taken from a boxful of Crozier's Finest Assorted, Genuine Glass, Imported at Great Expense from Her Majesty's Colonies. In the parlor Laura sat in her superb mourning that was so much a complement to a fair woman, and practiced her Chopin, since Mr. Edgeley was particularly fond of music.

25

*I expect that Woman will be the last
thing civilized by Man.*
George Meredith
The Ordeal of Richard Feverel

On a fine afternoon in late March, Laura hastily concealed a copy of the *Pall Mall Gazette* behind a cushion, hearing Kate's knock on the door. So stupid, she thought, to be forever pretending, and yet the habit of concealment died hard. Theodore forbade a copy in the house, because of Mr. Stead's articles on child prostitution.

"Come in, Kate."

And though I can now buy it for myself, and read it as openly as I wish, somehow I still hide it.

"Your afternoon tea, ma'am. Mrs. Hill has made an iced sponge as well as a cherry cake."

"See that Miss Blanche has a thin slice of each, will you, Kate?"

"Yes, ma'am. Is everything to your liking?"

The sandwiches rolled up, in thin brown bread and butter. The Earl Grey tea with slices of lemon and lump sugar. The several sorts of baked biscuits Laura never touched, but which were always punctiliously included. The cakes that Blanche would enjoy more, wafered into a silver basket.

"Thank you, Kate. Tell Mrs. Hill it looks delicious."

"Mrs. Hill says will there be anyone happening to stay for dinner, ma'am?"

"No, Kate. I am expecting Mr. Edgeley to bring his sister for an hour or so this evening. But wine and fruitcake, I feel, will do nicely."

Their eyes met: calmly, knowledgeably.

"Very well, ma'am. Will that be all for now?"

"Yes, thank you, Kate."

I had to read the articles secretly, by courtesy of Titus, and now Mr. Stead has left the *Gazette* and begun a new enterprise called *Review of Reviews.* I must buy myself a copy of that. So many ideas, such dynamism, so much stuffy nonsense blown to the winds, so much life. I wonder whether I dare—no, I could not ask for it!—that Socialist paper *The Link.* I wonder whether it would be possible to attend a meeting of the Fabians? Not unless someone I knew very well, someone respectable . . . Well, there is a time for everything. So very much more time than I have ever enjoyed before.

She lifted the silver teapot and poured. On the Common the sun shone, pale and fine and cold and gold. A spring afternoon, scattered about with children, festooned with shouting.

I need a year, Laura thought, to accustom myself to this freedom. Then I can consider freedom of a different sort: freedom from Titus finally, freedom from worrying about his ruining us, freedom from memory. I must somehow reconcile what I have been with what I wish to be. I must accept both the good and bad in myself. I must put the old behind me, in order to begin again.

Molly Flynn had been unable to resist wearing scarlet silk stockings studded with swallows. Finer, blacker swallows flew around Laura's wide black brim, displaying the merest touches of white. Beneath the black veil, sweeping to her feet, she created an atmosphere of withdrawn gentility. The two women divided the attention of the spectators between them: Molly on splendid display and Laura riveting the gaze by shrinking from it.

Lintott gave his evidence drily, precisely, impassively: stating that two letters had come to light, the others must have been burned; that he had traced Mrs. Flynn, a married lady who had wished to remain anonymous but now was prepared to give proof of the relationship between Mr. Crozier and herself.

The letters created a little stir in the cold room: a warmth that caused the ladies to compress their lips in outrage, and the gentlemen to finger beards and mustaches and glance covertly at Molly. By her side sat Flynn in his Sunday suit, conveying both threat and protection.

"Now, Mrs. Flynn," said the coroner briskly, crossing from passion to hard fact without difficulty, "we accept that a respectable gentleman of the late Mr. Crozier's status fell in love with you." His tone suggested astonishment and derision. "Nevertheless, one feels that some other pressure was brought to bear. Mr. Titus Crozier tells us that his late brother informed him that these letters were being used against him, to extort money from him. In short, he was being blackmailed."

"Blackmailed?" cried Molly. "Tell me what money ever passed between us? Ask the inspector here. He's been through everythink. The late gentleman's accounts, my husband's accounts. He's found nothink, and there was nothink to be found neither!"

"Why did you go to the gentleman's house so openly, Mrs. Flynn? Was it not to underline the threat of trouble, of scandal?"

"What else could I do, your honor, but take the letters myself?" asked Molly, injured. "I went veiled. I durstn't trust them to the post, and I couldn't hardly send them to his office in case they was opened. I put them in the hands of that there parlormaid and told her no one else was to touch them—and the huzzy went tattling to her mistress—"

"Yes, yes, Mrs. Flynn. Let us keep to the point. Why should Mr. Crozier say he was being blackmailed if he was not?"

"Ah, well, he would, wouldn't he, sir?" said Molly, confidential. "It's easy enough for a man to set a woman at naught, but he don't like it the other way round. Flynn had found out, your worship, and was threatening to shoot the pair of us. I run after Mr. Crozier's carriage, a-begging him to leave me alone, but he wouldn't listen."

She reached for an exceedingly embroidered handkerchief, wafted a quantity of musky perfume toward the coroner, and wept robustly.

"I tried and tried to send him about his business," she cried, "but then," with a flash of malice, "the poor gentleman wasn't getting it elsewhere."

Laura set her lips together in a fine line.

"I must ask you, Mrs. Flynn, to express yourself in a more seemly fashion. I do not wish to cause the late Mr. Crozier's widow more distress than she has already suffered."

And he inclined his head courteously to Laura's suffering, which she radiated in the crowded room.

"So you were not blackmailing Mr. Crozier?"

"Certainly not, sir, just a-giving him his letters back."

The coroner looked at Lintott, who shrugged.

"I am forced to accept your word for that, Mrs. Flynn. And I hope that, in the light of these tragic events, those in authority will keep an eye on this sort of thing in the future."

Again he looked at Lintott, and Lintott returned a perceptible nod.

"There is also the question of the anonymous letters," said the coroner, aggrieved. "So far the writer has not been discovered. They could be the random product of sick fancy, directed at a well-known family regardless of truth or consequence, in which case we may never trace the author. Inspector Lintott is holding this file open for future reference."

He cleared his throat, and glanced at Laura.

"But we may be sure that those letters had no bearing on the matter discussed here today. They happened to bring to light an unhappy situation which would otherwise have been shrouded in decent silence. No last message was left by the deceased, who doubtless wished to spare his family further grief. His health, as attested by the family physician, was poor. Dr. Padgett cannot be blamed for concluding, under these circumstances, that his patient died of a cerebral hemorrhage.

"I would say, therefore, that the late Mr. Theodore Crozier, under great emotional stress—and possibly under other pressures not proven—took his own life. I extend my condolences to Mrs. Crozier in her loss, and regret the undeserved ordeals inflicted upon her during these inquiries."

Flynn offered his wife the support of a stalwart arm. Dabbing her eyes, Molly swept out. The ladies nearest her switched aside their gowns, lest they be contaminated, and nudged their escorts to pay no attention to her. With Laura they were sympathetic, scandalized. But beneath their pats and whispers lay a faint contempt. She had never confided in any of them, never unbent. She had appeared to possess everything, and in reality possessed nothing of value. Her beauty was no challenge now, her wardrobe no cause for envy, her dignity no disturbance. They knew, simply, that she was incapable of keeping a husband faithful, was not even guilty of a grand passion with his brother.

Annihilated, she waited alone in her carriage outside the courtroom, while Titus paid homage to Mrs. Clayton's eighteen-year-old niece. The final twist of humiliation. Then out of the tide of spectators marched Lintott, Bollinger in hand, unnoticed as became his station in life. He nodded at her, once, twice, and spoke for her ears only.

"Rough, ma'am. Very rough. But satisfactory. Now, ma'am, keep a hold of yourself and don't mistake the shadow for the substance. Look neither to right nor left, and stay on course. You follow me?"

She inclined her head and tried to smile.

"That's all right, then," said Lintott, and nodded again, and strode off to more fearsome jungles.

Arthur Edgeley approached, and raised her gloved hand to his lips.

"I wish that my distress could ease your own, Laura. That was quite the most shocking spectacle of truth and justice I have ever witnessed."

"You are very kind," she answered automatically, bereft even of pride. "I feel nothing any longer, believe me. You need not mind."

"If it is any consolation to you, I should like you to know that I consider their justice was monstrously unjust to you, and their truth a monstrous lie. I thought I knew Theodore well enough. Now I know I did not."

"Nor, I fear, did I," said Laura, her femininity mortally wounded.

Her eyes were on Molly Flynn's red silk ankle, stepping into a hansom cab. So were many eyes: all masculine, covert, envious of pleasures unknown. High-colored, sensible, Arthur Edgeley turned his back on Mrs. Flynn.

"The city is littered with such women," he observed, divining Laura's wound. "Theodore would have been better advised to study the subtle instead of seeking the obvious. I am amazed he did not."

She flowered a little in his defense of her.

"Ah! Here is Titus at last!" said Arthur Edgeley. "It is of no use Mrs. Clayton's niece making eyes at him. He loves nobody but himself."

She looked at him uncertainly, and he smiled kindly, comprehending her loneliness.

"This spring will be a happier one for me than the last, Laura, and I did not think it possible at the time. Next spring will find you remembering with calmness what now seems insupportable. Titus! My dear fellow, do not leave Laura at the mercy of so many gaping mouths and busy eyes. She has had enough for one day, I should imagine."

"Why was Arthur Edgeley hanging round?" Titus demanded, unable to keep every woman happy at the same time.

"Protecting me from inquisitiveness, would you not think?"

He was not prepared to argue the point, intent on a new conquest.

"I shall not be able to call in this evening, after all," said Titus. "But we can see each other any day, Laura. And we must be careful after this furor!"

"I think it would be best," Laura began cautiously, "if we saw very little of each other, and met only in company. A quiet musical evening, for instance, perhaps while Mrs. Clayton's niece is staying here?"

He looked at her sharply, but she was detached and uncritical.

"I was thinking how lonely you would be, all by yourself, Laura."

"I have become used to being by myself. I shall miss you very much, Titus, but it would be sensible to give no further cause for gossip. Do you not agree?"

Why should he not? For this long chase was over, and he had grown tired of drama and scandal.

"Drive home, Henry!" Laura ordered, and settled back.

"I have been puzzling over the question of a manager,"

said Titus gaily. "You have a poor opinion of my business head, I know. So I am looking round. Indeed, I must. I cannot do two jobs at once, and I have been there at all hours since Theodore died."

"You must do as you think best, of course."

"Some hard-working fellow who won't mind earning his salary. Your own establishment, Laura, costs a pretty penny to maintain. And Theodore tied up a great deal of money in the boys' education, and some for Blanche in the event of her marriage. Laura, your dressmaker's bills are past comprehension, my dear!"

"You sound exactly like Theodore," she replied idly. "Has your tailor been paid, Titus?"

He shrugged and laughed, outmatched.

"We are so alike, you and I, Laura. We should have made a fine pair, should we not?"

"In one respect."

He glanced at her quickly and with some curiosity.

"And has that fire died?"

"I think this trouble has put it out for good."

"With me, you mean?" Vanity aroused.

"In every way," she answered, composedly. "One only loves once like that. Thank God, thank God."

"So you are not looking out for the chrism of love, Laura? Love's own crown?"

" 'With sanctifying sweetness'? No. I have my freedom, such as it is. I am not seeking further bondage. There is much else in life, and I begin to discover it. So you are my good friend and good brother once again, and I love you as I did in earlier years."

He was silent: released, but somehow disappointed. She laid a hand on his immaculate sleeve and smiled out of sheer affection.

"But I thank you for all the years, Titus."

He lifted the hand and kissed it, touched and pleased.

"That fellow Arthur Edgeley is a dull dog!" he observed, unconsciously on her wavelength, and interpreting it wrongly. "As a businessman I must pay him tribute, but as a man—"

"He and his wife were happy together," she said gently, turning his unspoken disparagement aside.

"That I find difficult to believe. How can one love the same woman for twenty-odd years? It is beyond my comprehension."

"They were always so mannerly with each other," she said, remembering. "One felt the loving kindness, and then they had many interests in common. Perhaps that is the answer."

"It would not be mine. I court fire."

His eyes glinted as though they stared into flames.

Fire can be rekindled, Laura thought. But did not say so.

"Should I clear away, ma'am?" Kate asked. "And Miss Nagle says shall she bring Miss Blanche downstairs now?"

"Yes, to both questions, Kate."

Laura rose, for musing had made her restless. But the smile she turned on her maid held contentment and promise.

"You have been my friend, Kate, for many years, and I shall be yours. Do not leave me yet, I beg of you, and when you do I shall buy your wedding dress. So think of it, Kate, because we must choose a pretty one."

"I wish it was Mr. Edgeley's butler that I was promised to," cried Kate, overcome, "but it isn't, ma'am!"

26

That shall be to-morrow
Not to-night.
I must bury sorrow
Out of sight . . .
　　Robert Browning
　　A Woman's Last Word

A few minutes later Blanche ran in to her mother, and
dropped the copy of *The Adventures of Herr Baby* written
by Mrs. Molesworth.

"What a careless little miss!" cried Laura indulgently.
"Here, let me smooth that page. The corner is quite
buckled."

She drew the child to her and they sat side by side on the
drawing-room sofa, fair head to fair head.

"Now be sure not to worry poor Mama, Miss Blanche,"
Nanny cautioned, without any of her usual emphasis. "She
has had a deal of trouble and must not be tired."

"You are not tired now, are you, Mama?" Blanche
whispered, one hand over her mouth, as Miss Nagle retired.

"Not in the least. I have been waiting for you, oh! so
impatiently. Now where were we up to, and what has Herr
Baby been doing since yesterday, I wonder? Here we are."

She read clearly and pleasantly, and Blanche dared to draw closer and finger the heart-shaped brooch at her throat.

"Papa gave you that," she observed, as the reading finished. "And he gave me my doll's house. He was very good to us, was he not? Only I was naughty and that did not suit him, because he was a good man."

Her gray eyes held a question.

"Papa loved you very much indeed," said Laura firmly, "but he found it difficult to say so. Gentlemen do not show their feelings as openly as ladies do. He may have seemed a little stern at times, but he loved you dearly and was very proud of you."

"Why was he? My pen wipers had to be washed, Mama."

"He was proud of you because you were so pretty, and he knew you meant to be good."

"It would have been nice," said Blanche wistfully, "if he had told me so himself. It is a pity that gentlemen do not say what they feel."

Laura had found the letters in the hidden drawer of his desk as he slept. Softly, skillfully, she drew them out, held her breath as he turned and murmured, began to read as he slept again.

From time to time she set down the pages and looked at that dark secret face on the pillow, which had totally eluded her for fifteen years. So this was what he could be? Tender and passionate, and sad of both tenderness and passion, and forgetful of his pride and righteousness.

Why did you not turn to me? Laura wondered. I could have been all of this to you. Why did you give yourself to her?

Then the discrepancies came upon her like phantoms, and she sat with the letters in her lap, pondering. For this was no buxom trollop, dark of hair and ripe of years, who would saunter up to a gentleman's front door in her finery. This was a very young girl of great sensibility. One would have said, a lady.

She mulled over every word Kate had said, and concluded that the woman had only been a messenger. Blackmail, perhaps? She reread all of them minutely, and a fearful possibility occurred to her.

Could Theodore be one of those men who procured a virgin, one such as Mr. Stead had exposed in his *Gazette* articles?

She looked again, picking up a clue here and another there, piecing them together in terrible fantasy. The girl had been a virgin, someone without protection but of good parentage who had taken up residence in a house.

That woman was the madam, Laura thought, and sickened to think that such defiled hands had touched this package.

The girl had not been the only one, either. Theodore spoke of others, taken and forgotten over a number of years. This alone had taken root.

And yet I fear the time when we may be parted. Then what dark roads must we tread? You with only the gift of making yourself pleasing to a man, and I with only the perpetual and degrading search for others who can never be to me what you are and could be. He will not let me see you, and I have been ill again. He even knows how much we mean, one to the other, and bleeds my pocket accordingly. But I should not mention this to you, since the money is of no importance. The money does not matter. Only you matter to me now.

If he so much as brushes against me I shall vomit, Laura thought, revolted. She was lost in darkness, seeing the drugged child lying in the bed, waking to nightmare.

She replaced the letters carefully in the package, and restored it to its hiding place. Theodore snored fretfully on.

"Mama! You have not one of your headaches coming on, have you?"

"No, my love. I have no headache at all."

"Perhaps," said Blanche, old and young at once, "you have a heartache because of dear Papa. Mama, I know my needlework is poorly done, but I should like to work a sampler for Papa, a big sampler."

"That should be possible, my love. What had you in mind?"

"Oh, a very big one, with birds round the edges, and a long verse, and the churchyard where he lies. In silk, Mama, not wool."

Laura stroked the child's pale hair and laid her cheek against the small face.

"That would take very long, and you would have to be particular as to the stitches. If you worked it in silk, we should need a fine linen, and one cannot pull out such thin threads without making a hole—should you make a mistake."

The child considered, swinging her legs, then put both arms around Laura's neck and whispered, "Please, Mama!"

"Well, I believe you want to do it so much that you will accomplish your task somehow. But I stitched such a sampler when I was a little older than you, and it took me two years to complete. Could you work so long and carefully and patiently as that?"

Blanche nodded hard, her bottom lip caught between her teeth.

"Have you thought of the verse, too, my love?"

"Yes, Mama. Shall I recite it to you?"

"If you please, my love. I should like that."

The child stood up as straight as if her slate were tied to her back, as it had frequently been under Nanny Nagle's dominion. Hands clasped behind her, gray eyes looking into some image of heaven, strapped shoes shining, she opened her mouth and then remembered something else.

"I feel it is only *right* that I should work a sampler for Papa, Mama. Do you know that sort of a feeling, when something is so right and proper that you must do it?"

"Very well," Laura replied gravely.

The quarrel over dinner had decided her. As the housemaid and kitchenmaid produced chaos and Theodore turned from ill temper to open tyranny, Laura hardened. His command to have her back again in their bedroom made up her mind. She could no more tolerate the accidental touch of his body than contemplate the terrors of which he had been so guilty. She followed him up the stairs, and took two capsules from her new bottle of sleeping pills.

"Theodore," she said submissively, "I know you are very angry with me, but believe me I do not wish you to be ill as well."

"My head, my heart, my cough."

"Dr. Padgett told me that you must not be excited in this fashion, since you are still weak from the influenza. He said that if you were to excite yourself too much you could suffer a severe—even a mortal—attack."

Transfixed, he stared at her.

"I beg you to go to bed, and I will carry out the remedy he prescribed. It is quite a new form of medicine," said Laura composedly, "and designed gradually to soothe and relax the nerves and constitution. Dr. Padgett has not tried it out before, but apparently it is all the rage in Vienna."

"Really? In Vienna? Ah, they know a thing or two that a stick like Padgett would never find his way about! What is it? Medicine?"

"A very rare pill. A series of pills. To be taken, two at a time, with water, every twenty minutes."

"That sounds quite new, most unusual. You must not fail to remind me of the time. How many pills are there altogether?"

"Eighteen. And I shall give them to you myself."

"Where is the bottle? I want to see it."

She laid a hand on his forehead and frowned as if to herself.

"Theodore, I do not wish to alarm you, my dear, but you really cannot fret like this without serious consequence.

I promise you that I shall come upstairs without fail, every twenty minutes, and give you the pills myself. You must lie very still and try to go to sleep. If you do go to sleep I can wake you sufficiently to give you the medicine, and I *shall.*" She looked into his face now without distaste or shrinking. "Do you believe me?"

"Yes, Laura. Yes," he replied, his fears temporarily allayed.

A child, he turned back the covers and lay down in the great four-poster bed. A child, he accepted the morphine capsules two by two, each time a little drowsier and heavier and thirstier. And Laura trailed up the staircase, every twenty minutes, until he had taken the last by midnight.

"Are you comfortable, Theodore?"

He stared dully at the mane of pale hair, the pale silent face, and reached clumsily for her hand. She shrank back, clutching the wrapper to her breasts.

"My—head. My—head," he said, slurring the words.

Obediently, she laid one palm on his forehead.

"You have no temperature. Does it ache?"

"Dazed—feel—dazed. Thirsty."

She gave him water.

"You are half asleep, that is all. Have you any pain, Theodore?"

"Arms—heavy—legs—like—lead."

"It is nothing that a good sleep will not cure," she said, and added for his benefit, in seeming desperation, "You should not have disturbed yourself so."

"Blood — pressure — Padgett warned — me — send — for Padgett."

"Do take one of my sleeping capsules, Theodore. Then if you cannot sleep we will send for the doctor."

She had been afraid lest he should not die, though Padgett's warnings over the pills assured her that a bottleful of them should be lethal.

She sank into the chair by his side, hands over mouth, and stared at the deathly mask. She was still sitting there, white and frozen, when the doctor arrived.

"I shall not go. I cannot go. Until you tell me," Laura whispered. "He is gravely ill, is he not?"

"No hope, I'm afraid."

Thank God, thank God, thank God, thank God, thank God, thank God.

Blanche cleared her throat, and began.

"Weep not for me, my children dear.
Let hope forbid the flowing tear.
What tho' on earth I am no more?
I am not lost, but gone before.

"Dear Lord, in thee I put my trust,
And Angels guard the sleeping dust."

He had mumbled dully as she sat well away from him.

"Dark road. Dark . . . road . . . dark."

"I never knew you," she whispered into the ensuing silence. "I never knew you. May God have mercy upon you and forgive you. Only He can. I cannot."

"Loved . . ."

He had surmounted his final word, setting it like a lamp on the last dark road of all.

"And then, down at the bottom, between the verse and the churchyard where dear Papa sleeps, I want to put *In memory of Theodore Augustus Sydney Crozier by His Loving Daughter, Blanche.*"

Laura sighed, smiled, and knelt before the child, holding her tightly.

"That will be most beautiful, my love, and I know you can do it. You will not make a single mistake, and then your children shall see how clever *their* Mama was when she was only eight years old."

"Are you crying for Papa?"

"I think I am crying for all of us," said Laura.

The clock, in its glass and gold-pillared seclusion, struck six times, soft and insistent. At the last stroke they separated, hearing Miss Nagle's gentler knock on the drawing-room door.

"I did not know, until Papa died, what a nice person you were, Mama," Blanche whispered, and kissed her, and held out her hand to the nanny so that she might be taken securely away.

Ah, you men, thought Laura, looking through her window onto the March evening, how you cover up for one another. You set that woman Flynn up as Theodore's mistress, and she lied for you. You allowed me to sit in that courtroom and suffer humiliation, so that he should not be exposed. But I knew, I knew, and I kept silent for the children's sake, And after all, your protection of him protected me too. Though, if they had accused me, I should have told them what I had discovered and what I had done, and cried shame on them all.

You make toys of us. Things to be possessed and then thrown away when you are tired of us. When will you understand that we have intellect and morality and passions even as yourselves? When will you use us not for what you want from us but for what we are? You give us only one chance to escape from the seclusion of childhood, and that is the seclusion of marriage. We embrace this lottery with rejoicing and total ignorance. You do not allow us to use our own money, nor often to reclaim it if the marriage fails. We have nothing of our own but our faces and bodies, and we are taught to charm with them so that we may be bought.

The Common became one vast golden space under the evening sky, and she hesitated to draw the curtains against such splendor.

I am grateful to be given a year of seclusion in which to find myself, Laura thought, and then I shall make up my mind.

You must make up your own mind, my love. Jealous, fearful, totally withdrawn now she would leave him.

So I am no more alone now than I was then, she pondered. And I shall be seeking out of experience what I once sought in blindness. I shall not be taken in by appearances, nor beguiled with presents, nor be deluded by compliments. I have put away childish things. I have looked in a mirror darkly. I have seen myself face to face.

Strength beneath sweetness, will beneath submissiveness, a justice executed without mercy. Adultery and murder mastering love and suffering.

Which must be forever between myself and God, and that shall be my expiation. One lays down the burden of others and takes upon one's shoulders the greater burden of oneself. One can demand nothing, expect nothing, only hope for redemption and be of service. Theodore. I shall temper his memory for the children's sakes, supply what he possessed—for her, at least—and could not give to them. They shall remember him with pride and honor, that is their need and their right. Blanche will mend his image in her sampler. Edmund will soften and Lindsey grow firm. Titus? Titus will never change, but in his way he cares for all of us.

And Arthur Edgeley? Gray-headed, thickening, well versed in adversity and the ways of the world.

He courts a better and a worse woman than he knows, thought Laura. Pray God I have the calmness to remember and the courage to forget, so that I do not fail either of us. I must not cheat him.

Look neither to right nor left, and stay on course. You follow me?

Well, every wandering is followed by a homecoming, thought Laura. And I have wandered far and into dark places. Perhaps I shall be given grace.

"You'll excuse me, ma'am," said Kate, softly imperative, "but I do think you should come and change before dinner. The lady and gentleman will be here directly after, and your new black satin is here from the dressmaker—by special delivery!"

"Ah, Kate, how practical you are. You deal only with the present, and that is the most important, after all. Let us inspect the dress!"